Feral Winter: Book One

INFECT

Benjamin Rempel

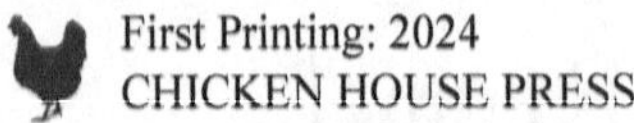

First Printing: 2024
CHICKEN HOUSE PRESS

Library and Archives Canada Cataloguing in Publication
CIP data on file with the National Library and Archives

ISBN trade paperback edition: 978-1-990336-73-7

Publishers note: Information on EEEV adapted and fictionalized from: Ontario Agency for Health Protection and Promotion. Eastern equine encephalitis: history and enhanced surveillance in Ontario. Toronto, ON: Queen's Printer for Ontario; 2014.

Author photo by Kimberly Vincent Photography

Chicken House Press
282906 Normanby/Bentinck Townline
Durham, Ontario, Canada, N0G 1R0
www.chickenhousepress.ca

To Amy, always
And Asia, also
And Will, of course

Other works by Benjamin Rempel

Short Fiction:

Last Shift
Small Town Monster
In Search of Damien
The Magician's Last Trick

This may be unpleasant…

INFECT

Benjamin Rempel

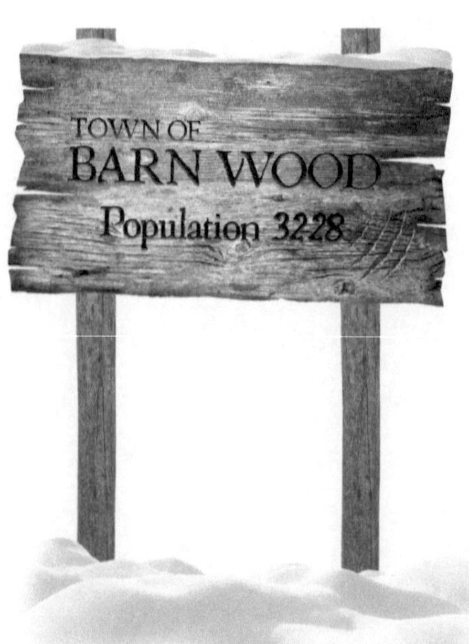

TOWN OF
BARN WOOD
Population 3228

Chapter One

March 1995
Day 411 | Late Afternoon

The impact should have killed the child.

Andrew heard the squeal of tires, the shatter of glass. He felt the shock of the seatbelt around his chest as his head cracked against the metal frame. He reeled around as the steel bumper struck the child, throwing her high into the air. Her head splintered the windshield and her neck snapped back, her limp body torn from the hood and tossed violently to the pavement.

Andrew shouldn't have seen the child; he shouldn't have been in the taxi at all. An hour earlier, just after his plane landed, he stood at the passenger pick-up scanning for his mother's rusted Ford truck.

"Where is she?" he huffed, sliding his sleeve up to see his watch.

He heaved his oversized backpack onto his shoulders, the weight of it bending his tall, athletic frame. He moved toward a line of pay phones and slid a quarter in. The phone rang several times before an automated voice answered: *The mailbox for Elizabeth Stone is full. Please try again later.*

He breathed through his teeth, slamming the receiver into its cradle. He paced up and down the line of cars, searching, the crisp winter air biting at his bare forearms. Eventually, he reached for his wallet and split the leather to reveal several green bills. Scowling, he raised his arm and whistled.

"Where to?" the cab driver asked as Andrew threw his backpack to the floor and piled into the backseat, the vinyl covering cool to the touch.

"241 Middleton Avenue," Andrew said.

"Where abouts is that?"

"Just head north. I'll tell you when we're close."

The driver nodded and sped away, the engine whining beneath the hood.

Andrew was still fuming that no one had received him at the airport. He knew his stepfather, Joe, and half-brother, Xavier, couldn't be bothered, but his mother had always been there for him.

He let out a heavy sigh, groaning as his fingers pushed into his forehead and temples. The flight had been traumatic and he felt knots constrict along his neck and shoulders. He closed his eyes and exhaled deeply several times, the strain of anger and tension slowly releasing.

As the car exited the turn-pike, he reached into his pocket and unfolded a piece of paper. It had a phone number on it and the name *Juliana* written in cursive. A small heart dotted the 'i' and a faint smell of lavender wafted up from the note. Andrew smiled, remembering the attractive redhead from the plane. He mouthed the numbers on the page as if committing them to memory. After a while, he folded the paper into his passport and crammed it into his backpack.

"That was quite a storm we had flying in," he said. He glanced out the window at the dry pavement. "Looks like it didn't come through here though."

"Nah, we haven't seen anything yet," the cab driver said. His voice was gruff, the sound rolling over his lips in a low rumble. "Been pretty dry here. Still a bit of snow but no rain yet. Not like the downpours we had a few years ago. Spring of '92, if I recall. You around for that?"

"I think so."

"Oh, you'd remember if you were. Half the forests turned to swamps. And then half the swamps turned to lakes!"

"Really?"

"Oh yeah, there were floods everywhere. Mosquitoes were insane too. And I remember lots of deer and horses died as well for some reason."

"When was this?"

"Like I said, it was '92. Late April, maybe May. Just a crazy spring, I suppose. Lots of weird nature stuff."

A squat man with thick arms and a smushed nose, the driver continued north along the wide country road, surveying the dreary terrain.

"The rains will come, mind you," the cabbie said. "It's still winter now but the rains will come. They always do."

Andrew ran his nails through his coarse brown hair, attacking an itch above his ear. His face was pale and hand-some, a faint scatter of freckles clutching to his pallid cheeks. He stretched his legs and adjusted his dark cargo pants and T-shirt.

He peered through the streaked window, the yellow rutted fields flying past. The muted hue reminded him of the flowers his mother would clip from their yard. She would take great care rinsing and displaying them in a heavy glass vase or scrubbed Mason jar. The house would fill with a subtle fra-grance, a pleasant mix of earthy flowers and his mother's own honeyed aroma.

When he was a child, the scent seemed to last the whole day and well into the evening as she would tie her dark hair up in a bun and lay down next to him. As night rolled in, she would hum softly, her warm fingers caressing down his back, her nails gently catching on each raised abrasion. With drooping eyes, Andrew would breathe in her scent and eventually drift off to sleep, vivid dreams beckoning him under, his matted curls tousled and mussed under the covers.

From the cab, Andrew gazed upon the snow-dusted grass and skinny alders set back from the road, the branches aching for their annual thaw, the grip of another harsh winter finally relenting. His eyes caught on the narrow creek angled away from the ditch, the icy current slow and cautious, moving deeper into the bush. He knew the creek well, a long channel which surged south during the summer months for countless kilometres, meandering through forest and peaty bogs. It was the same water that flowed beside the reeds and cattails lining the grassy bank mere steps from his mother's and stepfather's wrap-around porch.

As the minutes turned over, Andrew glanced at his watch several times, the driver fiddling with the radio settings, switching through different news channels.

"So, where'd ya fly in from?" the cabbie asked.

"I spent about seven months overseas," Andrew said. "Just finished third-year university."

"Third year, eh? You look a little young for that. How old are ya?"

"21. I turn 22 in June."

"Well, okay then. But last week of March is a little early to be done school, ain't it?"

"I fast-tracked. Took my exams early. The material was a little … it was kind of easy for me. A little basic."

"You some sort of genius or something?" the driver scoffed. "Some sort of Albert Einstein or that Microsoft kid making computers in his basement?"

Andrew smirked but said nothing.

"Fast-tracked, eh?" the driver said.

"It's not that big a deal," Andrew said. "I went mainly to get my mom off my back. I got an academic scholarship and it was all she could talk about for a while."

"My oh my, a scholarship," the driver mocked. "So, what'd you do at this fancy university?"

"I mainly focused on sciences like biology and chemistry. We studied germs, viruses, things like that. We looked at how humans adapt to viruses and how, well, sometimes they don't." He looked at the cabbie with a critical eye—as if he knew more than he was letting on.

"Well, I don't know much about that stuff but good luck to ya." The driver burped a potent mix of garlic and onions. And then: "Forests get pretty thick this far north, eh?" he mused, whistling at the vastness of the trees. "Seem to go on forever."

"Yeah, good for hunting but bad for long-distance relationships," Andrew said.

The driver chuckled. "And just the one road in, huh? If anything happened, you'd be penned in there pretty good."

"I suppose," Andrew said.

The driver drew quiet for a while longer before clearing his throat. "Where'd ya say you was going again?"

"Middleton Avenue."

"That in Rise Borough?"

"No, Barn Wood."

"Barn Wood? Oh, I didn't realize that. Well, I won't be dropping you there."

"Why not?"

"Because they're all going nuts over there!"

"Wait, what do you mean? Who's going nuts?"

"Something's going on in that town, for sure. Caught mention of it on the news just the other mornin'." The driver continued fiddling with the radio dial, trying to get a clear signal.

"What are you talking about?"

"Yeah, I guess they've moved onto other news, but I remember hearing something …"

"But I just spoke to my mom—"

But Andrew stopped short. He couldn't actually remember the last time he spoke to his mother. He had been so focused on cramming for exams and writing his papers that he hadn't actually checked in at home for several weeks. Maybe longer.

A pang went through him and it was then he realized he hadn't even spoken to his mother to tell her his flight details. He had only left a message on the answering machine several weeks ago, assuming she would get it and drive out to the airport to collect him.

"What do you mean they're all going nuts?" Andrew asked again.

"Hey man, all I know is what I hear on the radio," the driver said. "Something creepy is going on in that town. I even heard the cops are missing."

"What?"

"That's what I heard. The cops was chased away or scared off or somethin'. It sounds right screwy whatever's going on."

The tires rumbled as they crossed over a set of train tracks, the cabbie tightening his grip around the steering wheel. "There's an intersection about a kilometre up from here," he said. "I'm gonna drop you off there."

"You can't just drop me in the middle of nowhere!"

"That's as close as I'm gonna get."

"But we're more than twenty kilometres from my house! Can't you at least drop me closer to town?"

The driver glared through the rearview mirror, his dark eyes holding Andrew's. "That's as close as I get," he said again, each word slow and firm.

Andrew huffed and snatched his backpack from the floor. "Fine. But at least order me another cab. This is ridiculous!"

"No one will come," the driver said. "You see any other cars around?"

The question hung in the air as Andrew turned and squinted out the back window. Normally a busy street leading into the main part of town, the road was deserted. Not one car or pickup on it—just an empty road beside an empty field.

"But you can't just drop me anywhere you want! It's got to be against your company's policy or something."

"My *safety* is my policy!" the driver shouted.

Andrew folded his arms, his eyes darting around the cab as if searching out answers. "Well, what should I do?"

"I can take you back to the airport."

"I don't want to go to the airport! I want to go home!"

They crested a hill as the intersection came into view.

"Look, they have pay phones there so at least you could call someone to come get you," the driver offered. "But believe me, from what I've heard, you don't want to go anywhere near—"

Andrew never saw the child approach. The girl. But in an instant, she was there. The car hit her and the glass smashed and her body was thrown high into the air, making a vicious thud where she landed. The driver yanked the wheel, skidding to a stop along the gravel shoulder.

Andrew grabbed his bag and swung the door open, staggering to the front of the car. "What the hell happened?" he shouted.

"I - I didn't see her, I swear," the driver stammered, stumbling from the front seat.

Andrew glanced at the shattered windshield and then hurried to the girl. "Are you alright?" he said. She didn't move so he asked again, louder. "Are you okay?"

The driver hobbled up from behind. "Where did she come from? Was she in the field?" He wiped the sweat from his brow, his jaw quivering. "Is she - is she dead?"

Andrew stood over the girl but drew back when her body twitched. She made a noise in her throat, a raspy guttural exhale. She pushed herself from the ground and stared ahead, her eyes vacant and listless. Black scabs snaked up her arms, her lips cracked and flecked with dry blood. She was young— no more than 10—and the wide gash along her forehead burned red and raw.

"You're hurt," Andrew said, his eyes moving around the girl's face. "Why don't you lay down. I can go for help."

Gaunt with a sickly pallor, the girl turned to Andrew. She cocked her head, confused, as if listening to a foreign language. There was a peculiar quality about her, as though her eyes were misaligned or one side of her body didn't quite match the other.

She swiped her blonde hair away from the wound and

dug her thumb deep into it, carving out a soggy trench. Tugging it loose, she examined it, then lifted it to her mouth, her eager tongue lapping at the blood and flesh. Her skin parted to reveal a crooked grin, a grisly shape contorting across her face. She turned and snickered, a low chortle under her breath.

"What the—" Andrew whispered. He reeled back to the edge of the road, losing his footing on the shale and stone.

The girl's yellow eyes flicked from Andrew to the driver. Without warning, she turned and leapt into the fields, running north, a slight hitch in her step.

"Sh - should we follow her?" Andrew stuttered. He stared after the girl with wide eyes, his breath heavy.

"No way!" the driver said, fixed on the small silhouette bounding through the dry, tawny grass.

"But we should help her," Andrew said. "She's just a girl." But the words came out more a question than a statement.

"I don't know what that was," the driver sputtered, hurrying back to the car. "But that wasn't a girl. That was something else entirely."

Andrew looked where the girl had been lying. Her blood, which streaked the pavement seconds earlier, had turned black, bubbling like freshly poured tar. He leaned in for a closer look but jerked up when he heard the car door slam.

"Wait!" he hollered, but the driver was already shifting into reverse, forcing the car around. "Don't leave me here! You can't leave me here!"

Andrew sprinted to where he had dropped his bag, then spun back toward the taxi. "Stop! Wait for me!" he called out again.

But the cab driver didn't hear him, muttering under his

breath, franticly jamming the gearshift into drive.

Andrew stumbled through the ditch waving his arms but the driver had turned around, the car quickly moving away.

"Dammit!" he yelled.

Andrew was much too far from the airport to go back and the next town over was miles away, separated by vast forests and wide lakes.

He squinted over the fields one last time trying to find the child, but she was gone. He glanced up, the red sun falling closer to the horizon, the light quickly abandoning the sky. He turned in the direction of his home.

Something creepy is going on in that town.

A chill twisted up his back.

Warily, he shouldered his backpack and set off, nervously scanning the fields as he went. His trot quickened when he heard gravel ping the taxi's muffler and the screech of tires gripping pavement, the cab speeding faster and faster away from the town.

Chapter Two

March 1995
Day 411 | Dusk

Andrew made his way up the winding dirt driveway toward the family farmhouse. The tip of the century home could be seen from the road, but most of its grey brick and bay windows were blocked by the ash and ironwoods planted in the front yard decades ago.

He was out of breath, having jogged through forests and along abandoned rail lines from where the cabbie had deserted him. Throwing the heavy backpack to the ground, he leaned forward, gripping his thighs until his breathing calmed. He stood and pushed his hair off his sweaty forehead, glancing toward the overgrown, snow-dusted brush flanking the narrow driveway.

He cautiously moved up the lane, passing the creek out front, the black line flowing south, nubs of stone coating the river floor.

As he got closer, he noticed differences from when he walked away from the house last September. Leaves overhung the slanting gutters and the drainpipes were stained a rusted dull orange. Bleached and weathered, several cracks split the caulk between the brick and stone. Green algae crept along the foundation and a swampy stink burped up from where the water pooled.

"Must be a leak," he wondered aloud, nervously surveying the ground.

His eyebrows furrowed as he moved toward the detached garage. A black pickup truck laid on its side, all the windows smashed out of it, severed wires jutting out from underneath the dented hood.

Inside the garage, heavy tire chains were spread across the floor, along with rakes, a camping stove, a chainsaw, and a hatchet. In the corner, an overturned gas can leaned up against a rusted pickaxe. Thin sheets of plywood laid on the cement floor, a metal mallet angled against one of the boards. The shelves lining the rear of the garage—normally full of shovels, snares, and rope—were empty. He rustled a faded green tarp with the toe of his boot and the smell of mould and mildew caused his nose to scrunch.

Dust and boot prints lined the floor but when he crouched, he realized the prints weren't from a boot at all. They resembled something of an odd-shaped paw or crooked foot.

Andrew stood, then glanced at the house. He heard the nervous creak of the ironwoods moving with the breeze, as if leaning in for a closer look. He reached for the mallet, his quivering fingers winding tight around the rubber grip.

He shouldered his backpack and squinted into the yard. He couldn't see it—the plywood flush with the ground—but he knew it was there, sixty yards from where he stood. An un-used wine cellar when the family moved in nearly twenty years ago. The underground structure had been used sparingly since, haphazardly converted to store root vegetables and old hunting equipment.

Beyond the cellar were the neighbour's dormant fields where, come spring, wheat and corn would be planted. Barn Wood lived and breathed by the crops, by the constant feud between the farmers who planted them and the pests that took them. Overlooking the fields were the endless miles of blackened trees and gloomy shrubs, the dark hardwood forests and rushing waterways isolating the entire town.

Andrew turned away and hurried to the front porch. He noticed a window along the entrance was smashed, glass shards sprouting out from the damaged frame. Several axe marks punctured the front door, the brass lock and handle torn away. He ran his finger over the splintered wood but drew back when a sliver pierced the skin.

"Dammit!" he yelped. He bit down on the wound, his tongue hard against the slit, the tart metallic tang stinging the back of his throat.

Taking a step closer, he nudged the front door with his boot. He shuffled into the tiny foyer, the glow of the setting sun casting weak shafts of light onto the worn hardwood. He stepped toward the base of the stairs and tried the light switch along the wall but the circuit was broken.

"Mom?" he called up the stairs. Bumps formed along his arms. "Joe?"

He moved into the kitchen and tried the switch tucked along the checkered backsplash but it too failed. As he adjusted to the dim, he saw several cupboards hanging from their hinges, drawers pulled out onto the linoleum. A woodland painting of a stag teetered on the far wall, the glass shattered within the frame.

"Jesus, what happened here?" he breathed.

He pried the fridge open to find it empty, outside of a box

of baking soda and a wilted head of lettuce browning in the crisper drawer. Several documents were taped to the fridge: a hunting license, expired grocery coupons, a well-water inspection certificate, an advertisement for a flu clinic. There was a collection of pay stubs addressed to Elizabeth Stone, the last statement nearly seven weeks old, dated February 3rd, 1995.

Seeing her name, he called out again, louder. "Mom?"

In the rear mudroom, boots were scattered on the floor, a few raincoats hanging from cast iron hooks. He approached the red metal cabinet and mentally tallied the missing items: three rifles, ammunition, camouflage jackets, bowie knife, binoculars, a flashlight.

Staring into the empty cabinet, his mind travelled back three summers when he and Xavier went out for one last hunt before leaving for school. His best friend, Jeremiah Cook, had told him the deer were plentiful, so Andrew and Xavier prepared their rifles, woke up before the sun, and slunk into the bush. As the light crested the horizon, Xavier flanked to the left, as was his way, and raised his arm. It happened all at once but Andrew clearly remembered the startled doe bursting from the copse, how it turned and ran straight at him, and how Xavier, quick as the wind through the trees, raised his rifle and took the animal down.

"Still not as fast as me," Xavier snorted.

The brothers chatted quietly as they returned to the farmhouse. It was still early enough that their mother was just putting eggs in the frying pan when they bounded in through the mudroom, the earthy smell of roasted coffee filling the small home. It was a successful hunt and Xavier seemed to be enjoying himself. But that was before their mother proudly brought up Andrew's school plans again, fawned and fretted over him, and the resentment began to seep back into Xavier.

Andrew closed the cabinet door and the click of the latch echoed throughout the house. But it was another noise that caused a shiver to swell underneath his skin. A muted thud, over and over again, coming from upstairs.

"Mom, is that you?" he hollered, panic lacing his words. "Joe, are you home? It's me, Andrew."

His grip tightened around the mallet as he cautiously inched up the stairwell. He walked past the dated family portrait—he, his mom, Joe, Xavier—all squinting into the lens, a captured memory from years ago, from happier times. Several other portraits laid smashed on the ground and he stepped around them and edged into Xavier's room. Towels were crumpled on the floor, the bed frame pushed up against the wall. Andrew peered at the curious markings above the baseboards. There were shavings of sheetrock littered throughout the room as though a screwdriver had repeatedly punctured the drywall.

He moved to his mother's and stepfather's room at the end of the hall. Their oak dresser was on its side, the braided wind chime above the bed torn in two. He watched as the willow hoop moved up and down, bouncing off the ceiling, as if summoned to dance, and Andrew realized this was the noise he heard from downstairs.

He went to the window. There was a crack between the glass and sill and a draft was blowing in. He placed his hand over the gap and the wind chime abruptly stopped. Pleased to have found the cause of the noise, he paused for just a moment, listening to the faint tick of the bedside clock.

He stepped away from the window just as a horrific scream slashed through the air. He whipped around, racing downstairs and out the front door. In the frail light, he frantically scanned the patchy grass, his eyes flitting between the bushes and fescue, his shirt damp with sweat.

Seeing nothing, he turned to go back inside but caught a smudge of colour in his periphery. He wasn't sure if it was the trees swaying but as he squinted, a shadow broke away, and a contorted shape began slinking up the lane.

And then, just as sharp as the first one, a second scream split the evening air—a cutting, high-pitched trill, like the skirl of a child.

Andrew turned and sprinted to the back of the house and toward the underground cellar. Bloodroot and thatch had sprouted over the hinges so that he ran several yards beyond the entrance before realizing it. Circling back, he noticed a steel latch on the plywood door. It was unlocked, the metal bar lying beside the padlock.

With his breath hot in his throat, he yanked the door open and stumbled halfway down the creaky steps. He grabbed the handle on the underside and readied himself to slam the plywood but froze when he noticed a woman at the side of the house. She was tall and reed thin, her limbs bent and distorted. She blinked her yellow eyes and turned her head, her movements drawn out, slow and reptilian.

That wasn't a girl. That was something else entirely.

Andrew shifted and noticed a second person—a rounded man coming out from the trees. Wild grey hairs sprouted from his cadaverous skin and his fingers extended into mangled black claws. He moved gingerly, hunched over, with most of his cheek and jaw chewed away. Andrew felt the man catch his gaze just before he faltered and tripped down the cellar stairs, the plywood door slamming down hard after him.

The inside of the cellar was black and Andrew stayed deathly still for several moments. He drew a sleeve across his forehead, his cheeks flushed and red, his breathing heavy.

The space was damp with a rank mix of must and mould. He felt along the wall. The porous cement was rough to the touch until he came upon a storage rack and then the cold metal of a flashlight. Snatching it from the shelf, he fiddled with the switch until the light flickered. He scanned the concrete floor, the beam needling the dark, when a noise caused him to raise the light.

There was a shift in shadow and then something crashed into him, knocking the mallet and flashlight to the floor. He saw a glint of light and then a knife rushed forward. The blade stopped just short of his neck but the tip dug in, carving out a small refuge underneath the skin. His head was yanked back and Andrew felt the flat of the blade rest upon his Adam's apple, the cold steel hard against his windpipe.

He knew this motion. He had grown up watching his stepfather maneuver a slain deer the same way. Expose the throat and slit it wide.

Spittle flaked his lips and Andrew struggled to draw air in. His body flailed before he located a familiar smell: a sharp mix of forest oils and woodsmoke. The scent was always the same. Ever since childhood the musk had remained constant and it jolted his nerves to the surface.

"X!" Andrew gurgled. "X! It's me!"

The knife lowered and a brute of a man emerged from the shadows. His coarse hair was matted to his forehead, his hands calloused and blistered, soil caked under his cracked nails. His eyes were swollen and bloodshot, his pupils vibrating around the small space. He took a step forward, his dusty boots scraping along the concrete.

Andrew spun as shock travelled up him. "X?"

A set of dark eyes caught Andrew's as the stranger pawed at knotted hair, revealing thick stubble and bushy sideburns sprouting from his hardened face. His lips were crusted and chapped, his cheeks sallow.

"Xavier. It's me ... your brother."

Xavier sniffed the air. He leaned over and grabbed the flashlight from a pile of empty food tins. He pointed the light, the beam travelling up Andrew's sweat-soaked body.

"Why are you here?" Xavier said. His voice was gruff and cracking as if just waking from a deep slumber.

"Sc - school's done," Andrew stammered. "I finished early. I - I'm home now."

A long silence suspended between them until Xavier gave an awkward smile.

"Welcome home, brother," he said, still gripping the hilt of his knife. "Welcome home."

Chapter Three

March 1994
Day 30 | Morning

Angela Till handed the cab driver a ten-dollar bill and strummed her painted fingernails on the plastic covered seats.

"Sorry, are you waiting for change?" the driver asked. "The fare was $8.50. I just assumed …"

Angela huffed and continued strumming.

The driver dropped his head and rummaged through his pockets. The pieces clinked together as he counted out six quarters. He placed the coins in her outstretched hand. "Here you are, ma'am."

"I don't get a tip for what I do for a living!" Angela sneered. "What makes you so special?"

She flung the back door open and stepped out, her black heels immediately submerged in a mound of slush lining the curb.

"For Christ's sake! You're a horrible driver and you're even worse at parking!" she yelled as the cab pulled away. She bounded onto the sidewalk, flinging the sludge from her shoes.

Pushing through the revolving door, she scurried across the gleaming grey tiles toward the front desk. The expansive lobby was bright and spotless with new light fixtures lining the back wall, intricate crown molding etched along the crest of the freshly-painted ceiling. The sting of bleach and wood polish hung in the air.

A few patrons were seated in the foyer: a young mother with her anxious toddler, and a middle-aged man with a black raincoat draped over his arm, a dark Tilley hat cocked over his eyes. Angela whisked past them toward the pimply desk clerk dressed in a red sports coat and gold-plated name tag.

"Welcome to the newly renovated Main Street Inn!" the clerk squeaked. He stretched his arm toward a plaque displayed on the wall: *Main Street Inn – Refurbished March 1, 1994.*

"We had our grand re-opening earlier this month. You just missed it! Brand new flooring, renovated lounge and restaurant. Each of our guest rooms have been completely upgraded! I'm sure you will enjoy your stay with us. Are you ready to check-in?"

"Ha! I wouldn't stay here if it was free!" Angela chided. "I remember what this place used to look like—all musty and worn-out. There's still probably mould and whatever else behind those walls. You can't just slap new paint on and pretend it's a brand-new building!"

The clerk slunk behind the desk, averting his eyes as his cheeks became flush.

"I'm here for a meeting in the business centre boardroom," Angela said.

"Okay," the clerk mumbled.

"Well, where the hell is it?" Angela snapped.

"Oh, right, s - sorry," the clerk stammered. "T - top floor. That is, the fourth-floor, ma'am."

Angela pushed away from the desk, her wet shoes squeaking as she made her way toward the elevator bank. She tapped her foot impatiently as the glowing numbers slowly descended above the elevator doors. Eventually, the doors clunked open and she stepped inside.

"Hold the doors!" a young man called out as he crossed the lobby. He held a yellow notepad in one hand, a ballpoint pen balanced between his teeth. He stumbled as he swiped dishevelled hair from his eyes, the strap of his bulky camera slipping down his drooping shoulders.

"Hold the doors please," he yelled again.

Angela didn't flinch as the heavy doors snapped shut, the man drawing his arm back just in time.

Alone in the elevator, Angela studied her reflection in the steel door. She adjusted the collar on her blouse and pressed along each of her eyebrows, flattening them close to her dark skin. She smoothed her blazer but paused when she came across a ball of lint hidden on the fabric.

"Oh, for Christ's sake!" she said throwing the fluff to the polished floor.

She glided her tongue across her teeth, red lipstick along her incisors. In the blurry reflection it resembled a smudge of blood upon a set of fangs. She growled, rubbing the stain from her teeth.

The elevator jerked to a halt and a pleasant voice chimed overhead: *Fitness, Pool, and Business Centre – fourth floor.* Angela rolled her eyes as the doors opened. She slithered out and crept down the corridor.

"Dr. Till?" a voice hollered from behind. "I'm Brad Moseby from *The Chronicle.*"

Angela twisted and noticed it was the same young man who was running for the elevator in the lobby. He exited the stairwell, nearly out of breath.

"I have a few questions for you about the town's drinking water," he said, panting.

Angela ignored him and made a quick left down the hallway.

"There have been reports of potential tampering with the water supply," Moseby continued, struggling to keep pace. "Some residents are complaining of a metallic taste. Can you comment?"

Angela quickened her stride, the boardroom doors now in full view. She wiped her forehead, her ebony skin sheen with sweat.

"There are people who suggest staff at your health unit aren't doing enough to address these concerns," Moseby added. "Do you agree?"

Angela clenched her fists but continued her march.

"Some rumours are hinting at worse things than that," Moseby continued. "That the health unit may even be the *cause* of it."

Angela whipped around to face the gangly young man. Wisps of a patchy beard poked through his milky skin. A line of acne dotted his sweaty forehead.

Angela cocked her head, her glare digging into the budding journalist. "How old are you?"

Moseby swallowed, his parka hanging off his thin frame as though it were a size too big. "I just turned 22, ma'am. But what I wanted to talk to you about was the health unit's response to some unusual events—"

"Only 22?" Angela sneered. "And what paper did you say you were from?"

"*The Chronicle.* You may have seen our paper around town. We have six hundred regular readers—"

"Only six hundred? Jesus," Angela sighed. "I only give interviews to nationals. Not some two-bit flyer you write from your parent's basement!"

Moseby adjusted his glasses along the bridge of his nose. "But Dr. Till, *The Chronicle* is a legit paper and a reliable voice for community news."

"You're so naïve. Don't waste your time inventing stories. Stop bothering people and get a real job like the rest of us!"

Angela reached for the brass handle and swung the boardroom door open.

"Dr. Till, *The Chronicle* is a reputable paper, a voice of truth—"

The heavy boardroom door slammed shut as Angela adjusted to the dim. The blinds were drawn and the lighting poor, but she could make out a handful of men in grey suits and dark ties conversing along the back wall.

"Dr. Till!" a man with a velvety voice called from across the room. He was in a pressed three-button suit, his polished black loafers skimming across the glossy hardwood. "It's good to see you, so *very* good to see you," he gushed.

The commotion at the back stopped and the men moved toward the leather chairs surrounding the massive oval table at the centre of the room.

"Please do take a seat," the man with the velvet voice offered to Angela. "And how have you been since we last met?"

Angela rolled her eyes. "Small talk isn't exactly your strong suit."

The man coughed into his fist, the stubble hiding the red darkening his cheeks. "Perhaps not," he said. "My associates tell me I have a mind for business and not much else, I'm afraid. In any event, how long has it been?"

"I wasn't keeping track."

"Well, I was. It's been three months since we originally met. And that makes it almost two years since you suffered through your … your tragedy."

"I didn't come here for your sympathy," Angela hissed.

"Yes, but what a tragic story. I mean, your father dies of cancer before you turn 10 and then your mother—"

"That is none of your business!" Angela snapped. "You're a means to an end, nothing more."

The man pulled at his stiff collar and straightened his knotted tie. "Well, let's get straight to the point then, shall we? Why did you call us here for a second meeting? I assume you have some news to share."

Angela made eye contact with each person around the table. After a moment, she exhaled sharply.

"I initiated the protocol thirty days ago," she said.

The man's eyes widened. "Well then, that *is* positive news. That is positive news indeed! And well ahead of schedule I may add. Tell me, Dr. Till, what have you observed over the past month? What have you seen since you added the—"

"The timeframe is very short," Angela interrupted. "So, I wasn't sure if there would be a noticeable change. But I've completed the testing myself and … it's working. Slowly, but it's working. I predict nine or ten more months should be plenty of time to see the necessary effects."

"Oh, this is exciting! This is very good news indeed!"

He smiled and then motioned toward a lanky gentleman at the back of the room. The man grabbed something at his feet and then hurried toward Angela. He hoisted a thin burgundy briefcase onto the table and quickly retreated to the shadows.

The man with the velvet voice motioned toward the

combination keypad. "The numerical code is as you requested," he said, smiling.

Angela pressed six digits and the latch swung loose. She opened the briefcase and studied the contents for some time.

"You say you didn't come here for sympathy, Dr. Till. But I have found in my line of work, people seem to always come back for *that*," the man said, motioning toward the briefcase.

"It's much more complicated than that, Alan!"

"Alan? Well, that's a shift! It seems we are now on a first name basis!" he said, scanning the smirking faces in the room. "I didn't realize we were growing so close. Careful, Dr. Till. You and I might even become friends when all this is over."

He chuckled but drew quiet as Angela regarded him with a corrosive stare. She pulled at her fingers, the sound reverberating throughout the quiet room as each knuckle cracked.

Alan moved to adjust his lapel but returned his hands to the table, folded in front as if to issue a prayer.

A chill fell over the room.

"Let's get to the crux of it then," Alan said, clearing his throat. "My associates here have spent a great amount of time and resources gathering the contents which are before you. So, I will ask you directly—are you satisfied with our offer? Are you comfortable with the terms and conditions as they have been set out?"

Angela studied him. She snapped the case shut and nodded.

A toothy smile grew across Alan's face. "Terrific! Then everything is in place!"

He shifted in his chair toward a thin Korean man seated across from him. The elderly man adjusted a purple pocket square in his dark suit and stared ahead, stoic. He leaned on a slender walking stick, a gnarled and twisted head of a stag at its collar.

"Mr. Pak?" Alan said. "We move forward on your approval."

A single gold ring at the base of his pinky jostled as Mr. Pak strummed the table. He lowered his head, his lips set, his eyes squeezed shut. He tapped the metal tip of the walking stick, a rhythmic thrum in an otherwise silent room.

"Sir?" Alan said. "Do we move forward? Do we move into phase two?"

Eventually Mr. Pak opened his eyes and nodded.

"Splendid!" Alan said.

He spun in his chair to watch the other men smiling, murmuring excitedly, and shaking hands. He turned back to Angela.

"I do believe I speak for everyone here when I say we are pleased you have reconsidered our offer, Dr. Till," he said. "We are all *very* pleased you have changed your mind."

Chapter Four

March 1995
Day 412 | Dawn

Xavier jerked his rifle open and slid two bullets down the breech. He snapped it shut and checked the scope, his left eye squinting as he focused with his right. It was still dark out, moments before the sun would fight its way over the horizon to begin its daily chase of the moon.

Andrew climbed the steep steps of the cellar and joined his younger brother. Now that they were both out of the dim, Andrew inspected Xavier closely.

Since childhood, Xavier had been the larger of the two. Andrew sprouted lean with an athletic build, levelling off just under six feet. Xavier was broader across the chest and shoulders, climbing four or five inches taller. Even at 20, Xavier commanded a room, his husky size and gruff voice often surprising older adults. Still a young man, his father's co-workers would note, but one built of grit and power.

His weathered skin was coated with dirt and grime and he nervously rubbed along his square jaw. He wore a tattered camouflage jacket with brown cargo pants, the pockets bulging with matches, tape, and bullets.

Normally calm and measured, his eyes seemed to tremble under thick brows, continuously scanning and squinting.

Exhaling nervously, he was a knotted ball of tension. Xavier was not easily frightened and Andrew shuddered at the thought of what might have caused such a sharp change in his brother's demeanour.

Xavier turned toward the cellar. "Secure that bolt," he instructed.

Andrew fumbled with the heavy rod and slid it across the cellar door until it clicked. He slipped a camouflage jacket over his T-shirt and adjusted the bowie knife along his belt, items sequestered by Xavier from the mudroom days earlier. Andrew held a pouch of ammunition in one hand, a pair of binoculars around his neck. A cord of rope and water bottle were shoved deep into his pocket. He rubbed his hands together for warmth, shivering from the crisp morning air, then slung a rifle across his back, the leather strap resting along his spine. Xavier nodded and they began a brisk trot, moving past the farm fields and through the brush to the bleak, dense forest a few acres beyond their farmhouse. They traversed deeper into the bush and eventually arrived at the water. They waded through the shallow creek, the one which emptied into the river several kilometres away.

The cold water against his skin caused Andrew to recall when he and Xavier were teenagers. They would portage to the river's mouth in early spring, swollen after a heavy rainfall, and paddle the whitewater until their shoulders ached. Jeremiah would usually join them, his copper eyes wide with excitement, cackling and crowing as they cascaded off the rocks, threatening to tip them over.

Sometimes, when they had reached an eddy, Jeremiah would giddily jump into the shallows and put all his weight on the gunwales, the canoe pitching and rolling and filling with water. Andrew and Xavier yelled for him to stop, trying desperately to steady the sinking boat. But despite the immediate panic, they would always end up laughing, splashing each other until they were soaked through their clothes.

Until that last time, when something shifted in Xavier.

Andrew had dipped the paddle into the current and brought the cold liquid up over Xavier's shaggy hair and all at once he became enraged. He advanced so quickly, like a lynx over rocks, that for the first time Andrew was frightened of him.

That summer had been kind to Xavier, his body filling out with muscle and strength, another inch or two added to his already commanding height. Xavier had grabbed the bow of the canoe and lifted it clean out of the water, flinging it toward the shore, Andrew tumbling into the rapids.

Rattled, Andrew scrambled toward the embankment, clawing at the tangle of bulrushes lining the edge. Finally securing purchase on the slippery surface, he propelled himself out of the water. He turned to face his brother, river water dripping off his toque and ripped shirt.

"What the hell was that for?" he yelped.

"Sure, you're all school smart, straight A's in high school," Xavier growled, dwarfing his brother. "But out here? You'd be dead in an hour."

Andrew knew the statement wasn't true—he and Xavier had the same teacher when it came to wilderness survival—but he dared not challenge him. Because in that moment, he suddenly saw Xavier differently than he once had. Different even from when they had left the house earlier that morning, excitedly gripping their paddles, the squeaky mudroom door slamming shut behind them.

Now, in the forest, they quietly pulled themselves from the shallow creek. Xavier turned to Andrew. "I still have no idea what's going on," he said, adjusting the rifle strap along his back. "No idea where Mom is, no idea where Joe is. Hell, you coming into the cellar last night was the first time in weeks I've seen someone who didn't want to kill me!" His voice was deep and low, a grating sound, like sandpaper scraping along knotted wood.

"They definitely weren't in the house last night when I went through it," Andrew said. "You've got no clue where they could be?"

Xavier shook his head. "I've looked. Every day I look, but still no sign of 'em."

He nervously picked at his thick head of hair and Andrew noticed how oily it was, his beard coarse and patchy. Andrew rubbed his own cheek, his skin smooth and shaven clean mere hours before his flight.

They fell into silence, trekking through the yellowed lifeless brush, their eyes and ears alert.

"It all started to happen last fall," Xavier said finally. "About three months after you left for school."

"What happened?"

"That's what I don't know. I'm still trying to piece it together."

"Piece *what* together?" Andrew asked.

Xavier drew out a slow breath. "I guess it … well, something started last November. One night Dad and I made dinner for Mom's birthday. And around that same time I had this pull to be in the woods, like I needed the forest to heal something in me. So, I went hunting. Was probably in the bush for just under a week."

"You went without Joe?"

"I needed to be alone. When you left in September … well, it was a bit awkward around the house after that. I mean, *how* you left made it awkward. I just needed to get away to clear my head, to sort through it all."

Xavier coughed into his hand, a dry hoarse noise. He glanced toward his brother but Andrew kept his gaze low.

"Anyhow, sometime after I got back, James Bird came by the house," Xavier continued. "But he seemed off. There was something different about him."

Xavier slowed, the dry snap of branches underfoot. He squinted at the shafts of light straining through the line of poplars and pines. He adjusted the belt securing his cargo pants, his jacket hugging his muscular torso, his wide shoulders stretching the garment.

"He had this odd scent," Xavier continued. "Like burning aluminum. It was like you could smell the metal coming off him, right there as he sat on the couch."

"Like the smell of shop class in high school?"

"Kind of. But much stronger. Potent. And he was moody too. You remember him from high school, right?"

"Of course! He was one of the happiest-go-lucky kids around."

"Yes, exactly. Well, during this last visit something was wrong with him."

"How so?"

"It was like he didn't know how he got to our house or what he was doing there. I mean, he was polite enough to Mom and Dad but as he was leaving, he began checking out Mom, looking her up and down with this weird look on his face."

"Like he was into her?"

"At first, I thought it might have been like that. But the way his eyes were, they seemed vacant, like he wasn't really looking at anything at all, just staring at nothing. And his breathing was strange, it was this weird heavy rasp—"

A hawk squealed overhead and Xavier's hand moved to his rifle. Incredibly nimble, and yet he never seemed to be in a rush about it. This was the paradox Andrew grew up with. Xavier was always the quicker shot, the more accurate of the two. Shooting was an instinctive movement for him, like buttoning a shirt each morning. While Andrew needed constant practice, Xavier's reflexes were as natural and quick as lightning.

Eventually, Xavier lowered the rifle. "It wasn't only James though," he continued. "Over the next several weeks, other friends came to the house acting strange. And they always looked different."

"Different how?"

"David Morreau got boils all down his neck and started to speak with a slur. Julian Smoke started to walk with a limp, like both his kneecaps were swollen or broken or something."

Xavier drew quiet and knelt to examine some droppings, faint paw prints surrounding the mushy pile. He bent low, smelled the scat, and turned away.

"These are fresh. Keep your wits about you. We're close to a den, I'd imagine."

Andrew nodded. The sun had been in the sky for about an hour, casting long shadows on the forest floor. Despite the early hour and chill in the air, a line of sweat trickled down the front of Andrew's shirt, staining the fabric.

"Then what happened?" he asked.

Xavier cleared his throat, picking up the story again. "So,

then one day, I think it was January by this time, Mom's friend Meredith comes over. She was mumbling and confused, saying she needed to borrow some sugar."

"Really? Our houses are almost a hundred acres apart. She walked all that way for sugar?"

Xavier shrugged. "Anyway, as Meredith's standing in the doorway, just out of the blue, she lunges at Joe. I mean, fully bares her teeth and just goes at him."

"That's crazy! What happened after that?"

"Joe pushes her from the house, yells at her to go home. She left and it was quiet the rest of the night. Nothing else happened. But by the next morning, well, that's when things really started to get strange—"

Xavier dropped to a squat and raised a fist. Andrew swung the rifle off his shoulder, drew back the hammer, and brought the scope to his eye.

He knew Xavier's movements well. Something was out there.

Xavier peered into the dense underbrush, his mouth set. His fist unfurled, signalling they were close.

"Animal?" Andrew whispered. He lowered to one knee, his rifle pointed the same direction as Xavier's steely gaze. "Or human?"

A russet blur flashed through the foliage. Andrew trained his rifle on the shape and waited for Xavier's voice. The form rapidly made its way through the ground cover, Andrew's finger caressing the trigger.

Waiting.

Waiting.

"Animal!" Xavier shouted.

Andrew fired two quick shots, his shoulder absorbing the

energy from each charge. The shadow stumbled and then fell, a painful yelp cracking through the trees. Xavier stood and sprinted, drawing his blade from his belt. From his knee, Andrew yanked the rifle open and loaded two more bullets. He stumbled to his feet and began running, following the path of swaying branches.

"That school's making you slow," Xavier scoffed when Andrew finally caught up.

Andrew placed his palms on his knees, taking in great gulps of air. "I suppose. Unfortunately, there's not much time to hunt stray cats between classes," he chuckled.

"Goddamn classes at your goddamn fancy school," Xavier muttered under his breath.

"What was that?"

Xavier rolled his eyes. "Nothin'. Just pass me some rope, will ya?"

Andrew uncoiled the cord of rope from his cargo pants and tossed it to the ground. "What'd we get? A weasel?"

Xavier removed the blade from the animal's throat and began tying its legs together. "It's a fisher but you could never tell them apart, could you?"

"Fisher, weasel, marten. They're all the same thing, aren't they?"

Xavier grunted and hoisted the animal across his back, the twine tied tight around its paws. "At least you've still got your shot," he muttered. He glanced at the rifle still clenched at Andrew's side. "It's a good thing too. You'll need it with what's going on around here."

Chapter Five

March 1995
Day 412 | Dusk

Xavier cooked the fisher among the coals of a fire. After carving the animal into thin strips, he carefully turned them above the embers before he and Andrew returned to the cellar. When they arrived, he meticulously folded and placed each meat strip in a waxy cloth.

From the glow of the flashlight propped in the corner, Andrew could see racks lined with Mason jars. A few contained red peppers soaking in vinegar. Some had pickles with cloves of garlic bobbing in the brine. There were tins of black beans, peach slices, tomato sauce, and mashed peas. A near-empty jug of water sat on the bottom rack, sediment floating within the murky liquid.

Andrew sat atop a stool, knife marks carved into the stubby wooden legs. "How long have you been down here?" he asked.

"Two weeks. Maybe longer."

Andrew leaned forward, his forearms resting on the length of his thighs. He raised his eyebrows. "X, I've been gone for seven months. You've got to fill me in better than this! I mean, where is Mom and Joe? Why are all our friends acting crazy? You have to know a bit more about what the hell is going on here."

Xavier slowly raised his head. "For the first few days I was down here, I still went out every morning," he said. "I wanted to figure out what was going on. So, I stuck to the backroads, close to the tree-line, going through several of the neighbour's houses."

"For what?"

"Supplies."

"Find anything?"

"Most were empty. But I grabbed any food I came across." He waved his arm toward the back of the cellar, empty tins of beans and peaches piled sloppily in the corner.

"Some of the sheds had ammo in them," he continued. "A few had rope, batteries, blankets; stuff like that. I brought it all down here as I didn't know how long I'd be hiding."

"Hiding from what?"

Xavier pressed his lips together and shrugged. "I don't know," he muttered. "They're just … they're …"

His words faded and he stood still, staring into the dark for some time. Eventually, he reached for a large stone along the cellar floor and began whetting his knife, the scratch of rock grating along the steel. Gliding a finger down each side of the metal, he tested it, the blade now sharp and true. He began to pick at the hardened dead skin along the heel of his hand, pulling back when the tip went too deep.

Andrew moved closer to him. "Look, now that we have a bit of food, we need to go search for Mom and Joe."

"I'm always looking for them," Xavier said. "For any little sign of them, anything at all."

"Okay, but there are two of us now. So, we can cover more ground, be more precise about where we search, follow some sort of strategy."

"*Strategy?* You've been at the books too long. The only *strategy* out here is to just survive."

"But they can't be far, can they? If we start searching in a grid pattern first thing tomorrow, we should be able to—"

"Able to what, huh?" Xavier boomed. "You've been home one day and already you're gonna tell me how to do this? You don't know what's out there. You haven't seen those things! You've got no idea what's waiting on the other side of that door!"

"X, listen to me," Andrew pleaded. "If we can just think through this and make a plan—"

But Xavier turned away and went quiet, as if something dark wormed its way inside him, holding his secrets in.

Andrew shook his head. "It's crazy, man, everything you've told me," he said, after a while. "This whole thing sounds crazy."

Xavier let out a weighty sigh. "You can hear them, you know? Even from down here," he said. "The howling … the screaming. The noise travels across the fields. They're horrible sounds. Like someone being tortured."

"Who? Who's screaming? Who's being tortured?"

"I don't know. They're people, but … not."

"X, whatever's going on here, is it happening in other places? In other towns?"

"No idea."

Andrew jumped up. "None of this makes any sense!" he said. "I mean I was just on a flight yesterday and everything was normal. No one was talking about people turning sick, people acting strange, people acting all crazy! This girl I met on the plane—Juliana—she didn't know anything about this! Even the cab driver hardly knew anything, just bits and pieces he picked up from the radio."

Andrew shuddered at an uneasy thought. "Whatever's going on here, I just don't think anyone else knows about it. And if no one else knows about it …"

He drew quiet, several startling scenarios playing out in his head. "But X, when all this started, why didn't you just phone the cops?" he asked.

"When people started acting weird, I don't know, I just thought they were sick or something," Xavier reasoned. "People get sick all the time, do weird things all the time. I suppose I just thought it would pass."

"But not like how you're describing them—James, David, Mom's friend, Meredith—this sounds like more than a sickness. This sounds like people going insane!"

"I just never saw it getting this bad. And by the time I thought to call the cops, those people, those things, whatever they are—they took out the town's power, including the phone lines."

"Are you serious?"

"Yeah, nothing works. Ours and all the other houses I checked. The whole town's gone dark. I couldn't phone the cops. I couldn't phone anyone."

"Then why not take your truck? Hell, we could do it right now. Get out to the highway, drive out of here and find help."

"I tried that too. But by that time, things had really gotten out of control. Mobs of those crazy people were blocking the main road. They even barricaded the grocery store and co-op. There had to be hundreds. They had bats and spike strips and blockades up."

"Yeah, I remember seeing commotion on the road when I ran from the taxi. I ducked into the trees and continued through the bush, not sure what was going on."

"And those people—they were not in a good state."

"What do you mean?"

"I mean something was really wrong with them. Some had lost their hair—just these tufts of patches growing out of their head and neck. Others had all this loose skin dangling from their face, like their bones had shrunk or something."

"What the hell?"

"Yeah, and most of them were pasty and thin, like cadavers. And some had these long, sharp fingernails. All of them just looked sick, like not right at all."

"What'd you do?"

"When they approached my pickup, I panicked. I turned right around and came back to the house. But it was a stupid move."

"Why?"

"They must have followed me because later that night I heard them tearing the truck up, smashing all the windows, pulling the engine apart. I could hear them shrieking and nattering most of the night."

Andrew nodded, remembering seeing Xavier's truck smashed and turned over in the driveway when he had first arrived at the farmhouse. "So, what'd you do after that?"

"Came down here to the cellar. Figured I was way too exposed in the house. At least down here, I'm a bit safer. Or at least it feels that way. No one really knows about it."

"Okay, so your truck isn't an option. How about one of the neighbours?"

"I've looked for one that's not smashed or had the gas drained out of it. No luck yet."

"Okay, well, we'll just keep looking. Drive right out of here when we find one. Or we just hack our way through the bush to another town."

"You know how remote it is up here. We'd have to spend several nights in those woods just to get close to another town."

"We've done it before."

"Not with those things around. And what if it's worse in another town?"

"Worse than this?"

"We got no idea what's going on outside of Barn Wood. And besides, what if Mom and Joe come back? We need to stay here."

Andrew bit his lip and nodded, sitting down atop the stool again.

Xavier drew in a hasty breath. "You know, every so often you can see smoke rising from the middle of town."

"They're starting fires?"

"God knows what they're burning over there. Could be Vern's Hardware, maybe the feed store. I just don't want to be the one to find out."

"Jesus. This whole thing is crazy."

"Yeah, and listen, based on what I saw that night—when all those crazy people were blocking the main road—well, it got me thinking: maybe someone's behind this. And if so, they definitely don't want anyone to leave."

Andrew's neck jerked back as a scratch travelled along the wooden cellar door above his head. Reaching to his belt, he unsheathed his knife and held his breath. His heart thudded beneath his damp shirt, a chill surging up his spine. He crouched low, his eyes flicking around the small space.

Xavier already had his rifle in hand, shimmying toward the flashlight. He clicked it off just as a second scratch clawed at the plywood.

Andrew's thighs burned as he squatted, straining to hear any noises beyond the sound of chittering insects. After some time, he relaxed.

"What do you think that was?" he said.

Xavier raised a finger to his lips.

"But do you think it's one of them?" Andrew asked, his voice lowered.

"We're done talking," Xavier said.

He crawled past Andrew to the rear of the cellar and gathered a blanket to lie on, leaning his rifle against the concrete wall. "Whatever it was, it's gone now," he said. "Just keep your wits about you in case it comes back."

Andrew stood and stretched his legs, the blood coursing back through his thighs. He searched the cellar for a second blanket and laid down in the opposite corner. He adjusted his pants, sliding the long hunting knife from his belt and resting it beside his head. Every few minutes he reached out to feel for the leather case, his fingers confirming the blade was close.

He laid in the dark until he heard the raspy rise and fall of Xavier's chest—the scratchy inhale, the grating exhale—the sound still familiar from when they shared a room as children. He rolled away from the noise and stared up at the cellar door, beads of sweat cooling along his brow. He shifted his tired body, his shoulder cold against the cement floor.

He closed his eyes and eventually fell into a fitful sleep, his mind returning to yesterday morning and his flight home. He dreamt of the early morning take-off, the red-haired girl who smelled of lavender, and of the plane that fell from the sky.

Chapter Six

March 1995
Day 411 | Morning

Andrew's fingernails pierced the fabric of the armrest, the flesh beneath white from pressure. He twisted toward the oval window but drew back when a spear of lightning cracked, the rain lashing against the Plexiglas.

"Please return to your seats and fasten your seat belts. We are experiencing active weather," the captain bellowed over the loudspeaker.

Andrew's head jerked forward and he immediately tasted blood. He saw a flash of orange as a flight attendant fell to the floor.

"Take your seats immediately! The pressurization system is malfunctioning and—"

All at once the lights flickered out. Screaming erupted throughout the twin-engine airliner.

A loud hiss sounded above Andrew's head. He turned and saw tubes and what looked like suction cups drop from the ceiling, bouncing with the movement of the plane. He snatched the tube closest to him and pulled the strap over his hair, the silicone cup over his mouth. He breathed deeply—once and then again.

The quiet woman seated beside him whipped around to

face him. Her eyes were wide, her lips white and pressed together. She opened her mouth to speak but there was no sound and she lurched forward, wrapping her arms around her chest.

Andrew pushed her against the seat-back. He fumbled for the apparatus above and jammed the mouthpiece over her lips. "You have to breathe!"

Taut lines stretched across the woman's brow, curving toward her frightened green eyes. She began to twitch as Andrew slid the strap over her dense auburn hair.

"Listen to me! Take a deep breath!"

She nodded and breathed but her eyes glassed over and she began to convulse.

Andrew held the mask to his ear but heard nothing. He smacked the side of it and then noticed the tangle of knots above the woman's head. Springing up, he pulled at the jumbled mess but a shock of turbulence jolted the plane forward and he crashed into the seats in front of him.

After a few moments, his eyes shuddered open and he found himself in the aisle. He wiped the sweat from his forehead and reached for the armrest. From the faint glow of the illuminated floor strips, he saw the woman crumpled beneath the window.

"Dammit," he shouted. He lunged forward and grabbed her, hoisting her into the seat.

He clutched at the tubes again, tugging them into straight lines until he heard the stream of oxygen. His muscles tensed along his arms as he clenched the hard-plastic mouthpiece. He swiped the woman's red mane from her face and noticed her pupils had rolled back, a thin line of drool climbing down her chin.

He slapped the mask over her mouth and yelled into her ear. "Breathe! You need to breathe!"

He listened for a response but had trouble hearing beyond the noise around him. A young family huddled together on the carpeted floor, the mother praying loudly as the father brushed tousled bangs from his son's moist eyes. An elderly lady stood in the aisle shrieking. Others remained in their seats, wide-eyed, sucking uselessly at the cabin air.

In front of Andrew, the woman's hand fluttered and he straightened the mask over her pallid lips. He moved his hand along her cheek feeling for any movement and brought his face very close to hers. "You need to breathe now, okay?"

The woman's throat wheezed and Andrew felt her jaw tighten. Then all at once, she wrenched forward, clawing at the mask. She pressed it tight to her pale face and breathed. In and out. In and out.

After several seconds, her shoulders dropped and her breathing slowed. Her eyes met his and Andrew nodded encouragement. "That's good," he whispered. "Just keep breathing."

The plane levelled off and one by one the lighting above each row flicked on.

"We're fine!" the co-captain shouted, bursting through the small hatch at the front of the plane. He had a thick French accent and a toothy smile. "The captain has righted the plane. No more turbulence!"

Passengers rose from their knees and shuffled up the aisle to return to their seats. Quiet murmurs quickly grew into excited jawing.

The woman's lips quivered as she glanced at Andrew's hands still grasped around her own. Following her gaze, he slid them off her manicured fingers.

She turned and smiled nervously. "Would you excuse me for a minute?"

Andrew moved into the aisle to let her pass. He stretched his lean frame, adjusting his dark cargo pants, damp circles beneath his arms. His veins pulsed along his forearms, the lean muscle braided and taut.

"Pardon me," the woman said moments later, returning from the lavatory. She moved passed him and Andrew caught a whiff of lavender as her hair brushed up against his chin. He noticed how her jeans hugged her body as she took her seat.

She remained quiet, studying her lap, and then abruptly turned to Andrew. "I'm not sure what just happened but I feel I owe you a huge thank you." The words tumbled out quick and hectic, her voice infused with a faint Irish drawl.

Andrew smiled, the lids of his eyes drooping as if peeping out from under a window shade. "I'm not sure what happened either. I'm just glad this plane is flying forward and not down!"

"Isn't that the truth!" The woman adjusted her V-neck blouse, peach-coloured lines running down the front. "That was very intense!"

She looked away but after a quiet moment turned back. "What's your name?"

"Andrew." He reached across his body and she shook his hand, holding it in hers for a few seconds. "Andrew Stone."

"It's nice to meet you, Andrew. I must say, it seems odd shaking your hand after you just saved my life. I should be issuing you a cash reward or at least buying you dinner."

"It's quite all right," Andrew chuckled. "You would have done the same for me."

"I most certainly *would not* have done the same for you! I was terrified!"

"Well, it's definitely an interesting way to meet someone, that's for sure."

"If our positions were reversed, I would have kept right on clutching on to that mask and let you roll around in the aisle!"

"I hope not! But I think you'd help me."

"Ha! Well, you obviously don't know me at all!"

"When people are in scary situations it's impressive what they're capable of. The mind seems to have a way of calming itself and figuring out what to do."

"*Your* mind may work that way. *My* mind would be a mess! I would sit here and scream until someone came and knocked me out. Which, thinking about it, would probably be the best for everyone."

Andrew laughed and the woman smiled. She ran her finger along her neck and adjusted the silver pendant hanging just below her collarbone.

"What's yours?" Andrew asked. "Your name, I mean."

"Juliana."

"Juliana." Andrew pronounced the name slowly, rolling each letter around in his mouth. "It's nice to meet you, Juliana."

"Oh, yes, I'm sure I gave a great first impression. I was drooling the whole time and was a sweaty mess. I just needed to pee myself to make the entire introduction a complete disaster!"

Andrew smiled. He unscrewed the bottle of water tucked into the back-seat pocket just as Juliana's arm shot up, waving the flight attendant over.

"Let's replace that water with booze! That's what we need to calm the nerves," she said. "Wine, and lots of it!"

The flight attendant was making her way down the aisle, comforting passengers as she adjusted their seats and handed out blankets. She reached Juliana's seat and leaned forward.

"How can I help, ma'am?"

"I would like a *very* tall glass of your best white wine. And bring this fine gentleman whatever he likes. It's on me."

"I'm afraid we're not serving alcohol at this time," the flight attendant said. "Can I offer you water or juice instead?"

Juliana recoiled. "What? After what we just went through? Believe me, you need to get some alcohol flowing in here. You've got a plane full of people who just had their lives pass before their eyes. A lot of us are on edge."

The flight attendant pressed her lips together. "I'll see what I can do," she said coldly, and continued making her way down the aisle, pausing at each row.

Andrew turned to Juliana. "I suppose water it is then." He tilted the plastic bottle and took a deep gulp, the ice-cold liquid rushing down his dry throat.

"I guess so," Juliana conceded. "But if ever two people earned a drink, it was you and I and what we just went through. That was some crazy stuff! Have you ever been that scared before?"

"No way, not like that. I got lost in the woods once when I was young, but it was far less exciting than a plane dropping out of the sky."

"Lost in the woods? *That* sounds pretty scary!"

"I suppose. But my entire life didn't flash before my eyes."

Juliana shifted in her seat, tucking her foot under the other leg. She leaned forward. "Still, why don't you tell me about it? We've got nearly an hour before we land. Who knows, it might calm us after the crazy nonsense we just went through." Her laugh was loud and generous and Andrew immediately loved the sound.

"Pardon me," the flight attendant interrupted. "I checked with my supervisor and she said alcohol service may actually be a good idea at this point." She winked and handed Juliana a tall plastic glass of white wine.

"I definitely agree with your supervisor!" Juliana said. "There's nothing like a stiff drink after an ordeal like that." She closed her eyes and took a gulp of the cool beverage.

"And what can I get for you, sir?" the flight attendant asked.

"I'm good with water, thanks," Andrew said.

"You sure?" Juliana piped in. "If you don't get anything I'll end up drinking for the two of us."

Andrew smiled. "I'm good, thanks."

The flight attendant nodded and proceeded down the aisle.

"So, where are you coming from?" Juliana asked.

"I just finished my third year of university."

"You're still in university? Oh, my, you look older, I just assumed—"

"Yeah, heading into my final year in the fall. I'll be in the graduating class of 1996, if all goes well."

"Oh, well you're a few years younger than me, I'm afraid."

Andrew laughed and he held Juliana's gaze.

"So, what are you taking there? At university?" she asked.

"I'm interested in natural sciences, experimental sciences, that sort of thing. I'll be graduating with a degree in Epidemiology."

"Sorry, epi - what?"

Andrew chuckled. "I know, it's a mouthful. It's basically the study of diseases: how they occur and how they spread."

"And how they're cured?"

"Not really, funny enough. It's mostly the study of the *how* and the *why* of diseases. Maybe curing diseases is covered in fourth year!"

"Sounds interesting. And how did you like living overseas? Were you in a big city?"

"Yeah, and I have to admit, the city was really confusing at first. I'm from a small town—kind of a mix of rural farms with a tiny downtown square. I think we only have a few thousand people to be honest. Basically, my whole town could fit on the university campus!"

"There's nothing wrong with small towns. I quite prefer them over cities, to tell you the truth."

"Well, our town *did* just get a new community centre. We're all very proud of it."

"Sounds lovely."

"It makes sense for farming or hunting but totally sucked when we were younger and my mom sent my brother and I to a neighbour's house just to borrow an egg. We'd be gone for an hour just so my mom could finish her baking!"

Juliana chuckled. "What's it called?"

"Barn Wood—the *mighty town* of Barn Wood."

"Never heard of it."

"Like I said, it's pretty small and remote, off the beaten track. It's one of those towns you arrive at only if you're *really* lost."

"How long have you lived there?"

"My whole life, more or less. My father left just after I was born so it was just my mom and I for the first year or so. Or so she tells me."

"Oh, my, that sounds awful!"

"It was a long time ago and of course I was too young to remember any of it. She ended up meeting my stepfather, this guy named Joe. Pretty soon after they married and had my brother, or half-brother, I suppose. The four of us have been at the same farmhouse ever since."

Andrew took a long pull from his water bottle. "So, what do you do?"

"Oh, my story is pretty boring. I passed the bar about two years ago."

"A lawyer? Wow, that's impressive! What type of law do you practice?"

"The firm I used to work for focused on patents and copyrights, primarily with drug and pharmaceutical companies."

"Used to work for? You left?"

"Yes. It was complicated but some of the partners dabbled in … well, let's just say they were involved in a few shady dealings. After a while, I stopped trying to convince myself that it was fine and admit that what I was being asked to do was straight up illegal!"

"Geez. Sounds serious."

"Yeah, I definitely had second thoughts around the morality of what I was seeing. So, I left the firm soon after that and now I'm just trying to figure out my next move."

"If you're turned off that type of law, couldn't you work your way into something else like social law? Or you could become a human rights lawyer, or something like that?"

"I guess so. I'm not sure right now. To complicate things even further, my fiancé and I broke up a few months ago so

I'm taking some time to figure things out."

"Oh, I'm sorry to hear that."

Juliana waved his words away. "Don't be. I've had time to process it. It's probably for the best," she said. "I mean, it's definitely for the best. These things happen for a reason, right?"

She took a sip of wine and shifted in her seat. Her gaze caught the eye of the flight attendant and she emphatically waved her over. "Can I get a top up, please?"

The flight attendant nodded and refreshed Juliana's glass.

Juliana leaned closer to Andrew. "Now, tell me about that time you got lost in the woods."

"It's actually not that exciting."

"Shush, don't be silly. We just nearly plummeted out of the sky! If that happens again, you may be the last person I get to talk to. So, I at least want to know a bit more about you." She grinned and took a gulp of wine; her cheeks flushed, now the colour of roses.

"Well, it was my twelfth birthday," Andrew began. "I remember because the noise of my stepfather cooking breakfast woke me. I was excited that he was home because each June he went away for a month and always returned just in time for my birthday."

"Wait, he would leave for *a month*? Where on earth did he go?"

"Actually, I never knew where he went. Even to this day, I'm not entirely sure. Just one morning each June he was gone. His hunting rifle would be gone, his knife, his sleeping bag—"

"So, he went hunting?" Juliana interrupted.

"I guess. But a month in the woods is quite a long time, even for an experienced hunter. I always felt he must have gone somewhere else."

"And you never knew? Did your mother ever tell you?"

"I would ask her when I was younger but she would just become quiet. My brother and I just sort of accepted that every year he disappeared for a while. We just got used to it, I suppose."

"That sounds a little strange to me."

"It just became normal to us. I mean, I know he was hunting for at least *some* of the time because when he came back his truck would be full of game."

"And you guys would eat it?"

"Of course, we'd eat it! He brought all sorts of different meats home—deer, rabbit, pheasant."

"Oh, I don't know about all that. I just get regular meat from the grocery store!"

"Nah, it was good stuff. And Joe had an incredible shot, he was a gifted hunter. The tracking, the patience, the timing. He said hunting was in his blood, passed down from his father to him."

"Sounds like it was his passion."

"For sure. He loved being in nature, living amongst the trees. It made him so happy; you could see it on his face every time we went out. So, it wasn't unusual for him to disappear a few weeks at a time. And every June when he returned, he would have these beautiful homemade gifts for Xavier and me."

"Xavier's your brother?"

"Yes, half-brother. Sorry, didn't I mention him earlier?"

"I'm just trying to keep up with the story."

Andrew laughed. "So, anyways, Joe would bring these bright yellow and red rope necklaces and bracelets home with him. Sometimes they had our initials sewn into them or an outline of a bear or eagle or something. My mom would wear them above her ankle. But it was actually because of those bracelets that Xavier and I thought Joe was staying at someone else's house, at least for some of the time."

Juliana raised her eyebrows. "An affair?"

"We never thought that. But his clothes always smelled like laundry detergent when he came home. Believe me, if you've been out hunting for a month, you don't come home smelling lemon fresh!"

Juliana chuckled. She adjusted her blouse then fingered the ends of her hair.

"Sorry, I'm getting lost in telling the story," Andrew said. "Too many tangents."

"I don't mind. I like listening to you."

Andrew smiled, hesitating for just a moment. "So, I wake up on my birthday and Joe's in the kitchen frying eggs. And as we're eating, he tells me that turning 12 is different from *all* other birthdays."

"How so?"

"He makes up this thing that turning 12 is when a boy starts becoming a man and with that, comes more responsibility. At the time, I didn't think too much of it. But Xavier did. He never let me forget it because the rest of the day he kept saying things like: *You should climb that tree to the top—you're a man now, so you should be able to.* Or *I dare you to track those prints to see where they lead. You're a man now, so you should be able to.* Crap like that went on for most of the day."

"He sounds like a pest!" Juliana said playfully.

Andrew smirked and nodded. "Like I said, this went on for the entire afternoon. And without much notice, he and I got deeper into the woods as his dares became more elaborate."

"How long were you out there?"

"Well, our hunger should have brought us back to the house. But even at that young age we were used to ignoring it. By that point, we had already been out with Joe on several hunts and you have to learn to sometimes go a full day without eating."

Andrew raised the bottle and took a sip. "So, the night was starting to close in," he continued. "We had gotten turned around and couldn't make out which direction was home. I remember X found an outcropping of rock along a ridge and he made us take cover there. I wanted to keep walking but the light was nearly gone. It turned out to be a wise move. I mean, had we kept walking we would have been more exposed to coyotes."

"Coyotes? Oh, my. It sounds like your brother was a clever kid, after all."

"He's about a year and a half younger than me but even back then, he was still smarter in the woods than I was. He just had a feel for it, a natural instinct about him that I didn't."

"You don't think you would have made it back if you had kept walking?"

"Dark is different in a forest. In a city, you have streetlights, porch lights, things like that. In the forest, there's nothing. It's just pure black."

Juliana nodded, her eyes now wide with anticipation.

"So, we're both pretty scared at this point. I mean, we've been in the woods before but it was always with Joe. So, we huddle together in a cave. The coyotes begin their yelping.

And for a long time, we just lay awake, listening, not daring to move."

"Ahh! That sounds so scary!"

"Yeah, we were really scared, to tell you the truth. But one thing that happened was Xavier began humming the song *Happy Birthday*. I mean, we're two frightened kids lost in the woods and he still remembers it's my birthday."

"That's so sweet."

"We've had our differences since then, don't really get along anymore. But that moment still stands out to me."

Juliana shifted in her seat, touching her knee to Andrew's.

"Daybreak finally arrives and we get up and retrace our steps from the previous day," Andrew continued. "Then, we hear someone calling our names. We follow the sound and we run into my best friend, Jeremiah."

"How in the world did he find you?"

"We learned later that he and his father were out searching for us all night. Joe had called them to help. I guess when we didn't return for dinner, Joe figured something had happened."

"Oh, my. Good thing they found you."

"I remember Jeremiah was so proud for finding us that he ran ahead to tell his dad. We followed him out and as he's running over a stump he trips and falls and splits his lip open."

Juliana gasped. "That sounds awful!"

"He's just wailing, tears and blood flowing down his face. After a minute, we run into his father and the rest of the search party and everyone is panicked by all the blood but also excited to see us. It was a chaotic scene."

"Sounds like it."

Andrew nodded and pressed his lips together. He glanced

down at his lap and then back at Juliana.

"Wait, is that it?" she asked. "Is that the end?"

"That's it." Andrew swirled the remaining liquid at the bottom of his water bottle and drank down the last of it.

"What are you talking about? That can't be it? You can't end the story there! What happened to you and your brother?"

"Well, Xavier and I got in big trouble for wandering off. Joe and our mom were overjoyed to find us, of course, but we were still grounded for a month."

"And what about your friend, Jeremiah? What happened to him?"

"His dad took him to the hospital. He ended up being fine, but even to this day, he has a thick scar along his lower lip."

"Well, *that* is a good story. The ending needs work though," Juliana teased. "Still, I'm very glad I made you tell it."

"I don't tell that one much. It makes me sound like a wuss."

"Are you kidding? You don't sound like a wuss at all! It all sounded very exciting."

Suddenly, the co-captain came through the hatch at the front of the plane. "The speakers are still malfunctioning but the captain wishes for you to return to your seats. We will be making our descent momentarily and landing in approximately five minutes."

Juliana folded the tray table into the seat-back in front of her. She squeezed her eyes shut and gripped the armrest as the wheels moaned and jostled into their landing position. The plane hit the tarmac and soon came to an abrupt stop.

She uncurled her fingers and reached for her carry-on, then turned and smiled at Andrew.

"Listen, maybe you could tell me another story sometime?"

"Sure, that'd be great. It was really nice meeting you."

"Even though we almost died together?"

"Ha! Well, besides that part. But maybe we could grab a coffee sometime?"

Juliana smiled and slid a folded piece of paper into Andrew's hand. "That'd be nice," she whispered.

And then she shimmied past him and down the aisle, disappearing off the plane, a hint of lavender left in her wake.

Chapter Seven

March 1995
Day 413 | Dawn

Andrew climbed the wooden stairs and stepped into the smokey light. The hour was early—the hazy intermission between the moon and sun—and Andrew squinted nervously into the bluffs of poplar and shadowed pines stacked tight beyond the fields. He shuddered from the crisp morning air and gazed out upon a dusting of late-season snow. The wind had picked up from the night before and he watched as murky clouds and side-swept flurries skidded across the grey sky. Xavier joined him, slid his rifle over his shoulder, and reached back to secure the bolt on the cellar door.

They peered out upon the serrated line of tree and sky then moved quickly through the frosted grass toward the saplings, kicking up snow and twigs as they ran. Young stands created a jagged border around the shallow canopy of white birch and ash. Slowing to a trot, they leapt over felled trees, arriving a few minutes later amongst the dense hemlock and maples, buried deep within the thrall of bush and ferns. They stood silent, waiting for the sun to bleed out the darkness from in-between the trees.

Xavier moved to speak but stopped, something in the distance holding his attention. After a moment, he released a heavy sigh. "I told you about some of our friends and how they started acting strange," he began in a husky rumble. "Well, weird stuff like that kept happening."

"Like what?"

Xavier resumed his walk, his heavy boots crunching over the dulled mosses and deadwood along the forest floor.

"More and more people started to change," he said. "Both physically and mentally, something wrong in their heads. At the time, all we saw were a few neighbours acting weird and getting sick. That's all we knew."

His voice was jarring, a quick gravelly sound, the words coming out in punches. "Joe still went to the shop each morning. Mom did her nursing at the clinic. But then she came home late one night in February and everything changed—" Xavier stopped and cocked his head. He slid the rifle off his frame and dangled it loosely at his side. Andrew tightened the grip on his own. He glanced skyward at a line of hemlocks, much of the light blocked by the spidery branches.

"What is it?" he asked.

Xavier examined the peeling strips of bark as biting midges buzzed around his head.

"A little early in the year for these guys to be out," he mumbled, swatting at the insects.

He cautiously rolled the toe of his boot along the snow, followed by the crunch of his heel. The noise stirred something in the bush.

A flash shot through the shrubs and he raised his rifle with a smooth, languid motion. He fired twice between a dense stand of trees.

"Animal or human?" Andrew asked.

"Let's hope the former," Xavier said. He pulled the blade

from his belt and began rushing through the trees. "Although these days, it doesn't really matter."

Andrew ducked low branches and leapt over stumps to arrive where the bullet had stopped. A meaty hare laid still in the snow, its tanned coat smudged crimson red. Xavier bent and tied the hind legs together, hoisting it over his shoulder. They walked further into the trees for most of the morning, Andrew keeping pace a few steps behind.

Eventually, Xavier cleared his throat and continued with his story. "So, one night Mom came home and tells us the clinic is overflowing with patients. That night, she told me and Joe some God-awful stories."

"Like what?"

"Well, she said when people were waiting to see the doctor, some of them were calm, and then a few seconds later they would become furious. She said they would be nodding off in the waiting room one minute and then squealing at the top of their lungs the next. She told us most of them didn't even open their eyes, like they were in some sort of dream the whole time."

"What did Mom think was going on?"

"She had no idea. But two things happened that night to make her never go back to the clinic—"

Andrew reached out and squeezed Xavier's shoulder. Like a rehearsed scene, Xavier crouched low and held his breath, his eyes fixed ahead as Andrew reached for his gun. *One Mississippi.* Andrew slid the strap from his shoulder. *Two Mississippi.* The safety clicked. *Three Mississippi.* The rifle wavered, the sharp intake of breath. *Four Mississippi.* The blast from the shot. *Five Mississippi.* He yanked the bolt back and shot again.

At the second shot, Xavier stood and sprinted, disappearing amongst the trees. Andrew lumbered behind and when he arrived on scene, smirked and reloaded his weapon.

"Not bad for a city slicker, huh?"

"Just remember, I got the first one," Xavier huffed.

He finished securing the second hare and then tossed both rabbits to the ground. He looked up at the midday sky.

"It's getting later than I'd like," he said. "This may be all we get today. Let's cook and eat these here. The longer we stay away from the cellar … well, the more unpredictable it gets."

Andrew sat on a nearby stump with one of the rabbits. He surveyed the brown and white patches, rolling the limp animal over in his hands, pausing on the soft tufts of hair behind its neck.

Drawing his bowie knife, he nicked into the thick coat, a thin slit along the belly and up through the rib cage. Shimmying his hand inside the warm body, he dragged the innards out in one fluid tug. He peeled the fur back, beginning with the hind legs and then up to the shoulders, drops of dark red falling on the white snow below. With the knife, he severed the head, feet, and tail, and carved strips from the rabbit's meaty legs and torso.

Xavier kicked several rocks into a pile and dug a shallow hole with his hands. After placing some of the smaller rocks at the bottom, he formed a wide circle with the remaining stones. He gathered twigs and dry leaves from the forest floor, crisscrossing the thin branches at the base of the hole. With the matches from his cargo pants, he lit the dry leaves, tossing birch bark onto the heat as the flames began to catch. He crouched low as smoke billowed up, looking away from the fire, scanning the spaces between the trees.

"Should be hot enough now," he mumbled.

He blew on the embers and gathered the thin strips. They sizzled as he laid each piece on the heated rocks, using a branch to turn the browning meat every few minutes.

The smell reached Andrew's nose. It reminded him of his mother's rabbit stew, the gamey scent wafting out from the kitchen accompanied by the smell of boiled potatoes and onions, a twig of thyme thrown in the broth. She would whisper him over to dole some out from the iron pot, his hungry tongue slurping from the ladle. Sitting on the stump now, his stomach grumbled at the memory.

"So, what were you saying about Mom not going back to the clinic?" he asked.

"Well, we were at the kitchen table late at night," Xavier started again. "She had worked nearly thirty hours straight."

"Are you kidding me?"

"By that point the clinic was totally understaffed. She told us during her shift, this large man checked into the clinic and he became more and more agitated as he waited to see a doctor. Mom said he had only been there a couple of minutes when he starts writhing in pain and yelling for help. Then, all of a sudden, he runs up to the front desk and swings his fist down on the table."

Xavier grabbed a piece of the moist meat from the rocks and held it out. Andrew nodded his thanks and chewed around the gristle for a few seconds before swallowing. "And then what?"

"Mom said when he slammed his arm down ... well ... she said his arm just fell off."

Andrew drew back. "What do you mean, *it fell off?*"

"She said there was this ripping sound and then his arm slid off his shoulder and laid there on the floor. Mom said he was bleeding all over the place. And she said he didn't even notice! No one noticed! The clinic is packed, this guy's arm is lying on the floor, and no one even noticed!"

Andrew's mouth hung open, his eyes meeting Xavier's. He pulled his legs close to his torso, his hand hovering over his rifle.

Xavier continued: "The second thing that happened that night—"

"There's more?"

"Lots more. I can stop if you want."

"No, go on. I don't want to but I probably need to hear this."

"So, Mom said she finally gets some help to clean up the blood and they rush this man in to see the doctor. Then a few minutes later, an older woman comes into the clinic. She sits in the waiting area for a moment and then runs and lunges at Mom. This woman didn't say a word—just hopped the counter and jumped at her, snapping her teeth like she was trying to bite her."

"Are you serious? Was Mom okay?"

"Some of the nurses pulled the lady away. They told the security guard and he took the lady outside but it really shook Mom up. She clocked out and never went back."

"I don't blame her! What happened after that?"

"The three of us slept in the same room that night and for several nights after. We were all spooked! Joe and I took turns staying awake, listening for noises."

Xavier paused for a moment, drawing in a deep breath. "But then Mom and Joe started to get weird. There were small signs at first. Mom's skin grew patchy and she started having all sorts of bruises and cuts along her legs."

"From Joe?"

Xavier spun to face Andrew. "Just because he's not your real father doesn't mean he *hits* her."

"X, I - I didn't mean it that way. I was just wondering where the bruises came from, that's all."

Xavier took a bite of the meat, chewed, and then threw the remaining pelt in the fire. "I don't know where the bruises came from," he grumbled. "One day she was fine, the next there are all these purple spots running down her."

"Okay, I'm sorry," Andrew said. "What else happened?"

"Both she and Joe lost a lot of hair, it was constantly clogging up the shower drain. And Joe was losing weight—I could practically see every vertebrae when he changed his shirt each morning. And he would pace the kitchen mumbling a name over and over again. It would be mixed with other gibberish but one name kept coming up: Simon. Do we know a Simon?"

Andrew shook his head.

"Also, there were times when Mom would just stare at me," Xavier continued. "She wouldn't say a word. She would just stand and stare, her mouth wide open. Have you ever had someone look at you for minutes at a time? They don't say a word, just look you up and down as if trying to figure out who you are, and then, BAM! They just turn and walk away. It's creepy."

Andrew's eyes widened, his cheeks darkening.

"I stayed in the house with them but it started to get too iffy," Xavier continued. "So, I decided I was going to leave the next morning. I gathered a few things and called to them before I left. They didn't even respond, didn't even move. It was like they had forgotten their own names. Or had forgotten the sound of my voice."

"They forgot who you were?"

"I'm not sure if they forgot or they just didn't care anymore. They were in this fog all the time, this sort of confused state. It was like they were always lost in their own thoughts."

"That's when you left?"

"I was about to go when Mom came into the kitchen. She's standing there, staring at me, and all of a sudden, her eyes start to flutter. They're moving up and down like crazy fast but they're still closed. Then she opens them and it's like she just woke from a deep sleep. And she had this intense hatred in her eyes."

"Are you serious?"

"The next part happened so fast it's still a little hard to piece together. She was growling and punching at me, showing her teeth like a wild animal. I forced her into the basement and propped a chair against the door. I grabbed what I could before the chair came loose and she came at me again. I took off out the back door and ran."

Andrew shuddered and then reached for the last piece of meat. He lifted it to his mouth and chewed. He foraged around the tiny bones with his teeth and tongue, sucking at the marrow. The meat was tough and leathery and did little to satisfy the grumbling pains deep within his stomach.

"I went deep into the woods," Xavier continued. "I walked for the rest of that day and most of the night. I must have been twenty kilometres from any road, maybe more."

"But why did you leave? I mean, I know Mom and Joe were acting nuts, but you just left them there? In the state they were in?"

"I was scared. Not scared that I wouldn't be able to fight them off if it came to that but that I might be *forced* to. What if things got weirder and I would have to do something drastic? I didn't want to be in that position. So, yeah, I ran. At the time I figured it was the best thing to do."

Andrew nodded. "Then what?"

"I was away for about a week but was running low on bullets and water tablets. With the last of the winter melt approaching, I came back to the house. But by then it was empty. There was no sign of 'em."

"You still have no idea where they are now?"

"None. I came home to broken windows and smashed furniture but the house was deserted. It didn't feel safe, you know? Didn't feel right. It had this eerie feeling throughout it, like something dark had been there … or was still there."

Andrew swallowed and slid his hands down the length of his thighs. He gestured for Xavier to continue.

"Anyways, I slept in the cellar that night and ended up staying down there. It felt safer. Like when we would go down there as kids."

Andrew nodded at the shared memory but then looked up at his brother. "X, I know they were acting weird but we've got to find them. They probably need our help. Somehow, we've got to find them."

But Xavier went quiet, his attention elsewhere, his eyes drifting, his mind lost in thought. The sudden silence haunted Andrew. He felt like he couldn't breathe, not knowing where his parents were, as if the bare trees and huddled shrubs were pressing in, suffocating him.

He swallowed the last of the rabbit, spitting some of the smaller bones into the dying fire. "Those didn't last long," he said. "We'll need to hunt again tomorrow."

Wiping the knife clean along the stitch of his pants, he holstered his rifle and kicked snow onto the fire, the glowing embers quickly fading out. He turned to face Xavier but his brother was already far along the trail, returning to the safety of the trees, beginning the cautious walk back to the cellar.

Chapter Eight

June 1994
Day 119 | Morning

The bells over the front entrance chimed. Alan Mackenzie raised his head to see a man in a black raincoat enter the diner, a floppy Tilley hat shadowing his face.

"Welcome to Brenda's Bistro," the bubbly server said.

The man spoke briefly as he adjusted his glasses then followed her to a corner booth in the rear of the restaurant, a slight stutter in his step. He sat down with his back to Alan and pulled a menu close to his face.

Alan fiddled with his cufflink nestled within the stiff French cuff, the silver reflecting off the fluorescent lights. He was freshly shaven, the faint scent of nutmeg and sage along his throat. A shiny ring of baldness sat atop his head. He sipped at his coffee and glanced at his silver Rolex. He twisted in his seat toward the parking lot, making eye contact with his driver through the smeared windows.

The bells rang once again as a lean, muscular man walked in, a black goatee bookending his crooked teeth. He slid the tanned driving gloves from his massive paws and folded them in front of his grey overcoat.

"Any sign of her, Milton?" Alan asked.

"No, sir. Should we go? You have a full schedule today."

"Not yet."

Milton nodded and exited.

The squeal of tires caught Alan's attention and moments later he glanced up to see a lady enter. She spotted Alan and made her way over to him. She wore a tight black dress, heels, and a heavy necklace, a twisted locket at its centre.

"Far different digs than the last time we met, Alan. You've gone from a fancy hotel boardroom to this dive in less than three months!" the lady chortled, tossing a compact clutch on the table.

Alan glanced toward the black Porsche in the parking lot and smiled nervously.

"Far different mode of transportation since the last time we met, Dr. Till," he said. His tone was warm and velvety, yet more direct than their previous meeting. "I see you're enjoying the benefits of our … arrangement."

"Well, I can't keep taking cabs everywhere now, can I? Let's just say the first payment of our agreement went through." Her dark skin parted to reveal a smug smile.

Alan placed his mug on the table and scrunched his brow. The tracks along his forehead crisscrossed like lashes from a whip. "Yes, I can see that," he muttered. "Now, if I remember correctly, you are not one for chit-chat, so I will get straight to my points. We are both busy people with much work to do over the next few months."

Angela unbuttoned her fitted coat and draped it over the bench beside her. She flicked a fly from the air and Alan twitched at the movement.

"My clients are running out of patience," he said.

"Clients? You mean those baboons from the boardroom? I'm surprised they can feed themselves let alone sniff out an investment opportunity."

"Well, some are only involved for their deep wallets, I suppose that's true. But others are there for their brains—steering the whole thing from a distance."

"Like your boss, Mr. Pak? Seems like he's pulling the strings."

"He plays an important role, yes."

"So, he's got the biggest wallet?" Angela sneered.

"He's a coordinator of sorts, a facilitator. Mr. Pak brings together the right people at the right time."

"A facilitator or a puppet master? Seems like he's got you all tied up, Alan."

Alan waved the insult away. "As I was saying, my clients are beginning to ask questions. They no longer see the need in putting you up in fancy hotels or providing you with … further incentives." He motioned to the jewelry strung from her neck.

Angela's face tightened. "I have done everything asked of me!"

"Even still, my clients believe you are dragging your feet … or perhaps, the closer we get to the next phase, your feet are simply getting … *cold*."

"I am one hundred percent committed! Can you say the same for your clients?"

Angela waited for a response but Alan just shifted in his seat.

"Communication lines have been non-existent since our last meeting," Angela continued. "For Christ's sake, this is the first time I've seen you in months!"

"I can assure you my clients are working diligently and are fully committed to the project."

"And what about the other researcher? How do I know if

they're committed? I'm left to guess, left in the dark out here in this hick town!"

"That is not for you to worry about, everything is under control. Now, I would appreciate if you could stay on topic and answer the question."

Angela's brow furrowed but she remained quiet.

"My clients are not known for their patience, Dr. Till," Alan said. "I have worked with them long enough to know that when work arrangements become difficult, their ... *goodwill* is challenged."

"Goodwill? Ha! Is that what you and your friends call it? It seems you're confusing goodwill with greed!"

"We all have our agenda's, Dr. Till, hidden or otherwise. Goodwill. Greed. Whatever the motive is, it still doesn't change what needs to be done nor what everyone agreed to do. And perhaps I should ask: is your motive not the same as everyone else's?"

Angela dropped her gaze and placed one hand atop the other. After a few moments, she spoke. "I began making adjustments to the town water four months ago."

"This is something you have already told us. So, what has happened since?"

"The substance is very diluted. It needs to be that way to not raise any alarms or suspicion."

"Have any alarms been raised?"

"Early on, a few residents complained about a bitter metallic taste. Some hack journalist from the local paper—I think Moseby was his name—he tried to make a story out of it."

"Is it a problem?"

"No, we've reasoned it away. We went on record stating it

was a fluctuation in fluoride levels, so the papers have left us alone … for now. But still, we have to be careful to stay below their radar. Local news has a way of being picked up nationally and we definitely want to keep this under wraps. It's in our best interest to keep this well within the borders of Barn Wood."

"Agreed, that is imperative. And how do you know the adjustments are working?"

"My staff take routine blood samples through the regular work of the health clinic. What they don't know is afterwards, I take the samples and test them myself. I've observed the percentage of the chemical is rising. My guess is that it's similar in the general population. That is, anyone receiving their water supply through the town."

Alan leaned forward, lowering his voice. "And those that do not receive town water? What are you doing about them?"

"Some residents are on well-water, the older farm homes especially. But I wouldn't worry much about them."

"And why is that?"

A toothy smile grew across Angela's face. "I've already paid most of them a visit to inspect their wells, distributing fake water certificates. You'd be amazed what I can get away with flashing my credentials."

"How much longer, Angela? My clients need to know how much longer until we start seeing results. They are not enjoying this waiting period. They are anxious to move into testing the effects."

Angela clenched her teeth. "I never gave a guarantee of how long this would take! This is new territory—for everybody."

Alan added a second cube of sugar to his mug, stirred,

and raised the steaming liquid to his mouth. He dabbed a pocket square along his lips and clunked the mug back on the table. "Need I remind you this was the point all along? A lot of money has been invested in testing and monitoring the effects in a *timely manner*."

"The stuff we're talking about is measured in parts per million." Angela said. "Parts. Per. Million!"

"You've known this all along, Angela. Now we need to see results."

"Everything is moving in the right direction. I just need to be certain of specific elements. Yes, it's taking longer than even I predicted, but you can't hurry science, Alan!"

A shoe squeaked and Angela spun to see the server approaching. Angela turned back to Alan and lowered her voice.

"This would be easier if I could contact the other researcher. It would speed up the analysis. It would help me confirm some of my theories if I could just speak with them."

"The parameters were clearly explained at the outset of the project. Contact with each other is prohibited. I am your link. That is how this works."

"Anything for you, ma'am?" the server sang, stepping beside the small booth.

Angela waved her away, her eyes locked on Alan's. After a moment, Alan broke from the stare and turned toward the young server. "Just the coffee, dear," he said, his velvet voice returning.

"Sure. It's only a dollar. I'm going on break soon so just leave the money on the table." She skipped over to the other man seated at the corner booth who was still studying the menu.

With a shift of his wrist, Alan reached into his money clip

and placed a twenty-dollar bill on the table. Sliding his pea coat over his suit jacket, he began walking toward the exit but paused behind Angela's seat. Her perfume, an intense mix of wild orange and clove, tickled his nose.

"My clients have been very generous to you," he said.

He smoothed down his gelled hair and stared out the window where Milton stood waiting, perched beside the black Mercedes.

"But that generosity is not infinite, Dr. Till. They will need to see results and they will need to see them very soon. If *you* can't hurry science, Angela," he said, fastening the last button on his coat, "then we will find someone who can."

Chapter Nine

March 1995
Day 414 | Dawn

"I've been chased by those things, you know?" Xavier said.

Both he and Andrew climbed the narrow staircase leading out of the cellar. He sealed the opening and they began a slow jog toward the tree-line.

"When?" Andrew asked.

"My days are all messed up now but it was at least a week ago, maybe two," Xavier said. "I was going through Derrick Jackson's old place. The house was abandoned so I was looking for supplies. But I got this feeling like someone was watching me."

Andrew shuddered but stayed quiet, motioning for Xavier to continue.

"I went out and someone was just standing on the front lawn, staring directly at the house," Xavier said. "I wasn't sure if he saw me but I wasn't about to stick around to find out."

"What'd you do?" Andrew asked.

"I ducked back into the house and went for the back door. That's when I noticed a second man standing outside a window."

"Two of them?"

"Yeah, but the second one was turned away so I snuck to the back without him noticing. I was almost at the back door when the first one came through the front. This time, for sure, he saw me."

Andrew's eyes widened. "How'd you know he wasn't, you know … normal?"

"His eyes were dark yellow with loose skin under them. And he had this horrible burning metal smell coming off him. I felt like my throat was closing up, like I was having an allergic reaction or something."

Xavier unscrewed his water bottle. He took several gulps, wiping his moist lips with his sleeve. "The strangest thing was how he looked at me," he continued. "Like he knew I was there but didn't know what to do with me. Maybe like the first time a dog meets a cat. The dog keeps its distance, unsure if the cat is friendly or not."

"So, what'd you do?"

"I wasn't sticking around to find out if I was the dog or the cat! So, I bolted. But that got both their attention."

Xavier took another swig from the bottle then spat on a pile of ice and snow at the base of a tree.

"The guy ran after me, right through the back door," he said. "I sprinted into the field but then the second one saw me and came charging around the house."

"Are you kidding me?"

Xavier shook his head. "I just ran and ran, kept looking back. They were so quick at first, but by the time I ran about thirty seconds, they had already fallen back. I just kept running until I reached the cellar. I didn't know if there were more of them out there."

"Did they want to bite you or … kill you?"

"Honestly, they were hard to read—their awkward movements, their lack of focus. I think they were confused, if anything. Like they were deciding whether to attack or not."

"Were you scared?"

"Well, of course I was scared. You see those things running at you, you'd be scared too. But when I got back to the cellar, I realized I never reached for my gun. That's usually automatic for me if I'm spooked. So, it was weird. The whole thing was scary and weird."

"Have you seen any since?"

"No, after that it felt too dangerous to leave the cellar. I knew I needed to go up eventually but tried to stay below ground as long as I could. And that's when you showed up."

"I saw a few of them as well," Andrew said. "A young girl, a few hours after my flight."

"Where?"

"About twenty klicks from here, where the cabbie abandoned me."

"She was outside of Barn Wood?"

"Yeah."

"Hmm. Must have gotten out just before they set up the blockades."

"There was also a man and a woman later that night when I got to the house."

"They were at the house?"

"Yeah, at the end of the driveway. I was standing on the front porch and one of them—a woman—she started coming up."

"Did she see you go into the cellar?"

"I doubt it. I made it there pretty quick."

"How'd you know they weren't normal?"

"Like you said, they were awkward—walked funny, looked confused, had all these injuries. They never got that close, but even from a distance I could see something was wrong with them."

"Did they do anything?"

"One of them screamed. It didn't sound human or animal. It was something else, a noise I've never heard before."

Xavier nodded. "Yeah, I remember hearing screaming that night just before you came into the cellar. The noise seemed close but I didn't realize it was from our own driveway."

Andrew furrowed his brow, a thought forming. "X, why was the cellar door unlocked that night? Every time we're in the cellar you make sure I secure the bolt and put the padlock on. But that first night I just opened the door and walked right down the steps."

"Carelessness, I guess. I can secure it with the lock from the inside and it still holds without the outside fastened. But you're right—it should have been padlocked from the inside. I just forgot. At that point, I hadn't eaten or slept in several days and my mind wasn't firing on all cylinders."

He yawned and the two of them walked in silence for a while. Andrew reached into his pocket and pulled out the note with Juliana's number scrawled on it. He smiled weakly, remembering the redhead from the plane who had made him laugh. It was less than a week ago, but somehow seemed like a distant memory. He sighed and shoved the note back in his pocket, his fingers gently running over the ridges of the paper through his cargo pants.

He and Xavier continued to trounce through the trees until they came upon a clearing. Andrew didn't see them until they were close.

He made a noise in his throat and Xavier spun to see them too: a small group, maybe three or four, hiding within a stand of trees not fifty yards away. They were silent, squinting at the brothers. Xavier sniffed the air and raised his rifle.

"Hold on, X," Andrew whispered. "I think there's a sniper. Your ten o'clock. He's got eyes on you."

A young man was laying on the forest floor several yards from the rest of the group. A smudge of brown along the earth, he was all but camouflaged by a fallen trunk and surrounding deadwood. Only a slim ray of light reflected off the gun's scope and caught Andrew's eye. He reached out to Xavier's weapon and pushed down on the barrel.

"You sure?" Xavier said. "Whatever you're seeing, you sure it's a gun?"

Andrew focused on the fallen log, waiting for movement, but saw none. He screwed up his mouth. "Maybe not."

Xavier raised his rifle again to the small gathering among the trees and clicked the safety. "Good, because I thought for a second—"

There was the hard clap of a rifle as a bullet ricocheted off the tree beside Xavier, spraying bark into his matted hair. His breath caught and he dropped his rifle to the grass. Andrew followed, swinging the leather rifle strap from his own shoulder, disposing the weapon to the ground. They both lifted their palms and began slowly walking toward the group.

"Yep, there was a sniper," Xavier grumbled.

As they moved closer, the scene became clearer. There were three figures standing amongst the tall oaks. They were all women: a middle-aged White woman, short and dishevelled, with a frizzy mane of grey hair; a Black woman, tall and slender in jeans, many years younger than the first; and an Ojibway child with frightened hazel eyes, her long dark hair running down the length of her spine.

Several yards away from them was a young man lying in the dirt and snow, his rifle trained on Xavier. His skin was a deep russet like the child's and his eyes were wild, buzzing back and forth between the brothers.

"Still have your knife?" Andrew whispered.

Xavier nodded but then sniffed the air. His hand moved behind his back, hovering over the hilt tucked along his belt-line.

"What are you?" he called out.

There was some commotion among the three women. The short older woman swatted the other two away and stepped out from behind the trees.

"Are you infected?" she hollered back.

"What are you?" Xavier shouted again.

Andrew stepped forward and breathed in the smells of the forest and all of his senses came into focus. Trained on the sniper, Andrew's eyes peeled back the camouflage surrounding the young man. He could make out the boy's hands squeezed along the barrel, his sinewy frame rigid along the ground. The boy's hair was black and moist—a thick bundle pulled back, wispy strands tucked behind his ears. Although he looked young—perhaps only a teenager—Andrew feared something in him. He felt as if in that moment he was truly being hunted. And despite the warm morning sun, a cold shiver travelled up him, one he could not easily shake.

"I think they're okay," Xavier whispered from the side of his mouth. "I mean, they might be normal. We would have smelled them by now if they weren't."

Andrew exhaled slowly and turned his attention to the women. "We're not infected," he called out. "We came from town. We're just out looking for food."

After a few seconds, the tall woman joined the short one and they both began walking cautiously toward the brothers.

"There's a gun on you," the short woman called out.

"Yes, we're aware," Xavier mumbled, shaking remnants of bark from his hair.

The women stopped several yards away and the four of them stood still, studying each other. Andrew cleared his throat.

"I'm Andrew. This is my brother, Xavier."

The women said nothing, waited him out.

"We live just a few kilometres from here," Andrew added.

"How do we know you're not one of them?" the short woman barked. "One of those crazy ones?"

Xavier screwed up his mouth. "We can talk. Have you ever heard any of them speak?"

"Yes," she said resolutely.

She crossed her arms, her frayed sweater bunching up around her shoulders, and stared at them with steely eyes. She tilted her head and nodded as the taller woman bent and whispered something to her.

"It depends on how far along they are," the short woman continued. "Some seem to change quickly and others drag it out."

Xavier studied the ground and then raised his head. "They smell different from us—from normal people, I mean. Something's different with their blood. It's like something's missing from it."

"Or something's been added," Andrew said.

Xavier cocked his head. "Taken. Added. Makes no difference. They have a smell of metal or aluminum on them. The point is they stink and you can smell them coming."

"*You* stink," the short woman said.

Andrew smirked. "You've got him there, ma'am! But that stink has been with him his *whole* life." Andrew playfully shoved Xavier until he remembered a gun was on them.

The short woman stared coldly at the brothers then turned and whispered to the other—her companion quiet, nodding. The taller woman turned and jogged back to the others.

Andrew could see the young man coaxed from his hiding spot. He wore green cargo pants and a dark jacket, rips at the elbows and wrists. His worn boots rolled across the frozen dirt as he cautiously walked toward them, the stitching coming loose along the sole. He stopped beside the short woman and sniffed, his rifle raised and pointed straight at the brothers.

"We won't hurt you," Andrew said. His voice was louder than he had intended, a commanding boom against the quiet of the trees. "We're normal, like you," he added softly. "We're running, just like you are."

The young man whispered to the woman, clicked the safety, and lowered the weapon. He nodded and motioned for the brothers to follow. Turning, he glided toward the others, a leather cartridge pouch bouncing from his hip.

As they came upon the clearing, Andrew took in the makeshift camp. A few young poplars were bent and tied together with rope and twine. Three ratty sleeping bags were rolled out upon a damp carpet of icy mulch and snow. A sweater and several pairs of socks hung on a line a few yards away. A small pit lined with rocks sat at the centre of the camp, rounded embers smudged black from an earlier fire. He surveyed the few supplies scattered about the site. There was no food or water from what he could see.

He cleared his throat twice before settling on his question. "How long have you been here?"

"A few days," the short woman answered.

"All of you?"

"More or less." She picked at her mop of frizzy hair.

"You've all been travelling together?" Andrew asked.

"For the most part."

"What have you been eating?"

"We're getting by. It's not the Hyatt, but considering what's going on in town—"

"It's just such an odd group to be travelling together," Xavier interrupted.

The short woman turned on him. "Hey, we didn't plan for this! We walked into a horror show and this is the best we've been able to make of it!"

Suddenly, the young man turned to face the child. As he bent to whisper, Andrew caught a glimpse of steel along his belt-line. The young man reached down and grabbed the child's hand, the young girl anxiously staring back at Xavier with nervous eyes, a stain of dirt smeared across her cheek.

The short woman motioned to the child and as she stumbled toward a stump Andrew noticed a list in the girl's step and a swollen scar etched along her forearm. She pulled her sleeve over the marking and slid a toque over her hair. The woman sat beside her and leaned forward, rubbing the girl's back, humming softly.

"I'm Maddy," the short woman said finally. There was a hoarseness to her voice, like that of a smoker. Her silver fillings reflected the daylight when she spoke. "And that's Rachel," she added, motioning toward the other woman.

Rachel's greasy hair was drawn back, her jeans ripped along the knee. She nervously pulled at the sleeves of a dusty plaid jacket then fidgeted with something hidden in her palm. Andrew looked at her, puzzled. There was something curious about the woman, a murky memory he couldn't access. She was what the men in town might call a *looker*, with long, slim legs, alluring features, and a toned build. She held Xavier's gaze for a few seconds then looked away.

"This is Damien," Maddy continued, indicating the young man. "And the child here is Evelyn—Damien's sister."

Evelyn attacked an itch along her calf, jostling an anklet of bright yellow and red. Damien cleared his throat but remained silent.

Xavier turned to him. "That's quite a shot you have. You were only four feet off the mark."

Damien scowled at Xavier, his lips pressed together. "Had I wanted to hit you—"

"Now, now," Maddy interrupted. "Damien has a fine shot. He has taken good care of us since we've been out here. In fact, it's his gun that has kept us alive."

Andrew turned to face Maddy. "So, you've seen some of them? Those crazy people?"

"Oh, yes, seen plenty of 'em," Maddy said. "Disgusting things! We've been making circles in these woods because of them."

"You've seen them out here?" Andrew asked.

"Well, no, not since we've been in the woods," Maddy said. "But when we were out by the road some of them chased us."

"How'd you get away?"

"Ducked back into the trees. They seem hesitant of the forest, like they're not sure how to navigate it. I don't think they see very well either. Seem to always be squinting."

"When were you chased?"

"Oh, who knows, it's all a blur now. Damien had to shoot a few of them, but we got away. We headed back here as soon as it was safe. I'd imagine they know we're back here though, probably looking for a way to get at us."

"Have you seen any since?"

"No, but you can hear them, hear their screams once in a while. God-awful sounds."

"Do you think they're human, or …"

"Well of course they're human," Maddy snorted. "That's what makes this whole thing so sad. Half those people I've probably walked past on the way to work or seen at the grocery store!"

She stood and took a few steps toward Andrew. "But the way I see it, they're out to kill us. They're more creature now than human. And, for whatever reason, their minds have become warped, all thought bent on catching us."

A strange quiet fell over the group. The sun was beginning to fall lower in the red sky, the warmth of the day now fading.

Andrew turned to Damien. "What's your story?"

Damien held his stare for a moment before speaking. "My sister and I live on the outskirts. We came across this woman here who was lost." His voice was soft and low with a faint accent, like his tongue was trying to solve the shape of certain letters.

"After you fled to the woods? What happened then?" Andrew asked.

"We survived. As best we could."

"And after meeting the women?"

"We helped them, like she said."

"So, just you and your sister before that?"

"Yes."

"And besides these two, you didn't come across any others?"

Damien shook his head. "Just them."

"But before the forest—you didn't see any that were still normal?"

"I already told you what I saw," Damien said, growing impatient. "We ran into these two—"

"Yeah, but are you sure?"

The young man drew back, a sudden venom in his stare.

"Sorry, I - I didn't mean to pry," Andrew stammered. "I just meant, I just thought—"

A piercing screech came across the wind and Andrew's head twisted toward the noise.

"It's one of those things!" Maddy yelled.

She and Rachel sprinted toward the middle of the campsite. Like a rehearsed scene, they frantically gathered their belongings and shoved them into a large backpack, the sleeping bags scrunched into compact rolls.

"We need to find cover!" Xavier boomed. "Do you have another place we can hide? A back-up campsite?"

Damien dropped his gaze. "There's only this," he said. "We just have what's here."

"You haven't made a proper shelter? Just a few sleeping bags thrown on the ground?" Xavier asked.

"I hunt during the day while they rest. At night they keep watch while I try to sleep. That's all we've had time to do."

Andrew heard the scream again, the noise much closer. "X, we've got to move!" he said, squeezing his brother's arm.

Damien hoisted his backpack over his slender shoulders. "We'll go our way, you go yours—"

"But Damien," Maddy said. "They've got guns as well. We'll be safer with them."

"We've survived this long," Damien said. He nervously felt along the frayed leather of his rifle strap.

Andrew stepped forward. "She's right. You've got more gunfire with us. We're better to travel together, at least till we're out of range of those things. You can split off after if you want."

A howl rang out again, the noise bouncing off the stout trunks surrounding them, and then a snap of twigs less than fifty yards away.

"But we need to go now," Xavier said. "If you're coming with us, we leave right now!"

Maddy reached for Evelyn and threw the sleeping bags under her arm. She nodded to Damien. "We're safer with them," she assured him. "But we need to go now. We need to run, okay?"

Damien let out an exhausted grunt and nodded.

"Good," Maddy said. "I've got your sister. Now, let's move!"

They all sprinted through the dense brush and ferns, away from the shrill echo among the smokey trees. Andrew caressed the trigger of his rifle as his pace quickened. He looked over his shoulder every few strides, troubled at how odd it was to see his brother and a line of frightened strangers following close behind.

Chapter Ten

The moon was beginning to peek out as the group continued its quick pace through the brush. And there, just beyond the hill, Andrew saw them.

The first thing he heard was the shot—a violent explosion sending tremors through his core. He whipped around to find Xavier reloading, the barrel still smoking.

Xavier aimed and shot again, yanked the bolt back, and ejected the casing. He punched the bolt forward and peered down the scope. Exhaling slowly, he pulled the trigger then reloaded again. Andrew reached over to snatch the rifle away.

"What if they're human?" he yelled.

Xavier turned to him, his eyes manic, flicking from Andrew to the movement beyond the hill. "You can't smell that?" Xavier asked.

Andrew drew in a deep breath and all at once his senses were overtaken. The smell brought him to his knees as he choked on the foreign odour. His eyes began to well up as he vomited on the grass, pawing at the ground in search of his rifle. Xavier rolled beside him and unloaded both barrels, each shot bringing a body to the ground.

"Are you okay?" he shouted.

Andrew nodded, his outstretched hand finally locating his gun.

Xavier reached into his cargo pants, searching for the cold metal of a cartridge. He brought two rounds out and shoved them down the breech. He held his breath and swung his body over the ridge, emptying the rifle into an advancing woman. She squealed as the bullet went through her left eye and out the back of her skull, her body pitched hard to the icy clay.

Andrew wiped his eyes and surveyed the scene. Finally, he could see what was before them. "Oh, God," he whispered.

There were hordes of them, wild and deranged, screaming and frothing at the mouth. Many were rail-thin, their bones jutting out from beneath their clammy skin. Pus from burst boils leaked down their neck and arms, their hands ending in crooked fingers, nails sharpened to a point.

A line of them swarmed from behind the thick brush at the base of the incline while others barrelled down the steep bank lining the valley. Many were limping while some crawled on all fours. Still others were sprinting, charging toward the small group, their sadistic yellow eyes pulsing in the grey dusk.

"They're everywhere!" Xavier shouted, joining his brother on the lee of the hill.

Andrew raised his rifle but dropped to the ground as a booming crack snapped through the air. He rolled onto his back to see Damien on one knee. The boy took aim, pulled the trigger, swivelled, and shot again. Two victims crumpled to the valley floor about sixty yards out.

Andrew watched Damien's calculated press toward the creatures—his aim steady, his shot true. Something was familiar about his movements: the squint of his eyes, his loose stance, the way his fingers caressed the weapon like a treasured instrument.

"To the right!" Xavier shouted, jabbing his finger through the air. "Lots more down the right side!"

Damien spun the rifle over and ripped the bolt along the top. The rifle fit him perfectly; it blended in with his movements as though he had grown with it attached, an extra appendage from birth. He stood and fired, the recoil from the first shot meshing with the quick aim and release of the second.

One bullet hit an attacker in the lung, leaving it writhing and kicking on the ground. The second bullet exploded through another's throat, flesh flying out behind her. She let out a guttural yelp, fell to the ground, and did not move again.

"Andrew, they're coming to you!" Xavier hollered.

Andrew rose to a knee, firing two shots before ducking down below the hill. He peered over the crest once more, the setting sun casting shadows on the valley. Nearly half the attackers had been shot, but still, there were dozens more advancing.

"There's too many!" Xavier yelled. He grabbed Damien by the arm and pointed to the trees. "Take the others and run for it! We'll cover you as long as we can!"

Damien kept his mouth tight and nodded. He turned from the small cliff and then it was as if he was gone—vanished—reappearing among the trees seconds later. Andrew watched as the group sprinted away, their silhouettes quickly lost among the swaying branches.

The shot from Xavier's gun refocused Andrew and he rushed to reload.

"They're close, X! They're very close!"

He notched two more victims as Xavier climbed the small

hill and fired. One attacker took a bullet in the upper chest, the other in the centre of her face. Both fell and bled out.

Andrew crawled toward Xavier. "Time to move!"

Xavier nodded and galloped down the ridge, both of them sprinting toward the tree-line.

Andrew was a few paces behind, his breathing laboured, sweat pooling along his neck. After a few minutes, he slowed to a jog and glanced over his shoulder. Eight figures stood atop the bank squinting into the trees. Andrew stuttered to a walk, his lungs straining for air.

"I think we lost them," he gasped. "They can't see through the trees. It's too thick in here."

He peered toward the mount. The last of the light was leaving the sky but he could still make out the shapes pacing back and forth along the rise. He cocked his eyebrows.

"We better keep moving. The others won't be too far ahead."

After several minutes, they reached the group huddled within the trees. Evelyn was trembling with Maddy standing over her, the older woman whispering gently, stroking the child's hair. Damien emerged silently from the cover of trees, clinging to his rifle.

"We've lost them," Xavier said. "But we can't hang around here. There'll be others."

"Where can we go?" Damien asked.

"We need to find cover right away," Xavier said. "Do you know of a rock outcropping or a cave of some sort?"

Andrew shot him a look but Xavier avoided his brother's steely gaze and instead eyed the sliver of moon. "It will be pitch black in less than half an hour," he said. "Does anyone know where we can go?"

"X," Andrew said, but Xavier ignored him, turned his attention to the sky. "X?"

Xavier huffed and grabbed Andrew's arm. He yanked him through the brush until they both came to a small clearing just out of earshot of the others.

"I know what you're thinking, but it's too dangerous," Xavier hissed. "We're not taking them with us."

Andrew motioned to speak but Xavier cut him off.

"What if we're followed, huh? What then? Then those - those things will know where we are. The cellar is a safe spot, a good spot. I don't want to jeopardize that!"

"But these people, X. They're terrified. They've been living out here for God knows how long!"

"And?"

"I don't think the boy has even slept. Look at them. They're exhausted. They're starving."

"How is that my problem?" Xavier said. "Besides, they've survived this long. They'll be fine on their own."

"They've survived on luck alone! We leave them out here they don't last the night."

"But we'll give our position away!"

"Not if we're careful. Look, we have food in the cellar—not much, but enough. And first thing in the morning we can hunt for more."

"What did Dad teach us all those years out hunting? Don't let anything—human or animal—know where your shelter is."

"This is *completely* different!" Andrew exclaimed. "It's not like we're stalking deer or coyotes. We've got deranged maniacs chasing us!"

"And if we lead them to the cellar, they'll find us and

attack us there!"

"Well, there might be a way to help them. Maddy seems to think they're still human, maybe diseased somehow, like a virus working its way through them—"

"Keep your textbook nonsense to yourself!" Xavier seethed through clenched teeth. "If something as crazy as that comes running at me, I'm not thinking about helping it. I'm shooting it down!"

Andrew shook his head and scrunched up his face.

"What?" Xavier challenged. "You think a few biology courses make you an expert on this? ON THIS?" He swung his arms wide motioning to the hill they just ran from. "Mom always bragged about how clever you were. A perfect momma's boy, her pride and joy. She made sure everyone knew you were better than Dad and I—way smarter than the two dumb hunters in the family!"

Andrew tried to fight off the anger but it spewed forth all the same. "Whatever crap you and I gotta resolve we're not doing it here," he shouted. "This isn't about us! This is about helping those people survive one more night from those things!"

"It's *always* about us! Over and over again, you always made damn sure it always came back to you against me!"

Andrew held Xavier's stare, his face burning with heat, his breathing punching out in rapid bursts. He knew his brother's outbursts well, often smudging the line between loyal sibling and vicious adversary.

Andrew stepped back and turned his attention toward the group. He closed his eyes and unfurled his fists. Finally, he said: "They need to come with us."

Xavier stared into the trees; the sun was nearly gone, the

shadows growing longer.

"We grew up on these lands, X. We know them inside out. And you know as well as I do that there are no outcroppings or caves nearby."

Xavier grunted but said nothing.

"We would only run into danger and waste more time if we stay out here," Andrew continued. "Once night falls, we won't see those things coming. We'll be easy prey. And I remember Joe also telling us *that*! Enjoy the meal but stay smart to make sure you don't *become* the meal!"

Andrew glanced toward the sky. "Look, we have maybe ten minutes of light left. It's twenty to the cellar. There's nowhere else to go before night sets in. Taking them with us is the best option."

"The girl won't make it," Xavier said. "She walks with a limp."

"Then we'll carry her. We'll switch every few minutes if we have to."

Xavier looked to the horizon, the sky a dusky grey. A bat flopped overhead, beginning its nightly feed on mosquitoes and moths.

"It's not a smart move," Xavier said. "We give up our position and risk those things following us right into the cellar."

"You're right, it's not a smart move. But, it's the right move. This is the right thing to do."

A silence widened between them. Eventually, Xavier nodded.

The brothers joined the others among the brush and prepared to leave the area. Xavier shoved his cartridge pouch into Maddy's pack and hoisted it to his shoulders. Damien strapped two rifles to his back and another in his hand, the worn walnut stock suspended at his side.

Rachel held the sleeping bags under her arm. Maddy tied Evelyn's smaller bag to her hip then turned to Damien. "Let me have one of those rifles," she said.

Damien cocked his head but then slid one of the weapons off his body and handed it to her. He passed her several bullets which she shoved into her back pocket. She peered down the eyepiece, closing one eye to see through the scope with the other.

"I hate these things," she said. "After my father died, I swore I would never touch one again." She sighed deeply. "Desperate times call for desperate measures, I suppose."

Andrew bent to Evelyn. "How's your leg?"

The girl pressed her lips together but only made a soft noise in her throat.

"Listen, I'm going to carry you for a bit," Andrew said. "It will be faster this way, okay?"

Evelyn's eyes softened. She nodded and reached out to Andrew. She was scrawny and malnourished, much lighter than he had expected. He guessed she weighed no more than sixty pounds.

Xavier stepped in front of the group. "We have a safe house of sorts—an underground cellar—where Andrew and I have been hiding out. It's not much, but it will keep us alive another night."

"How far is it?" Maddy asked.

"It's twenty minutes south of here. We'll have light most of the way."

"And what if those things come back while we're running for this cellar of yours?" Maddy said.

"Be careful and smart and we have a chance to get

through this," Xavier said. "Don't kid yourselves, those things are still out there. Everyone keep your eyes and ears sharp!"

Maddy looked to Rachel, Damien, and Evelyn and nodded. "Okay, let's go," she said.

"I'll lead," Xavier said. "Damien and Maddy, you take the rear."

He turned and darted through the trees, fallen bark and stones jumping from the path. The others followed in silence, Damien at the end of the line, the clunk of his rifle slapping across his sweaty back.

After some time, Xavier yelled over his shoulder. "We're less than a kilometre now! Keep going!"

He rounded a broad pine when a flicker of movement rustled the tall grass several yards to his left.

"Ten o'clock!" he yelled. He spun and ran toward Maddy. "Start shooting! They're at ten o'clock!"

Maddy shook as she reached to click the safety. Damien was already aiming, his eye squinting down the scope, straining to make out the shape.

"Gun! Give me the other gun!" Xavier yelled, joining Damien along the tree-line. In a fluid motion, Damien slid the rifle from his back and tossed it at Xavier while still holding aim.

It was Damien's rifle which unloaded first followed by a squeal. "They'll be another one in there," Xavier whispered. "They seem to travel together."

Several yards away, Andrew stooped and released Evelyn to the ground. They huddled together, Rachel catching up to them a few seconds later. Andrew yanked the bowie knife from his belt. "Stay here! I'll be right back to get you."

He crouched and made his way toward Xavier and

Damien. Coming up a few yards behind them, he was struck by how similar they were. Even in the dim moonlight, he could see them both raised on one knee, rifles steady, drawn to the same height. Their breathing was measured, calm, and yet still burned with intensity.

Xavier was the broader of the two, his muscles like dense rope snaking around his thick bones. But kneeling side by side, their features seemed similar: same strong shoulders, same tilt of the head as they searched for sound. They were whispering to each other as if they had been hunting together their whole lives.

Without warning, Evelyn broke away from Rachel and began scurrying along the same path Andrew had taken moments earlier.

"Evelyn!" Rachel hissed and began moving in the same direction, crawling along the dirt and snow. "Evelyn? Andrew?" she whispered. She paused, as if listening for a response. "Evelyn, come back!" she pleaded.

She peered through the trees but the night had set in and she seemed to struggle to see but for a few yards. Rolling onto her knees, she felt along the forest floor and then stood on wobbly legs, bracing against a thick birch. She coughed, as though taking in a nauseating stench. Her head jerked back as something scurried among the shadows.

"Andrew?" she whispered. "Is that you?"

She bit her bottom lip, tears forming at the corner of her eyes. She hesitantly stepped forward into the foliage and was almost on top of it before she saw it: a squat form, a grotesque shape unfurling from the dark, its amber eyes piercing like a coiled snake. It drew in a wet, ragged breath and exhaled a raspy snarl.

Through the trees, Xavier heard the noise. He turned and fired less than a yard from where Rachel stood. A horrific cry filled the air.

"That's the second one!" he yelled. "Let's move!"

He tossed the gun to Andrew. "I'll take the girl. My bet is there are more of them still out there so we have to go quick!"

He swung Evelyn up into the air and held her close against his chest.

"Thank you," she whispered, shaking with fear. "Thank you for helping us."

Xavier swallowed. He opened his mouth to speak but struggled to find words. Instead, he turned to the others. "We're less than five minutes away. Let's go!"

Andrew ran to Rachel. "Are you okay?"

She shook her head, her cheeks flush and moist with sweat. Several of her tears released and dropped to the snow below.

"He saved me," she whimpered, choking on her words. "That thing, it was right there, right where you're standing. He saved me from it!"

"You're okay," Andrew said. "You're alright."

"It was so close I could smell it," Rachel sobbed, emotion taking over. "But your brother shot it. He saved me."

"I know, I know, but listen, we need to run now. Stay close to me. We're almost there, okay?" Andrew locked eyes with her until she nodded.

"Good. Now, let's go!" He bounded over the roots and rocks, Rachel following a few steps behind on shaky legs.

The stars were bright that night—bright enough that when he came out from the birch and maples, Andrew spotted the slight hump of snow surrounding the cellar. He was the first to reach it and he kicked at the latch, swinging the wooden door open.

Rachel and Maddy were the first ones down, Xavier close behind, still holding Evelyn tight to his body. Andrew motioned to Damien and the boy cautiously descended the steps into the dark.

Andrew twisted toward the farmhouse and then back to the forest, scanning the fields one last time. After a few seconds he moved down the steps, bringing the heavy cellar door down behind him.

Chapter Eleven

July 1994
Day 149 | Evening

Angela squinted through the mist and signalled left. She pulled the black Porsche onto the gravel lane, the windshield wipers moving the water off the glass. The rhythmic hum caused her thoughts to drift to two years ago, that spring when the rains seemed to go on forever. The sun hardly came out those months: *'precipitation levels dangerously high,'* the weather stations constantly reported.

From the car she glanced to her right to see expansive gated fields with horses pasturing, their snouts picking at the hay and loose grass. She remembered how the equestrian centre experienced great difficulties that same summer. It had seemed that each time she drove past, another dead horse was being harnessed and lifted onto the back of a truck.

Angela took the next left and saw the three-story building ahead. She hadn't visited it in some time but still knew the drive by memory. She twisted the steering wheel, one hand over the other, guiding the car along the winding driveway. After she parked, she stepped out of the car, reaching to the passenger seat for the thin burgundy briefcase.

A pair of older adults waddled by, each gripping an assisted walker while a tiny nurse barked orders behind them. A stumpy, middle-aged man sat perched on a bench, his black raincoat zipped up, a floppy hat low on his forehead.

The man looked to Angela and when she returned his gaze, his eyes grew wide and panicked. He glanced around nervously, fidgeting with his glasses, then pushed off the bench and scurried down the sidewalk.

Angela stared after him. She opened her mouth as if to call out but instead shook her head and hustled toward the entrance.

Inside, she took the stairs to the second floor, and when the orderlies turned, she slid into room 203.

The room was eerily quiet. A dresser and free-standing mirror stood in the corner, sky-blue bed sheets tucked taut along the firm queen mattress.

She lowered herself into the rocking chair at the foot of the bed, running her quivering hand over the yellow quilt folded at the base of the mattress. Her slender fingers squeezed and released the lumps of cotton gathered in one corner. She brought the comforter to her face, the fabric and stitching rough against her cheek. She breathed in the tart scent of orange peel and lemon and then placed it back on the bed, smoothing out the corners.

Eventually, she pulled the briefcase onto her lap and closed her eyes. She remained still, listening to the chatter from the nurse's station down the hall. She breathed deeply, the strong scent of bleach from the scrubbed linoleum scratching the inside of her nose.

She placed the briefcase on the bed and entered the six-digit code. The latch released. She drew out a thin black folder, '*CONFIDENTIAL*' printed in bold yellow lettering across the front, a smudged logo of an antlered buck near the top. She flipped through several pages. She had reviewed the documents nearly a dozen times already. And like so many times before, she focused her attention to the top of page three and began reading:

Transmission is through the bite of an infective mosquito. The virus is generally maintained within a bird → mosquito → bird enzootic cycle, with birds acting as the primary reservoirs and mosquitoes as vectors. This cycle has been observed in low-lying hardwood forests exposed to increased rainfall or flooding, along with swamps and bogs.

Studies have shown the mosquito can act as a bridge vector transferring the virus to mammals, mainly white-tailed deer and equines. The virus is almost always fatal with the risk of death extremely high, the disease killing the animal from encephalitis within one week of exposure.

The mammals have always been dead-end hosts.

Until recently.

Angela adjusted in her seat and flipped the page.

Emerging, ground-breaking research has

Someone cleared their throat and Angela's head shot up. A round woman in a blue smock stood under the arch of the doorway, blocking most of the hallway light.

"My staff have told you several times, Ms. Till, that you cannot just come into any room you please," the woman said. "This is a restricted-care facility."

Angela snapped the folder shut and returned it to the briefcase.

"Any room I please? Do you know whose room this is?"

"Ms. Till, I am well aware of who *used* to stay in this room. But she is no longer here."

"You are quite right about that! And that is all because of your gross negligence and the shocking incompetence of your staff!"

"That is not fair nor true, Ms. Till!" the woman shot back.

"*Doctor* Till, you imbecile! When you are speaking to me you will call me by my earned title!"

The nurse pressed her lips together, beads of sweat gathering at her hairline. Eventually, she spoke again. "Very well, *Doctor* Till. Regardless of how you wish to remember the past, the fact remains that you cannot saunter into this room and treat it as your personal study."

"I still pay the room fees, don't I?"

"Yes, but …"

"So, what's the problem?"

"You can't just come in whenever you like. Demand for rooms has been low so we've let you keep it for now but … well, there are protocols to follow."

"Do you have any idea who I am?" Angela yelled.

A second nurse poked her head through the doorway. "Is everything okay in here, Deborah?"

The head nurse folded her arms and cleared her throat. "Yes, Dr. Till was just leaving."

Angela scowled and remained planted in the chair.

"Dr. Till, we all share in your loss and our condolences go out to you and your sister," Deborah said, her voice softening. "But it has been over two years and … well … we can't have you coming around here as though she still lives here. You aren't permitted to just walk right in."

Angela stared blankly, as though unsure what was being said to her. Eventually, she shook her head as if coming out of a trance. She stood and spun around the room looking for something, but after a moment, she disbanded the search. She locked the briefcase and brought it tight against her chest. She turned toward the door and glared at the nurse.

Deborah motioned to speak again but something in

Angela's expression wouldn't allow it. Angela scanned the room a final time before rushing by the two women and into the dimly lit hallway, the nurses' blue smocks fluttering as she stormed past.

Chapter Twelve

March 1995
Day 414 | Night

Evelyn twisted side to side within the cramped cellar. A look of puzzlement came over her as she scanned the concrete walls and low ceiling. She turned to Xavier.

"How do you know when it's daytime down here?" she asked.

Xavier ignored the girl's question and continued to twirl his spoon in a tin of cold black beans. Every so often he raised a clump of mush to his chapped lips and sucked it down.

Andrew motioned toward the girl and cleared his throat.

"It's a good question, Evelyn. When it's daytime you can see shafts of light coming through, above here along the borders." He raised the flashlight to where the ceiling met the concrete sides. "The cellar was here when we moved in as kids and my stepfather tried to keep it in reasonable shape over the years."

Evelyn looked confused. "This is where you live?"

"Well, no, we don't live *in* the cellar," Andrew said. "We live in the farmhouse. Our mom uses this cellar to store olives and pickles, things like that."

Evelyn sniffed and then scrunched her face. "It stinks down here!"

"It does, doesn't it," Andrew chuckled. "I guess we got used to the smell when we were kids. Xavier and I would come down here sometimes to play. I'm guessing we were around your age. How old *are* you?"

Evelyn smiled weakly and pawed at her ratty hair. "I'm 12. Well, twelve-and-a-half."

"So, we were pretty close to your age then. We would play cards or experiment with chemistry sets down here. Sometimes we would pretend we were being chased by monsters—" Andrew paused and glanced toward Xavier. "Seems we don't need to pretend anymore."

Xavier stopped spinning the spoon. He stared ahead, stoic, as if remembering a secret from the past. "I think that's enough of the history lesson," he grumbled. He leaned toward Andrew and lowered his voice. "You talk too much," he said, a tension in his words.

Andrew gave a look but eventually nodded. "Probably for the best," he relinquished.

He turned to Evelyn. "Why don't you lie down and get some sleep? Actually, we should all try to get some sleep. We've had quite the night."

He stood, moving closer to the cellar entrance. "I'll keep first watch in case we hear something outside. X can take the second watch in a few hours."

Evelyn nodded and yawned and then moved next to her brother. Damien rummaged around, removing a few items from his backpack. He rolled Evelyn tight in a sleeping bag and rested her head on a balled-up sweater. She sighed and rubbed her tired eyes. He laid down beside her and both were asleep within minutes.

Maddy yawned and curled up in the opposite corner of

the cellar, a filthy sleeping bag draped across her legs. She was still trembling from the night's events but eventually her breathing became heavy and she too fell into slumber.

Perched on an upturned milk crate, Rachel leaned against the cold stone wall, staring into the dim. Her nose twitched at the musty smell of sweat and dirt prominent in the small space.

"I know it's tight in here but there might be room to lie down over there," Andrew said to her, motioning beyond the pile of tinned food.

"I'm fine right here," she said.

Andrew nodded. "Okay," he said softly.

Ensuring the safety of his rifle was clicked on, he leaned the gun against the wall. He adjusted his cargo pants, swatting the dust from the stitched cuffs. He sat at the base of the stairs, blinking up at the cellar door and then around the room.

Due to the lack of light, he couldn't see his brother lying in the far corner but still recognized his heavy breathing. He could see Damien and Evelyn clearly in the foreground and Maddy at the far end of the cellar, shifting and turning from an uneasy dream.

The room was quiet and for some time Andrew's thoughts ruminated on the terrifying night and the horrid things that had chased them. He recalled how each of the creatures looked different—marred and malformed—but almost in an individual way. They seemed to still have human traits, but the features were often distorted, and each had the same malice spewing from their fiery eyes. He shuddered, wondering if that's how the man at the clinic had looked when he yelled and charged at his mother.

He had also noticed the creatures hardly bled after they were shot. This was strange considering the close range and the number of bullets used to bring them down.

Eventually, he shook the disturbing thoughts from his mind. He stood and stretched, his tight thighs loosening with the sudden flow of blood.

As he walked over to rouse Xavier, he noticed Rachel had dozed off. He stood close to her and watched; her brown lids softened over her eyes, her head drooping to one side, her breathing light.

A sudden pang went through him. Taking in Rachel's features, he was sure he had seen her before. He stared down at her dark wavy hair, her taut skin. Even though she had been sleeping on the ground for several days, she was reasonably well kept. Her hair held a shine, her fingernails chipped yet still glossy with a splash of red polish. There was an odd appearance about her, something familiar.

She stirred and Andrew drew back. He stepped to the rear of the cellar and placed his hand on Xavier. "Your turn, X."

Andrew waited for his brother to shake the sleep from his foggy head before he laid down on the tattered blanket. His body ached, his inner thighs rubbed raw from the sprint back to the cellar, his knees still throbbing from carrying Evelyn most of the way. He tried to stay awake but almost immediately exhaustion pulled him under, vivid images from the past rushing into his tired mind.

He dreamt of a time three years ago, he and his mother sitting at the kitchen table, a vase of clipped lilies at its centre. Her thinning hair cascaded past her vibrant green eyes—a messy nest of brown and grey, several strands frayed from the heat. She was beaming as she read through the document in her hand and leapt up from the wobbly chair as soon as her husband walked in.

"Look, Joe! He got in!" She shoved the letter in front of him.

Joe's brow furrowed as he squinted to read the small font. An elaborate looping signature from the Dean of Admissions filled the lower third of the letter. His nostrils flared—a large mushroom nose mushed between his thick lips and narrowed eyes. He swatted the letter away and moved toward the fridge.

There were fresh cherries inside, rinsed and stored in a glass container. He grabbed a handful and plopped several into his mouth. As he bit down, a squirt of juice sprayed, the crimson drops coming to rest on his bushy moustache and then eventually down his chin.

He leaned against the wooden countertop and dragged a red checkered sleeve across his stubble, dabbing at the tart liquid. "Does X know?"

"Not yet, the letter just came this morning," Elizabeth said excitedly. "It says here Andrew has been offered a scholarship for a four-year degree at that renowned university overseas. He'll be leaving in a few months!"

Joe nodded and tossed a few more cherries into his mouth, pulling the stems out from behind clenched teeth. "Just let me be the one to tell Xavier, okay? I'll let him know when he and I are out hunting. Just so, you know, so he has a bit of time to digest the news."

"The *news*? Why do you say *news* like it's a bad thing?" Elizabeth said. "This is exciting! One of our boys is going to a distinguished university—the first of our family—on a scholarship! This is a big deal. We should be celebrating as a family—"

"X can be sensitive to this sort of thing."

"*This sort of thing?*"

"Oh, please, Liz, don't start," Joe barked. He shot a glance at Andrew, hesitating for just a moment. "Look, we all know Andrew is the smart one and no one is taking that away from him. I just think it's best if I—"

"This isn't a competition, Joe! They both have unique skills. This isn't something anyone needs to feel upset about."

"Yes, but … look, this is just another thing Xavier will come second in."

"What are you talking about? Xavier is amazing at a lot of things! He is very good at carpentry and you yourself have said he has one of the most accurate shots you've ever seen."

Joe's complexion deepened, his blood coursing through his neck and face. "Well, that's great isn't it!" he boomed. "So, *your* son will become a scientist or big-time university professor and *my* son gets to go out in the bush with his old man. Maybe he and I can put those carpentry skills to use and we can build a shed for all of Andrew's degrees!"

"Sixteen years of marriage and he's still only *my* son?" Elizabeth said, her voice wavering.

Joe breathed through his teeth and lowered his voice. "It's not what I meant, Liz. I didn't mean it like that. You're making it sound like—"

"You take Xavier hunting any time he asks, without hesitation," Elizabeth said. "Andrew has to *beg* you to take him. It's like he has to convince you to spend any time together!"

Elizabeth tried to make eye-contact with Andrew but he quickly looked away, his red-streaked eyes studying his lap.

His mother exhaled and dropped into her chair. She looked up at Joe.

"I'm proud of my sons—*both* of them," she said. "They each have incredible skills. They're kind and smart. We've taught them well and they will both grow up to be good men—good at whatever they choose to do, whatever they choose to be."

Joe spit the cherry pits into his cupped hand and tossed them into the garbage bin. He walked toward the dining room but paused underneath the wooden awning. He studied the leaves and flowers carved into the archway—an example of his handiwork seen throughout the aged farmhouse.

"Just let me tell him, okay?" he said. "He will take the … it will just be better coming from me. That's all I meant by it."

"This is happy news, Joe," Elizabeth said, her voice shaking. "You could at least congratulate our son."

Joe scrunched his flannel shirt up to his elbows, then dropped his arms, his scarred hands hanging at his side, squeezed into fists. He grumbled something under his breath and then turned away, a squeak from his boots as he trudged out the front door.

Andrew moaned and tossed on the cold cellar floor. In a sleepy haze, he slapped away a weight pushing down on his shoulder and rolled over. The pressure came again and his eyes opened to find Xavier hunched over him.

"You alright?" Xavier asked. "I think you were having a nightmare."

Andrew blinked, trying to focus. His cheeks were burning, a line of sweat dripping from his hairline and down his neck. He was trembling yet he managed to adjust the blanket which had been tossed aside in his sleep. He rolled up a corner of the comforter and laid back down.

"I'm okay," he said. But the studded crease along his brow remained.

"You look upset. You sure you're alright?" Xavier asked again.

Andrew continued to glare at Xavier but eventually nodded. "I said I'm fine," he said, rolling away from his brother.

He reached for his rifle, caressing the stock, laying his hand over the cool metal of the trigger guard. After some time, his eyelids began to droop and he dozed off again, sleep pulling him under until morning.

Chapter Thirteen

November 1994
Day 268 | Afternoon

Madeline Stover slid the blade from its casing and cut through the brown seal. One-by-one she pulled each vial out and placed them in a wire-framed tray on the storage cart. She wheeled toward the exit of the refrigerated storage unit but halted suddenly, a whiff of wild orange and clove on the air. She spun to see a shadow in the doorway.

"Hello there, what are you up to?" The voice was sweet enough but the cadence was off, something fake about the tone.

Madeline squinted. "Dr. Till?"

"Yes, I just came down to see how preparations were coming along," Angela said.

Madeline stood rigid. "Fine. Th - they're coming along fine," she stammered. "I must admit, I'm surprised to see you here. I mean, all the way down here in the basement. In the storage area."

"Sorry dear, I didn't catch your name."

"Oh, I'm Madeline, from the Family Health department. Everyone just calls me Maddy, though."

Angela stared blankly.

"I work in Kevin Midas' section," Maddy sputtered. "I

report to Sajee Kassan."

"Okay, so listen," Angela said. "I wanted to check how the vaccinations are being transported from here to the clinic. The ones on your cart here—where were these taken from?"

Maddy pointed to a row of identical grey coolers. There was a prominent black and white logo on the container with *Ministry of Health* written in large bold font.

"From right over there," Maddy said.

"Ah yes, I was afraid of that," Angela said. "You see those are the *old* vaccines. The ones we actually want to use are on that shelving unit over there, along the other wall."

Angela spun and led Maddy toward several blue metal racks. They were lined with dozens of slimmer coolers, almost hidden from view.

Maddy tilted her head to read the writing engraved on them.

"BioHealth Pharmaceuticals?"

There was a grey logo underneath the lettering. She couldn't quite make it out but it seemed to be a stencilled image of a buck staring straight ahead, stoic. The ink had run and the borders were now smudged producing black globs dripping from the antlers, the snout of the animal smeared and blurred— a wrathful face melting in the sun.

"Yes, here they are," Angela sang, motioning toward the stacked containers.

"These ones? Direct from a pharmaceutical company?"

"Yes, these are the ones. Now let's bring your cart over here and replace the ones you have with these—"

"But, Dr. Till," Maddy interrupted. "We've always used the vaccinations from the Ministry of Health. Why would a pharmaceutical company ship right to us? Everything needs to be tested and vetted through the Ministry. We only get our shipments through them."

Angela forced a smile. "Perhaps there has been a change in protocol this year. I'm not sure, I don't pay much attention to these administrative details, these trivial matters. Those are dealt with at your level."

Maddy shrunk and remained silent.

"Regardless, I know for sure the vaccinations we are to use are these ones," Angela continued. "The ones on the blue metal racks."

Maddy gave a nervous look. "Perhaps just let me verify the change with my manager—"

Angela turned on her. "You will switch these immediately!" she barked.

Maddy took a step back, her cheeks growing hot. She pulled at her sweater, staring forward, needing several seconds to recover from the outburst.

"Madeline, I have been very patient with you," Angela said. "But as leader of this health unit, I am telling you to return those vaccinations and instead, fill your cart with these ones."

Angela twisted her spidery arm and pointed forcefully toward the blue racks. "Is that clear?"

Maddy hesitated as she reached for the cart. She looked to Angela but quickly averted her eyes as a flash of anger rippled across the doctor's face. She pushed the cart to the back of the room and began returning the vials to the grey coolers.

"Dr. Till?" Sajee Kassan appeared at the door of the walk-in freezer, squinting toward the two figures inside.

"Dr. Till? Is that you?" Sajee took another step forward. "Oh, it is you. I didn't recognize you at first. You don't normally come down … I mean, what a nice surprise to see you. I just came to check on Maddy. Is everything okay? Is there anything I can help you with?"

Angela's gaze remained fixed on Maddy, her stare digging into the woman's back as the nurse slipped each glass tube into its original sleeve.

"We're fine," Angela said coldly. "I was just confirming with Madeline here that we're all set for the flu clinics later this month."

"Oh, we certainly are!" beamed Sajee. "But Dr. Till? I don't mean to be forward but I provided our preparation updates at yesterday's logistics meeting. It's great you have an interest in our work, but … well, I mean, can I help you with anything further?"

Angela remained silent, her back still turned. Sajee's heels clicked as she took a step forward.

"Well, do let me know if we can do anything more for you," she said timidly.

Angela cocked an eyebrow. "Actually, there is one thing you can do," she said.

"Certainly!" Sajee exclaimed. "Anything at all!"

"Notify the rest of your staff that the vaccinations we are using this year are the ones on the blue racks. The ones Madeline is putting back seem to have … well, they are simply not the right ones. Some mix up with the Ministry, most likely."

"Really?"

"You know how disorganized they are over there. They can't even lace up their shoes without mucking it up!"

Sajee's face dropped. "Oh, my, was there a problem with the ones delivered? I signed for them myself."

"No, no, we're just … we're just making a switch, that's all."

"I still don't understand … when we processed them, they met all the receiver criteria."

"Like I said, someone likely screwed up," Angela said. "Sometimes these things happen."

"Oh, I feel awful."

"We'll dispose of the old ones shortly but in the meantime, notify your staff they are to only use the ones on the blue metal racks. Only those ones are safe."

"But Dr. Till, there is a long list of protocols to follow. I mean, this is unusual, to make such a significant change so close to the clinics' opening."

Angela turned to Sajee and stared at her scornfully. "You do want to help me?" she said. "Right?"

Sajee swallowed. "Yes," she said hesitantly. "Of course, Dr. Till."

"Then notify your staff they are to only use those ones," Angela said, pointing.

"Yes, of course," Sajee said. "I'll send out a memo right away."

Angela kept her attention on Sajee, producing a crooked smile. And in that moment, Maddy slid a handful of vials into her sweater pocket before pushing the empty cart further into the freezer toward the blue metal racks.

Chapter Fourteen

March 1995
Day 415 | Morning

Maddy stretched her stubby legs, yawned loudly, and announced: "It reeks down here! We all stink!"

Everyone started to rouse from sleep. Evelyn wiped the crusted nuggets from her eyelids as Damien rubbed his shoulder where the rifle had repeatedly recoiled the night prior.

"Yes, I suppose we all do," Andrew said, methodically folding his sleeping blanket and placing it in the corner.

It took Xavier some convincing, but eventually everyone agreed it was likely safe enough during the daylight to tiptoe across the yard to the farmhouse and, one after the other, everyone could shower.

Andrew stood watch for the hour as each of the four strangers cautiously crept through the grass and into the house. Andrew showered last, the faucet only churning out lukewarm dribbles as the well and last of the hot water tank reserves struggled to keep up. He wasn't fussed by the low pressure though, the water still refreshing after several days without it.

He held the bar of soap to his nose and inhaled deeply. The sharp aroma of lavender reminded him of Juliana, her red hair bouncing off her shoulders, the scent of her perfume suspended between them for the entire flight. He smiled at the thought of her as a week of sweat and dirt swirled around his feet and down the metal drain.

"We all smell like a wedding party fresh from the salon," Andrew chuckled when he returned to the cellar. "Hopefully those creatures' sense of smell is as bad as their eyesight or they'll be able to sniff us out. Best if we lay low today anyway."

Maddy nodded in agreement. "Or at least until we start to stink again," she said, her mouth upturned into a smirk.

Andrew hung his damp towel on one of the metal racks to dry then distributed some of the remaining food: beans in maple syrup, a jar of pickles, a few tins of sliced peaches.

Evelyn opened a peach tin and raised one of the fleshy pieces to her lips. She gobbled it down, the sweet juice running down her chin, and quickly stabbed her fork into another. Andrew reached behind to one of the racks and unfolded a wrapped waxy cloth. Within it were thin strips of cooked meat resembling jerky. He offered a piece to Evelyn.

"What's this?" she asked.

Andrew winked. "Probably best if you don't know."

Evelyn bit down, chewed, and swallowed. She smiled as she reached for a second helping.

"Where'd you get this food?" Maddy asked, digging her spoon into a can of beans. She hungrily shoved the mound into her mouth and swallowed.

"Xavier stocked up several nights ago," Andrew said. "When things started to get strange, he took what he could from our house and some of the neighbours."

"Looks like you scored!"

"Well, don't be fooled. Most of those tins in the corner

are empty. We haven't tidied up yet. I guess next time, we have to steal a broom!"

Maddy nodded and hummed to herself, moving her foot through the tins. Many of them toppled over, the metal clanging along the cement floor.

"Still, thank you for sharing," she said. "We haven't had much to eat for some time now. Damien tried his best to hunt but besides an occasional rabbit, there wasn't much food to go around."

"How long were you in the forest?" Andrew asked.

"A little over a week. It was soon after I noticed a lot of people phoning in sick at work. I felt fine so I kept going in, but some of my co-workers seemed confused or not sure what they were supposed to be doing."

"What do you mean?"

"Well, many of them just walked around, in and out of boardrooms, like they didn't know where their seat was. This one guy, Gavin, came in one day with no pants on!"

"What? Are you serious?"

"And as weird as that sounds, what was even more strange is that no one seemed to notice. Or even cared. Everyone was in some sort of daze, like a constant stupor."

Maddy paused to put the last spoonful of beans into her mouth, licking the utensil clean. She brushed her damp hair from her forehead. "Then one morning, our receptionist, Lydia, gets up and walks out of the building," she continued. "Walks right in front of an oncoming truck! Boom! Dead on impact."

Andrew scrunched up his face in horror. "What?"

"People were saying Lydia did it on purpose but others said it was an accident. And some couldn't even remember who Lydia was. They just shrugged when they heard the news."

"That's unbelievable," Andrew said.

"There were rumours about all sorts of strange things happening," Maddy said. "But you didn't know what was true and what was nonsense. Until you went to the hospital."

"What do you mean?"

"People were being admitted for all kinds of strange things: bones poking through their skin, horrible head wounds. And it was constant, happening all the time. That's when I knew without a doubt that something was off."

"What'd you do?"

"I told my husband and son to leave town. I didn't want them to get caught up in it, whatever was going on. I wanted to go with them but felt I needed to stay back and help with the clinics."

"Oh, you're a doctor?"

"A public health nurse. But our training includes responding to emergencies so I often volunteer or get redeployed to the clinics."

"Our mother helped at one of the clinics," Andrew said.

"She did? Which one?"

"The one off of Main, about a block west of Hickory."

"Oh yeah, I know the one," Maddy said. "I don't get called to that one much, but I know of it. Where is she now?"

Andrew's shoulders slumped as he glanced at Xavier. "We're not sure. But we're looking for her—her and my step-father. But before she … disappeared, she told X some crazy stories about the clinic."

"Oh, there are some crazy stories, alright," Maddy said. "During my last shift there was this short fella who walked in, even shorter than me. I noticed right away that his head looked way too big for his body, like it was swollen or something. And then right there in front of me, I could see his head getting bigger. It was slow at first and I thought for sure I was imagining it. But sure enough, when I looked again, I saw it growing."

Evelyn sat down next to Maddy. "That's disgusting!" she said.

"What'd you do?" Andrew asked.

"The other nurses and I just stood there," Maddy said. "It was terrifying. We were frozen. I mean by this point we had seen some crazy stuff but nothing like this. This was completely different—like a mutation happening right before our eyes."

"What happened to the man?"

"We tried to get him in to see a doctor but we were so backed up. After a few minutes, he screamed how painful it was and then just began smashing his head against the wall." Maddy repeatedly slammed her fist into her palm. "He just pounded his head over and over again."

"That's so scary," Evelyn said.

"Eventually, his head went right through the drywall," Maddy said. "It must have hit a support beam because the whole clinic shook. The sound his head made against that steel post was horrible, just awful. He fell to the floor and didn't move again."

"Was he—was he dead?" Evelyn whispered.

Maddy drew quiet, Evelyn's question answered within the silence. "That was it for me," Maddy said after a moment. "I had seen enough. I walked right out of there and never went back."

"You left the clinic?" Andrew asked.

"Absolutely. I walked right past the security guard who was dragging that same fella to the back of the building. There was blood all over the tiles."

"What'd you do after you left?"

"I didn't know *what* to do. It was all too much for me. I mean, before he banged his head against the wall, he begged me to help him," Maddy said, her voice beginning to tremble. "But I couldn't. All I could do was … watch him die. I mean, in the end all I could do was walk away, you know? So, I walked right out to my pickup and drove like hell."

"Where'd you go?"

"I was trying to meet up with my husband and son. I had sent them to his parent's place, my in-laws. They're a good three-hour drive from here. But the road was blocked. There had to be a hundred people out there that night and they had those steel lines that puncture tires."

"Spike strips?"

"Yeah, those things. And these massive barrel fires were set all along the ditches. There's only the one road out of town so I—"

"Went into the woods?"

"Well, not at first," Maddy said. "First, I drove back home to get some things I thought I might need and then I went into the forest. I wanted to move around those barricades but within the safety of the trees. I figured it would take me less than a day to get beyond the town limits and find some help."

Maddy flinched as she reached around to the back of her neck. She squished a small spider between her fingers, flicking it to the cement below.

"But it didn't pan out that way," she continued. "I got

turned around and lost my way and had to spend the night out there. It was so cold. As soon as the sun came up, I started walking again. But in the woods, it's hard to figure out direction. I spent a second night lost out there …"

She sniffed, her eyes becoming red and moist. "I wasn't sure if I was going to make it or not. I was scared and I missed my boys so much."

She ran the sleeve of her shirt across her eyes and then raised her arm and pointed at Damien and Evelyn. "Thank goodness I ran into these two!" she said. "They gave me quite the scare sneaking up on me but I was very glad to see other people. I mean, other people that weren't going nuts! I travelled with them for, oh, I don't know, seven, maybe eight days?"

She looked to Damien and he nodded.

"He and Evelyn had come from the east, just beyond the town limits, and said things were getting strange out that way as well," Maddy continued. "Their parents are missing too so we decided to stay together and hunt for food. Decided to set up camp until we could figure things out, you know?"

Andrew nodded but stayed quiet.

"When we were out there, I kept thinking the cops would come and rescue us," Maddy continued. "But they never came. No one came."

"Is that when Xavier and I found you?"

"I suppose so. It was around that time."

"And when did you run into Rachel?"

"Oh, well, Damien spotted her running from town. She was with us for only a day or so until we spotted you two fellas."

A sudden silence came over the cellar as Maddy drew

quiet, nibbling on the last of the tinned peaches.

Throughout Maddy's retelling, Rachel regarded the small woman with piercing eyes and a set mouth. When the silence settled in, she shifted, closed her eyes, and leaned her head against the cement wall. She exhaled loudly, a quiet restlessness about her.

After some time, Evelyn spun to face Andrew. "Are there any more of those meat sticks?"

Andrew grimaced. "I'm afraid not."

Evelyn's shoulders slumped. She moved to one of the blankets and laid down, looking up at the ceiling.

"You know, my mother makes the best kabobs," Andrew said, sensing the girl's disappointment.

Evelyn bit at her lip, confused. She sat up.

"Meat sticks!" Andrew said. "Kabobs are just another name for meat sticks."

Evelyn nodded as Andrew repositioned himself along the concrete wall, his outstretched legs splayed across the narrow room.

"Anyway, my mom's kabobs were the best! She would use this spicy rub on them and man-oh-man would they jump with flavour! She probably made them once a week in the summer when my stepfather had the barbecue going."

"Sounds delicious," Evelyn said.

"But one morning—I'm like 11 years old or something—my mom is making kabobs at the sink," Andrew said, his voice now animated with the story. "She cuts the beef into strips, puts the rub on them and then puts each one onto a skewer. She leaves them in the fridge to marinate. But on that day, my stepfather decides to prank her. He prepares his *own* skewers. Except they're not made from beef."

"What were they made from?" Evelyn asked as she nervously pulled on her lip.

"Snake."

"SNAKE?" Evelyn screeched. She squirmed on the floor but motioned for Andrew to continue.

"Yep—snake. I don't know where in the world he got it from! He was always bringing weird things into the house, usually from his hunting trips."

Maddy chuckled as Evelyn screwed up her face. "That's so gross!"

"So, he chops the snake up the same size as my mom had done with the beef, uses the same spicy rub and everything. He even uses the same red-coloured Tupperware my mom used and he puts the kabobs in the fridge."

"Oh, that's sneaky," Maddy said.

"Sure enough, my mom comes home and thinks nothing of it. My stepfather goes ahead and barbecues and we all sit down and eat. My friend, Jeremiah, was over for dinner and even he gobbled them down. It wasn't until after dinner that my stepfather admitted what he had done."

"What'd you do?" Evelyn asked.

"My mom ran for the washroom. X, Jeremiah, and I stuck our fingers down our throats trying to make ourselves throw up. My stepfather just kept laughing, having the time of his life. In hindsight, it actually didn't taste that bad. But on that night, we kept giving each other the Heimlich, trying to get the damn things out!"

Evelyn stuck out her tongue in disgust. "I definitely don't want any snake! But I wish there were more of those other meat sticks."

"Here." The voice was rough and unexpected and caused

Evelyn to turn quickly. Xavier stood and leaned toward her. He handed her a piece of jerky then crumpled the empty cloth and tossed it back on the rack.

She nervously looked up. "Thank you."

Xavier grunted and shuffled to the other end of the cellar, moving his boot through the empty tins.

"We're almost out of food and water," he said. "We'll have to go out tomorrow."

"You think it's safe?" Andrew asked.

"We probably have enough for only one more meal down here," Xavier said. "We don't have much of a choice."

Andrew nodded. "Looks that way," he sighed.

"I can take Maddy, Rachel, and Evelyn and hit some of the neighbour's houses," Xavier said. "You and Damien go back into the woods and try your luck at hunting."

"You want us to go back into the forest?" Andrew asked. "We just got chased out of there!"

"I know. But they seem to come out closer to nightfall, closer to dusk. We might be okay if we all leave right in the morning. It'll be bright, so if there's anything out there, we should see it coming."

Xavier slid a dusty milk crate from the wall and plopped his tired body down with a thud. He drew out his knife and ran his finger along the length of it. He accidentally nicked the skin, the flesh parting, the red sap oozing over his fingernail.

"Besides," he muttered, staring at the syrupy blood stringing from the sliced digit. "We won't last long down here without more food and water. Won't last long at all."

Chapter Fifteen

March 1995
Day 416 | Dawn

The morning was met with a torrent of freezing rain, hard and heavy. It drenched the frozen dirt and sickly weeds as a thin mist circled the group atop the cellar's entrance. After a brief exchange, Andrew and Damien holstered their rifles, turned and trounced across the damp grass, frozen droplets spraying up from their boots, bent blades left in their wake.

Xavier pointed beyond the detached garage toward the gravel country road. "We'll head that way," he said.

"What's over there?" Maddy asked, her voice hoarse from a restless night.

"A few farmhouses," Xavier said. "I'm hoping for food and bottled water. Maybe something for sleeping. We're running low on bullets as well."

"What else should we look for?"

"Anything useful," Xavier said. "Batteries, rope, scissors, knives—anything with a sharp edge, really."

"How many houses are this way?"

"There's four or five along this road but they're all spaced hundreds of acres apart. I've gone through most of them but may have missed some things the first time around."

"Will there be more of those scary people?" Evelyn asked.

"I doubt it," Xavier said. "It's daylight, so we'll see them coming if any are around."

He drew the zipper up his raincoat, the teeth clicking together until they rested against his scruffy neck. He exhaled into the cold air, the steam from his breath clouding his stoic expression. He noticed Evelyn staring up, her wide brown eyes peeking out from beneath her wool toque.

"Just stay close to me," he said. "You'll be okay."

He headed east, flanked by Evelyn and Rachel. Maddy followed a few steps behind, humming nervously to herself.

They trudged through the ditch hugging the gravel road, staying low to the ground. The rainwater sloshed around as it streamed from one storm culvert to the next. They passed a stray border collie rummaging the ditch for food. Her ears perked when the group approached, but she cowered and slunk off when they got within a dozen yards.

"Why can't we use the road?" Maddy called out. "My shoes are soaking! There has to be half a foot of water in this ditch!"

"We'll be easy markers on the road," Xavier grumbled.

"To who? There's no one even out here!" Maddy yelled back. She drew her hood up over her frizzy hair and swatted the wet bangs off her forehead. Her rose-coloured sweatshirt had turned the colour of blood where the freezing rain had soaked it. "We could cover more ground if we used the road. It's starting to come down in sheets!"

Xavier ignored her as the group laboured on, passing several abandoned cars on the shoulder of the road. Every so often, he would creep toward one and check under the sun visor or floor mats for keys but he came up empty each time. Most of the cars were smashed and had flat tires, their wires pulled out from beneath the hoods, hoses and spark plugs littered on the ground.

They slogged on for nearly an hour longer. The sound of water rushing through the ditch became louder and louder to the point that no one heard the car approaching until Xavier whipped around.

"Get down!" he shouted. He dropped to his knee, guiding the rifle from his shoulder.

"They might be able to help," Maddy said. She began climbing out of the ditch, her arms waving above her head, until Xavier pulled her back down to the ground.

"We don't know who's in there," Xavier said.

"What, you think those creatures are driving now?" Maddy shot back.

"Given what we've seen, anyone that doesn't have a rifle strapped to their back is very suspect," Xavier said as the car roared past, wet scree and gravel spraying the yellow grass lining the ditch. He raised his head and watched the black Porsche continue its push toward the centre of town.

Maddy jumped to her feet. "They could have helped us!" she said. "They could have driven us right out of this nightmare!"

"Do you think they saw us?" Evelyn asked, her shoulders shaking through her threadbare coat. "Was it one of those crazy people?"

"I doubt it but we'll never know now," Maddy said. She turned and marched off through the ditch, her boots squelching as she trounced away.

"Better safe than sorry," Xavier grumbled under his breath. He readjusted his cargo pants and shook the water from his hair. He turned to face Rachel and Evelyn. "Let's keep moving," he said. "There's a house just up ahead. Just stay low and keep your ears tuned."

The group soon came upon a red-bricked farmhouse as a strong breeze drew up from the north. The hinges squealed as the screen door slammed over and over against the frame, the latch and handle torn off, laying in the grass a few yards away.

Xavier examined the claw marks along the damaged frame. "They've been here," he announced solemnly.

"They've been here or they're *still* here?" Maddy asked, her voice low.

Xavier looked back at the markings as a shudder grew across his shoulders. "Evelyn and I will search the kitchen and rooms upstairs," he said. "Maddy—you and Rachel check the main living area and any rooms toward the back of the house."

"You want us to split up?" Maddy asked.

"What I want is for us to be in and out of here as quick as we can!" Xavier chided. "We don't want to stay here any longer than we need to."

He and Evelyn cautiously walked down a narrow hallway and into the kitchen. Most of the cupboards were dangling from their hinges, the breakfast table overturned, wooden chairs splayed to each side of the room.

Xavier stepped toward the rear of the kitchen, his heavy boots shuffling over the aged floorboards, and peered out the glass sliding door leading to the back deck. He noticed the barbecue tipped on its side, the propane tank smashed and dented. He surveyed the door frame, deep gauges splintered along the curved wood.

"Something was trying to get in," he mumbled to himself.

He moved toward the pantry but then spun to examine

the wood again. His fingers fumbled over the coarse indents and he noticed the markings were only on the inside of the frame. The outside was free from damage.

He exhaled sharply. "Or something was trying to get *out*," he whispered.

He moved deeper into the kitchen. A well-water safety certificate hung on the fridge, signed by the region's Medical Officer of Health. *PASS* was displayed across it in green lettering with the date of *April 1994* squished at the bottom. An expired electricity bill was tapped to the fridge, a handwritten note scribbled across it: *Mary, please remember to pay by Friday!*

Xavier shifted and noticed a photo of a man and a woman seated at a picnic table. The couple wore jean shorts and tank tops, squinting toward the camera. This same man was in a second photo, beaming. His arm was wrapped around a brute of another, scars down his cheek and a missing front tooth.

Xavier leaned in closer. "That's Tony *the Tank* MacAvoy!"

"Who's that?" Evelyn said from across the room.

"He's a retired hockey player—a hall-of-famer."

Xavier noticed the date stamp on the photograph: *November 21, 1994*. Behind the gentlemen in the photo were rows of desks, several women in white smocks sitting at each one.

He yanked the fridge open and breathed in the pungent smell. Everything had spoiled. A murky film covered the black olives, translucent milk bags lumpy and congealed.

He moved around the kitchen, rifling through several drawers. His fist closed around something solid and he drew out a roll of sticky duct tape. He dug further but only found scattered notepaper and a few thumbtacks. The drawer whistled shut as he moved onto the next one.

"Check those drawers over there," he instructed Evelyn.

She cautiously shuffled across the kitchen and pulled drawers open one by one. "What are we looking for?"

"Like I said before, anything that can help us: knives, ropes, bullets—"

"You think they keep bullets in the *kitchen?*"

Xavier turned and grunted.

"How about a stapler?" she teased, holding one up.

"No, not a stapler," he said. "Just keep quiet and keep looking. If we don't find anything here, we'll head upstairs."

In the den down the hall, Rachel was routing through a wooden desk. Maddy knelt on the floor beside her, rummaging through stacked cardboard boxes. She raised a dated edition of a well-thumbed newspaper.

"Do you read this paper?" she asked. "*The Chronicle?*"

Rachel turned to look at it then shook her head.

"This Brad Moseby guy," Maddy continued, pointing to the front-page article. "He's just a local columnist but fancies himself a big-time writer."

"Never heard of him."

"Yeah, well, he's always hanging around our office, asking the strangest questions about water sanitation and if every town buys their chemicals from the same supplier. I mean, how am I supposed to know what other towns do?"

Rachel smirked.

"A bit of a cowboy if you ask me," Maddy continued. "Not sure many people liked him snooping around but I guess he was just trying to do his job."

After several minutes, the two of them had accumulated a modest pile of supplies to bring back to the cellar: batteries, scissors, a blanket, a roll of toilet paper.

Maddy pushed another heavy box aside. "There are only tax documents in this one, nothing useful to us."

"I'm not finding anything over here either," Rachel grunted.

She continued flipping through some of the papers on the table when she paused on a flyer advertising flu clinics. The flyer had bright bold lettering along the top: *Get your flu shot and photo with your favourite hockey stars! Games and music for the kids! Free face painting! November 20 – 30th, 1994. Come see us at the brand new Community Centre or Main Street Public Library.*

She held up the flyer as Maddy strained her neck to see. "Seemed like a lot of hoopla over getting a flu shot," Rachel mused.

"Oh, yes, I remember that," Maddy said. "They made a big deal of the clinics. There was a lot of excitement around the events, a lot of gimmicks to get people inoculated. Did you get your shot?"

"No, I never made it. My birthday is in November and my sister surprised me with roundtrip tickets to Sarasota."

"Wow, that's quite the birthday present! All I got for my birthday were socks!" Maddy said. "I would have loved to have been in the sun and out of here for a few weeks—especially in November! What dates were you gone for?"

Rachel pointed to the flyer. "Funny enough, it was these exact dates. I flew out the morning of the 20th and returned late on the 30th."

"Did you end up going to another town for your shot?"

"No, it's one of those things that you keep putting off and then spring comes and you realize you never got around to it."

Rachel continued to shuffle through the documents but jerked her hand away as a drop of red stained the papers. She put her finger to her lips, sucking the wound, but it was still bleeding when she removed it from her mouth.

Maddy scrunched up her face. "That's quite the paper cut. Bring it here."

She wrapped some of the toilet paper around the wound, squeezing tight for several seconds and then looked up at Rachel.

"You know, you look familiar."

"Oh?" Rachel whispered softly.

"I noticed it when we first met. It's like I know you from somewhere but can't quite place my finger on it."

"I don't think so." Rachel mumbled. "Maybe we've just passed each other on the street? It's quite a small town, after all."

Maddy opened her mouth to speak again but Rachel yanked her hand suddenly, the bloodied toilet paper falling to the floor.

"Well, it's still bleeding quite a bit," Maddy said, examining the wound. "Let's go—maybe the others found Band-Aids."

A sudden noise came from overhead as though someone was shifting their weight from one leg to the other. There was a long pause as both women tuned into the sound. Maddy followed Rachel's stare toward the ceiling.

"It's probably just old floorboards," she whispered nervously. "Let's look in the dining room. There's nothing useful in here anyway."

Upstairs, Evelyn pushed on the door of the primary bedroom. A ball of flies buzzed frantically in the corner as she stepped around the queen-size bed. She bent over from the smell but jumped back when she spotted the woman coiled on the floor. She tried to cover her mouth but failed to muffle her own scream.

In a shot, Xavier was in the room. He scooped up the girl, carrying the wailing child down the hall to the landing. He turned back toward the room but Evelyn thrashed and flailed, terror swarming her eyes as she clawed at his chest and arms.

"Don't go! Please don't leave me here! Don't leave me!"

"It's okay. It won't hurt you," Xavier said. "I just need to go back and check something." He paused for a moment, looking down at the child, and then scrambled back to the room.

The woman's face was the colour of smoke, the texture of her skin thick like glue. Bags sagged under her eyes to merge with her swollen cheeks, one eye frozen open, fixated on the floor. Her limbs were knotted and deformed, her nails yellow and cracked and sharp as knives.

Xavier moved closer and noticed a red line across the woman's neck, crusted blood coating the wound. A clump of wet dark matter congealed out from one ear.

He heard Maddy hustling up the stairs so he turned and yelled into the hallway. "Have you come across another one?"

"Another what?" Maddy hollered.

She finally reached Evelyn on the landing and placed her hand on the girl's arm. Kneeling down, she rubbed Evelyn's trembling shoulders. "You'll be okay," she said. "Everything's okay. We'll go very soon."

Xavier shuffled back toward the staircase. "What did you find?" he asked.

"A few bottles of water, a blanket, toilet paper, scissors—"

"Good. Bring it all. We have to leave!"

"Why? What's in that room?"

Xavier turned to face her and his look caused her to draw back.

"It was strangled," he said. "Very recently. And if *one* of those things is around a second one's not far off."

Xavier's shirt was soaked with sweat, his hand tight around the stock of his rifle. "We need to head back to the cellar. We've gathered enough for today."

Maddy nodded and the four of them bounded down the stairs and out the front door, sprinting the length of the driveway.

Evelyn struggled to keep pace, her one leg weaker than the other, her neck swivelling as she frantically searched for movement in the surrounding fields. "Will we have enough food for tonight?" she called out.

"Hopefully the other two had more luck," Xavier yelled over his shoulder. "It doesn't matter though—we're heading back now. Without Andrew here, I don't want to get in another shoot-out with those things!"

"Was she dead? Was that lady dead?" Evelyn asked, her voice shaking.

"Yeah, she was dead. But it's not her I'm worried about."

Evelyn shook and made a noise in her throat, her skin sheen with sweat and tears. She reached up to Xavier, her outstretched hand trembling. Xavier grabbed it in his.

"It's okay," he said. "It'll be okay. But you need to move. We need to hurry!"

The rain had subsided and the sun was out now, bright and piercing. It was so bright that when Evelyn turned back toward the house, she couldn't fully focus. The glare was so vivid that even when squinting she couldn't make out the outline of the figure standing by the bedroom window. She didn't see its excited pacing nor bloodshot eyes, its sharp stare following her every step.

"Any luck?" Xavier asked atop the cellar later that day.

Damien solemnly shook his head and heaved the cellar door open, clunking his boots down the wooden stairs to join the women.

Andrew sighed. "Sorry, but we'll have to go out again tomorrow. We'll have better luck with all of us." He kicked at the ground. "Any sign of Mom or Joe?"

Xavier lowered the cellar door to block their voices and turned to Andrew. "No, but we saw one, right up close. It was in one of the houses we went through."

"What? Did it chase you?"

"It was dead. She had been murdered."

"Murdered?"

"Strangled. Looked like they had used a thin rope. But I don't think she had been dead for long."

"How do you know?"

"The whole scene was … was fresh. Like it had happened just before we arrived. And the smell in that room—the smell was so strong. It was that burning metal smell, that horrible aluminum smell."

"Who do you think killed her? Someone like us? Someone who isn't crazy, I mean?"

"Maybe, but we didn't see anyone else."

Andrew's eyes widened with a new thought. "Are they killing each other now?"

Xavier wiped at his beard. "I have no idea. Evelyn saw it

too. She came across it first."

"Is she okay?"

"It really spooked her. She hasn't said much since we ran from the house."

"It's a lot. This whole thing is a lot."

"She was beyond terrified. No kid should have to see anything like that."

"Never mind kids! *No one* should have to see any of this, period! This whole thing is a nightmare!"

Xavier reached down to lift the cellar door but turned back to Andrew. "I can't get the look on her face out of my mind. I keep seeing it over and over."

"Of the dead lady?"

"No … Evelyn's."

Andrew sighed. "It's just fresh in your mind. Don't worry too much about it. In time, she'll get over it. She'll be okay."

"Maybe you're right."

"Let's head down. I'll take first watch tonight. Once you get a good sleep, you'll forget all about today. Or the worst of it, anyways."

They joined the others in the cellar and after eating the last of the food tins, everyone laid blankets on the floor and drifted off to sleep. Everyone except Xavier. He tossed and turned much of the night. And more than once, Andrew woke to find Xavier pacing, his face long and anxious, staring down at the child as she slept.

Chapter Sixteen

January 1995
Day 328 | Night

Dressed in a starched-white lab coat, Angela pulled up to the bench and twisted a glass slide from the box. She seized the rubber bulb of a nearby dropper and dipped its pointed end into the pipette beside her. The glass container showed two images along its label: a skull-and-crossbones lined the top while a picture of a buck with full antlers sat beneath it.

Angela dripped several drops of the liquid onto the slide and jimmied it into position under the microscope. Staring down the eyepiece, she mumbled to herself, jotting down chemical names and percentages in the yellow notepad. She thumbed to where additional calculations were strewn across the pages. Studying the figures, she pursed her lips, prominent creases running along her brow.

She reached into the burgundy briefcase and removed a metal cylinder, a yellow bio-hazard symbol emblazoned on the side. With steady hands, she cleaned the dropper and transferred a small amount of the solution. She smeared the crimson substance onto the same slide then lowered her head toward the microscope.

For some time, the soft hum of the sequencing machines

was the only noise in the muted laboratory. Angela remained hunched over, occasionally pawing at her nose, the astringent burn of bleach and peroxide irritating her.

Eventually she sat up. She rubbed her temples, slight indents along her forehead from the hard plastic eyepiece and head cradle.

Meticulously washing the slide and station, she repositioned the microscope into its original place. She returned the container of clear liquid to the back room and the metal cylinder to the briefcase. She jotted down several additional figures in the notepad, a faint smirk teasing at the edges of her mouth.

She scanned the work area one last time before heading for the exit. Although no one else was there, her eyes lit up and her mouth knotted into a jagged smile—stained lips and big teeth—just before the light flicked off.

Chapter Seventeen

March 1995
Day 417 | Morning

Damien and Andrew shuffled through the undergrowth as the orange sun crested the eastern horizon. They came upon a hill beside the lee of a jagged stone and both laid prone in the damp grass. Damien removed a pair of binoculars from their casing and peered through them.

"Recognize this place?" Andrew asked.

Damien swivelled to gaze upon the fields in front of him. He shook his head.

"It's the same hill we shot down all those maniacs the day we met you guys. It's a great place for hunting—elevated with fantastic sight lines."

Damien squinted into the brush and could see a few bodies lying motionless, an arm or leg spread lazily across a fallen trunk.

"X and I would often hunt from this very spot," Andrew continued. "Mind you, we were usually hunting deer, not mutated crazy people."

Damien snorted. "Do you think they'll come back here?"

"Let's hope not. But I have been thinking about them. Trying to deduce clues, trying to see any patterns."

"And?"

"I don't have much to go on, to be honest with you," Andrew sighed. "None of them are right in the head, we know that much."

"Yeah, that's obvious," Damien said.

"But still there are differences. Like some are really far gone and others still seem to be with it, you know? Like they're experiencing different phases of a virus or something."

Damien looked through the binoculars again before turning back toward Andrew. "Are you scared of them?" he asked.

"They're resilient, I'll give them that. But they don't appear to be very clever. I mean, take the other night right here on this hill. They just kept running toward us. There was no strategy in their attack."

Damien fiddled with the angle of the lens and spotted his sister, a small speck in the distance walking hand-in-hand with Maddy.

"As Maddy said, they're likely all from around here," Andrew said. "She's even scared she might recognize some as friends or co-workers. So, it wasn't that long ago they used to be regular people, used to think and act like normal folks."

"Do you believe that?"

"I don't think those human traits are that far from the surface. But who knows? It's just a theory, I suppose."

"Maybe … Maybe you're right."

"You disagree? You think they're too far gone?"

"I just don't want to be the one to test your theory."

Andrew chuckled and they both laid in the grass for some time, the sun's heat warming their backs. Lying only a yard apart, Andrew could see Damien had lost weight even in the short time they had been together. The boy's jacket hung off his slender frame and he constantly pulled at his pants to sit atop his shrunken waist. He shifted again, scratching at something down his back, and Andrew noticed a line of pinpoint scabs along the boy's spine just before Damien lowered his shirt.

Andrew rotated onto his side and pulled out the piece of paper with Juliana's name and number on it. He had been thinking of her lately, her kind eyes, her vibrant laugh. He had spoken to her for less than an hour on the flight but for some reason she had carved something special into him, a welcomed knot in a plank of wood. He ran his finger over her name, the small heart over the 'i', then folded and put the note back in his pocket.

He tilted toward Damien. "See anything worth shooting?"

Damien lowered the binoculars and smirked. "That could mean anything nowadays."

Andrew laughed, his eyes half shut, the skin beneath them sagging. He too was leaner than even a few days ago, his jawline more prominent, tufts of dark hair sprouting from his cheeks and throat.

"Listen," Andrew said. "I want to apologize for when I first came across you in the forest, asking all those questions right off the hop."

Damien waved the words away. "Don't worry about it," he said.

"I was just trying to understand what was going on, where all these creatures were coming from. We hardly knew anything then."

"I don't think you meant anything by it."

"It was insensitive, none-the-less."

"Like I said, don't worry about it."

Andrew pressed his lips together then let out a tired

breath. "You know, you remind me of my best friend, Jeremiah."

"Oh yeah?"

"Quiet mostly, and patient. You kind of look like him too."

"He's Ojibway?"

Andrew nodded.

"Yeah, me too," Damien said. "Well, half. White dad, Ojibway mom."

"Yeah, that's what I figured—"

Suddenly startled, Damien sprang to his feet. "I don't hear her anymore!"

"Who?"

"Evelyn. I don't hear her voice."

"Could you hear her before?"

"Yes. It was faint, but I could hear her." He raised the binoculars, scanning back and forth across the field.

"Do you see her?" Andrew asked.

"I see Rachel and Maddy—they're a few hundred yards south of us. But I don't see Ev."

"I'm sure she's there. I don't think she'd stray far from Maddy."

Damien lowered the binoculars. "I'm telling you she's not there!"

"Alright, well let's head over and check it out," Andrew said. "It's not like we're having any luck here anyways."

It took them several minutes to reach the others. The ground cover was thick to jog through and they needed to navigate an icy bog; the stale, decaying odour caused Andrew to gag as they crossed over it.

"Where's Evelyn?" Damien asked as they came upon

Maddy and Rachel.

"I'm not sure," Maddy said. "She must have drifted off toward the trees."

"When did you see her last?" Damien asked anxiously.

"I don't remember. I'm sorry but I'm just so tired, I haven't been paying much attention. It's been, I don't know, maybe five minutes … maybe more."

As the words left her mouth, Maddy began to tremble and she cupped her hands to her mouth. "Evelyn come back, sweetie! If you can hear me, please come back!"

She frantically called out several more times, pausing to listen, but heard nothing. "Damien, I'm so sorry," she said. "I'm just so hungry and not thinking clearly. We must've misplaced each other."

Damien spun to face Andrew, a look of panic across his face. "Wait, where's Xavier?"

Evelyn's small hands struggled to force the bolt open. She laid the rifle in the grass and tried to pry it loose a second time. It finally wriggled free and she placed a cartridge into the breech, pushing the bolt closed, forming a smooth line from stock to barrel.

"How far is that tree?" she asked.

Lying in the snow and damp grass beside her, Xavier tilted his head, his gaze following her pointed finger. "Forty yards … fifty at most."

Evelyn breathed deeply. "How far can this gun shoot?" she asked.

"A hundred and fifty yards. An experienced hunter might

get two hundred out of it."

"How far can you shoot?"

"Me? Well, I've been doing this since I was very young, even younger than you. My father taught me to hunt and I took to it right away."

He produced an awkward smile. After so many weeks of fear and tension, the movement seemed almost foreign to his cheeks and jaw.

"My father was raised right here in this same town so he knows these forests, knows this land," he continued. "He taught me to respect it so most of the time I only hunt when he and I are stocking up for the winter."

"Or when crazy people are chasing you?" Evelyn said. She brushed her knotted hair from her eyes and smiled.

"That's a good point. I only shoot for food and to avoid *becoming* food!" Xavier laughed. It was a gravelly bark—a distinct sound Andrew heard often growing up and a noise that now caught his ear on the wind. He motioned to Damien and they turned east, following the faint echo.

"So, how far can you shoot?" Evelyn asked again.

"I could peg a beaver sunning on top of its dam three hundred yards away if I needed to," he boasted. He rolled next to her. "Now, are you ready?"

She nodded and held the rifle close to her face, her skin blending with the tanned wood.

"Okay, press your cheek into the stock," Xavier instructed.

Evelyn shrugged, balancing the rifle between her chin and shoulder. The wood was polished smooth, worn down from years of use.

"That's it," Xavier said. "Now hold the gun steady. Place one hand near the trigger and the other one along the base of the barrel. You don't want any muzzle sway."

"Muzzle what?"

"Muzzle sway. Basically, you don't want the gun to move too much after you've shot it."

He pointed to the apparatus snapped atop the rifle. "Now, don't worry about zeroing the scope for now. Just stare down it until you see the front site in the middle of the crosshairs— that sort of ball at the end of the barrel. See it?"

Evelyn repositioned the gun and nodded.

"Wherever that front site is pointing is where the bullet will go, so line that up with your target. Now I want you to click the safety with your thumb."

"This button here?"

"Yeah. And now when you're ready, pull the trigger back, like a squeezing motion. The rifle will move after you shoot so be ready for some kick—"

The air exploded and a sour smell drifted up around them. Fifty yards away a knotted piece of bark flung off a skinny red maple.

"Ha! What a shot!" Xavier crowed. "Are you sure your brother's never taken you hunting?"

Evelyn's cheeks flushed pink. "No, he's never even let me hold a gun!"

Xavier reached out and tousled her hair. "That's a shame because you're a natural!" he said.

Evelyn smiled a toothy grin, an array of baby and adult teeth fighting for room in her small mouth. But then staring at the rifle she suddenly became quiet.

"Xavier, do you think Damien and I will find our parents?" she finally asked.

Xavier swallowed, adjusting the snug hunting jacket along

his shoulders. "Yes, of course we'll find them. Why would you even ask that?"

"It's just that … well, you and Andrew are missing your parents, and Damien and I are missing our parents, and Maddy is missing her family, and I just thought because so many people are missing other people then maybe, well maybe they won't be found."

"Listen to me, okay? Everyday Andrew and I look for our parents, no matter where we are, we're looking for signs. And that includes *your* parents as well. We're going to find them. All of them, okay?"

Evelyn hesitated but eventually nodded.

"Now, that was quite a shot you just did, you should be proud of that," Xavier said. "But let me see your hand."

The young girl stretched out her arm as Xavier examined her palm, turning it over in his.

"You see, sometimes you'll get red marks or small cuts along your palm if you're gripping the stock too tight. When my dad taught me to shoot, he would run his finger along my hand after each shot."

Xavier slid along Evelyn's fleshy palm, through the main divot in the centre, and up her pointer finger.

"He was looking for signs—a blister or something—that showed I was squeezing too tight or holding the gun wrong. He would say *'keep your grip loose and you'll bag a moose.'* It was a stupid saying but Andrew and I laughed at it when we were younger."

"My uncle used to say the same thing," Evelyn giggled.

Xavier stared at her. "Really? I thought that was something my dad just made up." After a moment he cleared his throat. "Anyway, should we try again?"

"That's enough!" said Damien, suddenly coming upon them. He reached down and yanked the rifle from his sister.

"Hey!" Xavier said. He pushed himself from the ground and lunged for the rifle but Damien swung the weapon over his shoulder and out of reach in one fluid motion.

For a moment they both stood silent, eyes locked on one another.

"She asked me to teach her," Xavier said. "There was no harm—"

"I said that's enough," Damien growled.

"Oh, Evelyn! I'm so glad we found you!" Maddy said as she caught up with the rest of the group. "Did you get lost? Is everything okay?"

Evelyn scurried toward Maddy but Damien cut her off and grabbed her by the arm, trouncing through the yellow stalks, pulling the child roughly behind him.

"Is everything okay?" Maddy asked again.

But Andrew and Xavier said nothing. They were already walking away, following Damien and Evelyn at a distance.

Chapter Eighteen

March 1995
Day 417 | Late Afternoon

The sun descended in the overcast sky as the group walked in silence for most of the afternoon. Damien and Xavier didn't reach for their guns once, each with their head down and quiet. Andrew fired at a weasel slinking among the bulrushes, but he was too noisy in his approach and the clever animal dropped into the water before he could load again.

As the day drifted into early evening, he pulled Xavier out of earshot of the others. "Why would you disappear like that?" he asked, the words more forceful than he intended.

"I was just teaching her how to shoot."

"You know everyone's on edge, X. What did you think was going to happen?"

Xavier snorted but said nothing.

"His sister is suddenly gone so naturally he thought the worst," Andrew continued. "It was only when I heard you laugh and the gun go off that we knew where you were. But a gunshot these days means one of two things: you found something or it found you!"

"I was showing her how the gun works. Someone ought to with what's going on around here!"

"That's not up to you! Besides, you're still a stranger to

him. You don't say much in the cellar, he still doesn't know what to make of you. When he's calmed down you should try to talk to him."

"I didn't ask for your advice," Xavier shouted. "But you keep giving it. Time and again, you keep telling me how to live my life!"

"Whoa—what the hell is that supposed to mean?"

Xavier exhaled sharply, muttering something under his breath.

"Listen, you're on edge, I get it," Andrew said. "Is it because we haven't found Mom and Dad yet?"

"No, it's not because we haven't found Mom and Dad," Xavier sneered. "And besides, he's not your dad!"

It must have been something in Xavier's voice, the cut of it, the hoarseness of it, because all at once, the memories flooded back to Andrew. He was young, maybe 10, his bedsheets held tight to his neck. His mother sat opposite his bed, leaning forward in her chair, a mix of sprigs and wildflowers on the nightstand.

"Tell me again why he left," Andrew asked, his voice cracking with emotion.

"Come now," his mother said. "Let's not get into that. Your father had his reasons and none of them had to do with you, okay?"

His mother reached out to him and tucked an orphan strand of shaggy hair behind his ear. Andrew looked up with wet eyes, a wide gap between his front teeth. She brought him to her lap and began to soothe him, whispering, gently rubbing his back. When he had calmed, she eased him back under the bedsheets, tucking the heavy quilt taut along the mattress.

"Joe is a good man," she said as if reading his thoughts. "I know he's not your real father, but he's just as good a dad as one could have. You go to sleep now, okay?"

She kissed his forehead and left the room.

After a few quiet moments, Xavier rolled over from his own bed jutted into the corner.

"He's still not your real dad," he said coldly.

Even at a young age, Xavier had such a strong, hard way of looking at people. Andrew's stomach twisted and his body felt like an open wound. He rolled away from Xavier, lying awake most of the night, his tears silently snaking down his flushed cheeks.

Among the trees, Andrew balled his fists. "I haven't had it easy either," he said. "Your life is hard, I get that. But mine hasn't been a walk in the park."

Xavier turned away and began walking in the other direction. Andrew followed at a distance for some time to let his anger subside. After several minutes, he moved to within a few yards of Xavier.

"Listen, I know you're frustrated about not finding them yet but they're still alive. I know it, I can sense it," he said.

"So, we're working off a sense now? A hunch?" Xavier said, turning on his brother. "There hasn't been one sign of them since I fled the house three weeks ago!"

"Look, at least I'm trying," Andrew said, the fury in his voice returning. "I don't have much to go on but yeah, this is me trying!"

"So, now you're gonna start trying, huh? Start trying to be a big brother?"

"What the hell does that mean?"

"You left me!" Xavier shouted. "Last September, you left

and never looked back!"

"I went to school, that's a pretty normal thing to do. Besides, we got in another huge fight that day, so yeah, I just left."

"But you were never around! Even growing up you never had time for me."

"What are you talking about? We did lots together. We even shared a bedroom for Christ's sake—"

"And where were you when all of this happened, huh?" He lunged forward, jabbing a finger into Andrew's chest. "You left Mom and Dad and me to fend for ourselves. We needed you and you weren't around!"

"I had no idea about this freak show, you can't blame me for that!"

"Oh, but of course you weren't here. It's always *school, school, school,* and *look how smart Andrew is.*"

"Is that what this is all about, huh? That I'm good at school and you're not?"

"You've always thought you were better than me!" Xavier screamed and his body shook as if exorcising an ancient demon.

Andrew froze. His legs became weak and shaky as he tried to steady himself. He was suddenly nauseous, his head spinning, and he gripped his chest, a feeling like he was being pummelled by fists. Gasping for air, he waited for the pain to pass, but still it lingered. He opened his mouth to speak but Xavier jumped forward.

"You figured long ago that you were better than me," Xavier growled. "And then you left … just up and left and disappeared, leaving me to deal with all of this." Xavier stared at him long and cold. He turned suddenly and stormed into the trees, his eyes cast down for the rest of the afternoon.

Andrew kept his distance as the group trudged through the forest and it was dusk by the time the cellar came into view.

Andrew lifted the heavy door and the group made their way down the familiar steps into the dark. Reaching behind him, he pulled the door shut, flicking his flashlight on. He sniffed at the air, but by the time the scent reached him it was already too late.

Evelyn's scream was cut short as two thick arms reached out from the shadows, clawing at her throat. A raspy cry strained out of her until the heel of Xavier's rifle smashed against the intruder's head. The dark form recoiled for a moment but then pounced again.

"Look out!" Andrew hollered, shining the light toward the noise.

Xavier swung the rifle again, the stock crushing the creature's skull against the cement wall. It went limp and collapsed, blood and bile pooling beneath it.

Steadying himself, Xavier swung the rifle again as a second creature charged. It screeched and grabbed the gun, throwing it to the ground. Stumbling, Xavier crashed into one of the metal racks, toppling several empty Mason jars and the mallet. The creature wailed and bared its teeth, forcing itself upon him.

"X!" Andrew yelled.

Xavier reached for the mallet and swung, hammering a deep dent into the creature's head. The beast shook for a moment but then lunged again, landing forcefully on top of Xavier. A loud clink sounded as Xavier went limp, the metal mallet dropping to the cement floor.

"No!" Maddy shrieked.

She grabbed the pair of scissors, raised them high into the air, but the monster swiped at her and she fell hard against the far wall.

The beast turned to face Xavier once again but then howled in pain, flailing and twisting its crooked back. Andrew stood behind it, turning the hilt of his knife over and over again.

The creature squealed, hissing in short bursts. Andrew threw it to the floor and jerked the knife out and then back in through its collapsed lung. He stepped away and looked down at the crumpled shape, his shoulders heaving with adrenaline. His eyes dropped as he wiped the knife along his ripped pants.

Xavier rolled over and fumbled for a second flashlight, feeling for the cold metal. He shone the light around the cellar, searching the corners.

"Are we clear?" Andrew asked.

The light bounced along the walls and up the stairs. Xavier exhaled, trying to steady his breathing. "We're clear, that's all of them," he said. "Is everyone okay?"

"I think so," Maddy trembled. "How about you?"

Xavier nodded then flashed the light toward his brother, a shudder moving along Andrew's shoulders, a faint murmur on his lips. Xavier shone the light back toward the thing lying dead on the floor and he slowly started to recognize its features: the almond-shaped copper eyes, the lanky frame, the thick scar along its lower lip.

"Oh, God," he whispered.

"What is it?" Maddy asked.

Xavier exhaled deeply. "His name is Jeremiah Cook. Andrew and I grew up with him. He was Andrew's best friend."

Maddy covered her mouth. "Oh no," she whispered.

She leaned toward the body. It was littered with knife wounds, dark stains dampening the over-sized shirt. The blood seemed to be congealing along the lines of the wounds. Even the liquid pooling on the floor seemed to be moving and curling into itself, like a snake slithering, seeking out its own tail.

There were grey markings on the boy's left wrist. It appeared to be a temporary tattoo of some sort—a deer with antlers jutting out. But the image was smudged and faded, looking more like beads of black blood dripping off the animal's long face, its eyes hollow, the logo smeared into something unnatural and grotesque.

She turned to Xavier just as his head snapped up.

"Evelyn, come here!" he shouted.

He grabbed her by the forearm, turning it over. A spot of blood sat idle on her skin. It was murky—a colour closer to black than the normal red hue. And then the blood began to move. Not down her arm the way gravity would pull at it, but up it. And as the blood climbed it began to vibrate, a slight quiver to it.

"Is that *your* blood or—"

Evelyn met his eyes and swallowed.

Xavier turned to the creature curled on the floor and then back to Evelyn.

"Maddy, grab the first aid kit from my bag!" he shouted.

Maddy struggled to unclasp the buckles. She yanked out a bulging pouch with a red cross strewn on it.

"Give me a cloth and anything with strong chemicals in it!" Xavier barked.

Maddy peeled a sling from its wrapper. She twisted the

cap from a small vial of antiseptic and soaked the thick cotton with it. Xavier grabbed it and wiped the blood from Evelyn's arm. He crumpled the sling on the floor and began rubbing forcefully with a second cloth.

"I think she's good now," Damien said.

Xavier snapped the lid off a second bottle of disinfectant and doused Evelyn's arm with it. He rubbed her arm, leaning into the motion, the skin turning red, white flakes of dead skin shedding to the floor. Evelyn winced and tried to pull away.

"She's good now!" Damien said.

As if in a trance, Xavier kept rubbing, pressing harder and harder, his thumb digging into the muscle. Evelyn yelped and Damien lunged forward and threw Xavier's head against the wall.

"Leave her alone!" he yelled.

Xavier rolled onto his side and shook. His eyes narrowed as he jumped to his feet, pushing past Damien to grab Evelyn once again.

"But she's had their blood on her!" he cried. "We don't know what will happen. We need to watch her, make sure she doesn't turn—doesn't turn into one of those—"

"She's fine," Damien shouted.

Xavier released Evelyn and the room fell quiet. Damien guided his sister as they both moved to the opposite side of the cramped room. Maddy and Rachel joined them in the shadows.

Sweaty and exhausted, Xavier awkwardly plunked down on the milk crate and dropped his head in his hands. It was quiet throughout the cellar for some time, only the occasional mumbling from Xavier. "I'm sorry," he muttered, so softly it was almost to himself. "I'm sorry."

Then Andrew's voice came from the dark, muffled and aching. "He was at my seventh birthday party."

Xavier raised his head and turned toward Jeremiah's body. "I know, Andrew, I know. But he attacked us. What were we supposed to do? I know it doesn't make sense but—"

"And my eighth. We went to that tiny pizza place on Main, remember? He ended up spilling pop all over his lap and had to wear a plastic bib the rest of the day."

"Look, none of us wanted this," Xavier said. "But we're surviving, okay? We're doing the best we can."

"He bought me a Lego set for my ninth—"

"We didn't know it was him!" Xavier shouted. "None of this is our fault! We walked into a goddamn nightmare and we're just trying to survive it! One day at a time and one night at a time. That's it! That's all we know! One day. One night."

"And what if Mom and Joe are like him?" Andrew said. "Like the rest of them? What if they hunt us like he did? What if *they* want us dead too?"

"We'll find them," Xavier said. "We'll track them and we'll find them. We just have to figure this all out. We need to think it through and piece it all together—"

"Wait!" Andrew said. "Jeremiah knew about the cellar. I mean, before he turned into that thing—when he was normal—he knew about this place. He knew where we would be. Even after he changed, he somehow knew we'd be here."

Andrew paused to let his voice catch up with his thoughts. "X, a lot of our neighbours know about this cellar. If Jeremiah found us here then … well … what's stopping others?"

Xavier pressed his lips together, the creases on his damp forehead tightening. He stared at his brother, his chest pulsing up and down.

He stood suddenly, grabbing one of the creatures by its collar. He heaved the body up the steep steps and through the cellar door, dragging it along the snow and slick grass and pitched it behind the rotted garden. He returned and did the same with the second body, his heavy boots clunking back into the cellar a few seconds later. He turned his attention to the others, his eyes pausing on Evelyn's forearm—red and rubbed raw.

"Andrew's right," he announced. "Our position is compromised. We're not safe here anymore."

"You want us to leave?" Maddy asked.

"We don't have a choice. Down here we're stuck in a hole with only one way out. If they find us again—"

"Three days ago, we were chased out of the woods by those things!" Maddy said, her voice rising. "We barely escaped! And now you want us to go back?"

"We can't stay here. It's just not safe."

"It's not safe out *there* either!" Maddy shouted.

Xavier peered down at the last few dozen hollow points scattered along the floor, the empty food tins in the corner.

"We have to go," he said firmly. "We're out of food and nearly out of bullets. We don't have a choice anymore, we're out of options." He gave a tired sigh, as if the weight of the world was on his shoulders. "We leave at first light."

Chapter Nineteen

February 1995
Day 367 | Night

Angela's head shot up from the microscope. After mixing the red liquid with the clear one, the resulting substance was sequencing far different than it had the previous month.

She pulled the yellow notepad from the burgundy briefcase to recheck the values. This time, the ratio was different.

She slunk to the sink and vigorously washed the slide. She studied the streaks, the fluids still visible on the clear surface. She scrubbed it again but the stains remained and she eventually tossed the slide into the trash.

She removed a second slide and began the process again, the one she had repeated month after month: two drops of blood drawn from a vial stored in the briefcase mixed with four drops of clear liquid, extracted from the biohazard container from the walk-in fridge.

She looked through the eyepiece and waited.

The concoction sat still for a while but then twitched. The blood droplets folded onto themselves, squirming away from the clear liquid. She dragged a stir-stick across the slide. Immersed in the liquid, the blood turned a deep red, then brown, and then black. Its texture changed from a porous trickle of fluid to a dense gel, like wet tar on a humid day.

And then the same thing happened as the previous slide. The blood droplets—thick and dark as oil—began to shake, and then all at once, turned to ash.

A shiver ran through her. She reached for the notepad again but stopped when a large figure darkened the doorway.

"Good evening, Dr. Till," the figure said, his face shadowed. His voice was gentle, a stark contrast to his tall, imposing stature.

Angela jumped off the stool and squinted into the dark. "Alan?"

The figure stepped through the doorway and shook his overcoat loose from his broad frame. "I hope I didn't startle you," Alan said, although something in his voice seemed to suggest otherwise.

"You did give me quite a fright," Angela admitted, her breathing beginning to calm. "What on earth are you doing here at this hour?"

"Just a routine check-in," he said, adjusting the Windsor knot in his tie.

"But it's nearly midnight."

"Yes, well my clients are curious about your progress."

"You mean Mr. Pak sent you, don't you?"

Alan huffed. "I do have some authority in this whole thing, Angela. Give me a little credit."

Angela turned back to the microscope and her notes. "Actually, it's good timing you're here," she said. "I've been studying the substances further and … well … the reactions are changing! I need to keep testing but the last two sequences have caused the blood to … to … well, I don't even know how to explain it. The chemical effect, well, I've never seen it before. The sample transforms from a liquid to a dense substance and then to a type of—"

"Slow down, I'm not a scientist."

"I'm aware. This is why it would be easier if I could just contact the other researcher to discuss my findings."

"You know the terms."

"The terms don't make sense! It's like I'm conducting experiments in the dark or with one arm tied behind my back."

Alan waved the suggestion away. "You're smart, that's why we approached you. Figure it out."

"But these reactions should still concern you, Alan. The blood changes! When it's exposed to higher concentrations of the water—*our* water—it changes from a liquid form to some sort of ash—"

"Just get to the point. What does it all mean?".

"What it means is that the chemical in the water supply, when mixed with the activating agent, is multiplying. Up until now, we had full control over concentration levels. But now the chemical is increasing on its own."

"Mutating?"

"Sort of. It's changing, even after we stopped adding to it!"

Alan cleared his throat. "If it's changing on its own, then I don't see how we are responsible."

"We issued the virus months ago. Of course we're responsible!"

"No need to panic. We have protocols for situations like this."

"Yes, I'm aware of the exit plan. But this is beyond that now. If I can just meet with the other researcher, maybe I can compare analyses or—"

"You can't meet!" Alan bellowed.

Angela stumbled backwards from the sudden outburst and drew in a hurried breath.

"*You* work alone! *He* works alone!" Alan barked, his face red, exasperated.

He drew a pocket square across his damp forehead then rubbed his hands together nervously.

"More importantly, the investors won't be pleased with this new information," he said.

"Well, I'm sorry for your investors but this is the situation we find ourselves in," Angela said, maintaining her distance. "No one wanted this but the experiment is now out of our control. I can no longer predict the effects of—"

"Nothing has happened that alters our course," Alan said. "This thing is changing—so what? Maybe it's changing on its own. We didn't allow for this. It wasn't us."

"But we did allow for this. It *was* us," Angela said, her voice catching. "We allowed for this to happen."

Alan exhaled in frustration. "There are plenty of safeguards in place," he huffed.

"But Alan …"

He struggled into his overcoat and plodded for the door. "Just do your job and we'll all be rich."

"But Alan, there's more I need to tell you—"

Alan marched through the doorway and down the dark hallway.

"Alan?" Angela called after him as he disappeared within the shadows. "Alan? Are you still there? Alan?"

Chapter Twenty

March 1995
Day 418 | Dawn

The rifles were cleaned and loaded. Andrew hoisted his backpack crammed with the last few bottles of water, a first aid kit, a compact shovel, a flashlight, a cord of rope. He glanced around the cellar at the others, his gun clenched tight by his side.

"Ready?"

Evelyn studied him with worried eyes, her lips pressed tight together, her skin flush and moist.

"It'll be okay," Andrew said. "We're going to find someplace safe. And then we'll find help, alright?"

Evelyn nodded as Andrew turned and bounded up the stairs. His nose wriggled, catching a familiar scent, but he was already pushing on the plywood, his body up through the cellar door.

The brightness of the early sun surprised him and caused him to squint, just long enough to miss the shadow passing over him.

Maddy was the second one up the steps. Her rifle was raised to the east but the clawed hand came from the west, gripping her throat and throwing her to the ground. A second hand dug into her chest, a splatter of red darkening her shirt.

Andrew spun as Maddy's high-pitched shrill shocked the morning air. He saw a second attacker lunge at the woman, smashing its enormous fist against Maddy's nose and jaw. A crooked finger wormed its way into Maddy's ear, slicing the eardrum, blood bubbling out from the opening. The beast wrapped its palm around her skull and pounded it against the hard earth.

"Maddy!" Andrew yelled.

He raised his rifle, clicked the safety, and fired. The beast twisted to the ground from the impact but rose again, lurching toward Maddy. Andrew fired a second shot square in its chest and the beast fell and laid still.

There was a loud bang and Andrew whirled around to find one of the beasts atop the cellar door. The creature slid the bolt across the plywood as Andrew had done many times before.

A sting shivered up his neck. *They've been watching us,* he thought.

Andrew aimed at the creature and shot. But as he moved to reload, he noticed just how many there were. Three, maybe four dozen, all charging toward the cellar. Some were listing forward, drooling and hunched over. Others scurried off the back deck of the farmhouse, stirred by the commotion, their yellow eyes wild and hungry.

They've been watching us, Andrew thought. *This whole time they've been watching us.*

He shifted his weight as the infected began to swarm, circling, penning him in like a pack of wolves. They were more animal than human now, he could see that. He stepped toward the cellar door but several of the beasts hobbled forward, blocking his path. Crusted blood lined their lower lids as their feverish eyes trailed each of Andrew's movements.

The one creeping up from behind was salivating, its teeth grinding back and forth. It reached for Andrew but the hunter in him sensed it, and he turned and fired, the shot travelling through the creature's throat.

Andrew lurched forward but two others jumped at him. One of the monsters swiped viciously, causing Andrew to stumble, his tailbone bouncing off the cellar door. The creature growled, thin lines of red saliva pulsing from its mouth.

"Andrew!" Xavier yelled from underneath the locked wooden door.

One of the creatures dug its nails into Andrew's side. He wailed as the beast drew its arm away, flesh ripping from Andrew's abdomen. Gritting his teeth, he swung his legs, kicking at the monster. He flopped onto his side, slid the backpack off, and drew his knife. Rolling to a crouched position, he sliced one along the thigh, then stood and stabbed another between its ribcage.

"Where the hell are my parents?" he yelled, adrenaline overriding his fear. "Where the hell is my mom?"

"Andrew!" Xavier yelled again from beneath the earth, a constant banging coming from the underside of the cellar door.

Andrew rolled on top of the metal bolt and gripped the lever but he couldn't slide it. He shook so that each time he shifted the latch, his tremors would snap it shut again.

Four beasts pounced on him then, squealing, dragging him off the plank and onto the trampled grass. They dug their claws into him, their blunt teeth rooting down on his neck and throat. Andrew writhed, kicking one of them off, but the other three held him down with their weight. He inhaled the heat and decay from their breath, the rank smell floating over him as they tore pieces of skin from muscle. One bore down on him, leaning its weight on Andrew's leg, nearly crushing the tendons which ran out from under the knee. Andrew wailed, but slowly, the pain began to subside.

Andrew could see the beasts on top of him—their drool and blood mixing with his own—but oddly he could no longer feel the pressure of their weight, the tear of their claws. And their movements now seemed sluggish, their downward thrusts gradual and drawn out. He noticed one of their arms rise up but it seemed to take ages for it to travel back down, smashing into his chest, over and over again.

Exhaustion washed over him and his eyes became heavy. His thoughts travelled to a time when he was running through the backyard as a child, the yellow grass tickling his bare legs, the summer sun beaming down. Xavier was there too, laughing his big laugh as he always did when he was younger.

In the vision, Jeremiah appeared at the side of the house. He chased Andrew through the field, pretending to shoot at him with a long stick. Carl Henderson was there as well: the older redneck that sought out and bullied younger kids. Spurred by the noise, he too came running around the house and caught Andrew fleeing. Carl pinned him to the ground, braying with laughter. He punched and slapped Andrew hard across the face, scratching and clawing at the boy, bits of red seeping out from between his teeth.

The image switched to later that evening. Andrew was hunched at the table, a long gash down his cheek, his eyelid purple and swollen. His stepfather also sat at the table, the sleeves of his checkered shirt rolled up, his veiny forearms splayed out, his chiselled wrinkles sitting at odd angles.

Xavier was explaining why he had ripped the boy off his brother and beat him to a pulp, his mother running from the house to break them up, and then Carl running home squealing. Andrew had watched Xavier put his hands around the boy's neck, muttering and slurring in a possessed rage, lit-up and kinetic, as if all his synapses were on fire. For months afterwards, Andrew wondered what would have happened to Carl Henderson if their mother hadn't shown up.

Joe pushed away from the table and gazed out the kitchen window. Thrifty and frugal, he was a simple man but one with a temper. The faded jagged line winding down his forearm served as a reminder of that—teenage wounds that followed him into adulthood—and he ran a finger along the ridges of the faint scar. He rubbed at his black stubble, a thick moustache over his lip, the faint smell of sweat and earth oozing off his skin. A wry smile began to sneak across his face. He reached over to Xavier and tousled his dirty black hair.

"Only for him, okay?" Joe chuckled, pointing across the table at Andrew. "You hear me, X? You're only allowed to fight if it's for him."

All at once, Andrew shook the image from his mind as he heard Xavier howl from the cellar. He held his breath and using the last of his strength, heaved one of the creatures off. Extending his leg, he grimaced and kicked at the latch with the rim of his boot. Shifting his body, he turned the angle of his foot and the latch slid open, a gentle clunk as the metal bar came loose.

His eyes fell shut just as the door flung open and all at once Xavier was upon them.

He violently threw one of the beasts to the ground, repeatedly stomping its head with his boot. He tackled a second one and then sprung up, the creature squirming and kicking as Xavier stood on its throat until it went still. A third one ran for him, but he already had his knife drawn and cut the monster open with one sweeping slash.

Damien followed Xavier into the daylight, emptying his rifle into the forehead of a creature, then turning and firing into the chest of another. He shot with such speed and precision that nearly a dozen creatures were strewn across the yard by the time he had reached the top rung.

"Don't move!" he yelled down at Evelyn before flipping the cellar door shut on top of her.

Both she and Rachel scuttled to the rear of the cellar, listening to the war unfold above.

Damien jerked the gun to his left, drew the bolt back, and fired, a bullet catching the inside leg of an advancing creature. It hobbled a few steps before crashing to the ground. An acrid sour smell drifted through the air as Damien reloaded and shot again as another massive creature collapsed among the bushes a few yards away.

Xavier plunged his blade deep into the shoulder of a beast, spun, and then suddenly stopped. He stood still, staring upon a creature much smaller than the others. A child. Her skin was bronzed with knotted hair below her shoulders. A deep gash split her forehead.

Xavier shuffled away, lowering his knife. "It's okay. Y - you don't need to do this. I won't hurt you."

She circled him and yipped several times as if calling out in a foreign tongue, her teeth grating back and forth, her amber eyes burning with hatred.

"It doesn't have to happen this way," Xavier said.

The girl lunged at him, snapping her teeth along his neck.

He pushed her to the ground and stepped away as she jumped up from the sleet and ice.

He raised his palms. "Please. You can run. You don't need to do this! You can go! You're too young for—"

The girl shrieked, exposing her pointed teeth, and pounced once again at Xavier. She dug her nails into his forearm and clawed her way up his body toward his throat.

"Please," Xavier pleaded.

Biting hard into his bottom lip, he held the girl tight, turning his head away as he twisted her neck. He gagged as the lifeless body dropped to the frozen earth.

There was a loud thud as Damien called out in horror.

"Some of them went down there!" he shouted, pointing at the cellar. "But my gun's jammed!"

He tried to wiggle the bolt, the hollow clink of the cartridge deep inside. Xavier refocused and reached for the strap along his own rifle, tossing the weapon to Damien.

"Use this one!" he shouted. "Where's Evelyn?"

"She's still down there!"

Xavier bent and jerked the cellar door open. It was Evelyn's scream that propelled him down the steps so that at the rear of the cellar he stabbed all three creatures in a possessed rage until each body fell to the cement floor. He knelt on the chest of one still breathing and wrapped his thick hands around its neck. The monster shrieked, kicking its legs as Xavier pressed down, grunting with exhaustion. The creature's neck collapsed under his firm grasp. And then the black blood flooded out.

"We need to go!" he yelled.

He reached for Evelyn and yanked her up the stairs, Rachel following close behind. At the top of the stairs, he spotted Maddy's rifle upon the snow. He sprinted toward it, loaded the weapon, and pushed it into Evelyn's arms.

"There's too many of them. Damien and I will try to hold them off as long as we can. But we need every gun firing! You understand?"

Her frightened eyes met his. She attempted to raise the rifle but it was heavy, the barrel vibrating within her grasp. Xavier placed his hands over hers, wet and smeared with blood.

"You'll be fine," he said. "Just remember what I taught you."

Evelyn raised the gun, her fingers crawling over the smooth metal.

"Safety?" Xavier said.

Evelyn slid her finger along the length of the rifle until she heard a click. Her lips trembled as she repeated the instructions. "Safety."

"Scope?"

Evelyn closed her left eye and peered through the glass with her right. "Scope."

"Target?"

Evelyn moved the rifle to the right. A giant of a man, well over six and a half feet tall, turned and spotted her. He already had a hole in his chest with blood dripping from the wound. He stumbled toward her with a cannibalistic glare.

"It's just like shooting bark off a tree," Xavier whispered.

Evelyn swallowed. "Target."

"Breathe. Just breathe," Xavier said. "Feel for the trigger. Wait for the shot."

Xavier cried out as the bullet flew through the beast's neck. It collapsed and laid motionless on the ground as Evelyn closed her eyes and exhaled.

"And again," Xavier shouted, drawing his knife and springing up. "Reload and shoot again—again and again and again!"

He stabbed an advancing creature through its lungs as he made his way to Damien. He knelt at the boy's boots, spinning the jammed rifle around, cranking the bolt back and forth. On the third try, the casing sprung loose, and he reached inside the cartridge pouch for extra rounds.

"We're getting low on bullets," he said. "Only kill-shots from now on."

"All I ever shoot are kill-shots," Damien said.

Xavier loaded his weapon and stood, his back foot resting against Damien's. They looked like shadows of each other, guns drawn, one facing east, the other west. Damien would fire, then Xavier, in what seemed like a rehearsed dance.

"How many of these things are left?" Xavier shouted.

"I've shot down at least twenty," Damien answered. "But they keep coming!"

Andrew was on his feet now, his hand pressed firmly along his ribs. Blood streamed through his fingers, the pasty liquid running over the back of his hand. He hobbled toward Xavier with his bowie knife gripped at his side.

Xavier turned to him. "You okay to move? If you need to, will you be able to run?"

He hesitated at first but eventually Andrew nodded.

"Okay," Xavier said. "We can't hold them off much longer. We're in the wide open here. We need to try and lose 'em in the trees."

He turned to Damien and motioned toward the shallow canopy a hundred yards out. "You'll have to carry your sister,"

Xavier said. "I'll take care of the others."

Damien shot two more rounds, nodded, and sprinted for Evelyn. Xavier tossed Andrew his rifle.

"We may need some cover!" he hollered as he ran toward Maddy.

When Xavier reached her, he recoiled. She was nearly passed out, humming and mumbling to herself, her body quivering in a heap of blood and dirt. Her chest was punctured by what appeared to be dozens of knife wounds. Her right ear was shorn from the side of her head, a stream of yellow mucous dripping from the other. Her face was almost unrecognizable, the creatures having trampled and eaten much of it.

Rachel was kneeling at her side, her eyes brimming with tears. "She's coming with us."

A look of uncertainty crossed Xavier's face and he stood motionless for a moment, rooted to the spot.

"She has a pulse and is breathing and she is our friend so she is coming with us!" Rachel shouted.

Xavier nodded, then bent and scooped Maddy into his arms. He gathered around the others and squinted beyond the field.

"The forest confuses them, we know this, that's how we lost them before," he said. "So, we need to get there."

Rachel nodded and hoisted the backpack. Damien swung two rifles over his shoulder and heaved Evelyn into his arms, her left leg hanging limp down her side.

Xavier spun as several creatures came up behind him. "Go!" he shouted. "We need to move now!"

The group ran through the long grass as the creatures continued their advance. Andrew turned back and fired upon one, a stream of black fluid sputtering out the top of its head. He and the others soon closed in on the clasp of young saplings along the edge of the forest. He stumbled and grimaced, blood dribbling from his chest and side.

"Stay with me!" Xavier yelled, spinning to face him. "You hear me? You stay with me! We're going to make it!"

Andrew slowed as they reached the wide trunks of the oaks and maples. He glanced back through the crowded limbs and jagged twigs, the creatures dropping further behind, the group shielded now from the things that hunted them.

Chapter Twenty-One

February 1995
Day 387 | Night

Angela breathed deeply trying to slow her heart rate. Her dark skin glistened with sweat as she curled her fingers into fists, her filed nails digging into her moist palms. She stood trembling with her eyes pressed shut outside the chamber door.

She was still shaking from the evening's events. She had walked into her mother's former nursing home and stumbled upon the creature by accident. She had parked her Porsche and cautiously entered the building. Stacked linen carts and full medication trays lined each nursing station, abandoned just days earlier. The rooms were nearly empty, most of the residents relocated when rumours of a mysterious virus began to take root.

Angela took the stairs to the second floor. When she entered the dimly lit stairwell, she hustled up a few more steps before the strange detail struck her. She paused on the landing but then began moving back down, the click of her heels echoing within the confined space. At the base of the stairs, she could hear breathing—a raspy gurgle every few seconds.

Her head shot up, her ear now trained to the sound. She looked passed the crumpled shape to the stairwell exit less than eight strides away. She hesitated for just a moment and then sprinted, flinging the metal door open. On the other side, she lunged for the nearest nursing station, fumbling to stretch a pair of latex gloves over her trembling fingers. She turned and yanked an empty laundry sack from the trolley.

Swinging the stairwell door open again, she grabbed the sleeping creature by the neck. In a flurry of movement, she shoved it into the oversize cloth bag, heaving and tugging at it as quick as she could, sealing the drawstrings at the top.

The creature woke and struggled as Angela hauled it across the tiled floor to the parking lot. Adrenaline coursing through her, she reached down and hoisted the bag into her trunk and slammed it shut. She started the engine and sped away, racing the short distance to the health unit laboratory.

The creature had stopped moving by the time she arrived. Angela struggled to drag both the laundry bag and her burgundy briefcase toward the elevator and across the fourth floor. She pulled and kicked at the bag until it rested in the middle of a large hexagonal chamber encased with shining shatter-proof glass. She left the bag and fumbled through the briefcase.

"Where are they?" she mumbled to herself.

Soon, she produced a needle and small vile from one of the zipped pockets. She filled the needle. Shaking, she felt along the bag for the creature's pointy vertebrae. She pushed the tired beast to the floor, digging the needle in, emptying the syrupy liquid through its knobby spine.

The creature woke with a start, wailing and thrashing, a thorny claw ripping a hole through the bag. Angela turned to run but one of her heels slipped and she stumbled. The creature dug at the hole, now large enough for its nose and mouth to push out. It was snuffling at the air, saliva foaming along its gums as its red tongue flicked side to side.

Angela kicked off her heels, dragging her frozen legs toward the door. She dove for the exit but had to stretch back, pawing and fumbling for the briefcase. The creature ripped free from the bag and stood hunched and trembling in the middle of the enclosure. It frantically scanned the area, stopping on Angela, and for a moment it seemed to settle, casting its gaze to the side, as if recalling a memory.

Angela yanked at the door handle and the creature shook awake, pulling out clumps of its hair, wailing in pain. Seething, it hissed and lunged at Angela just as she slammed the door and sealed it with the pressure airlock.

The creature shrieked and pounded on the glass, stumbling from one end of the cage to the other. After a few moments, the noise subsided and the creature collapsed at the furthest point of the chamber.

Angela studied it through the glass: a ball of claws and bushy hair, shoulders heaving up and down, its lungs straining for air. After some time, it rolled onto its side and raised its head toward the door. Angela gasped and covered her mouth.

The creature's face—mostly hidden by its shaggy hair and deep scars—now looked like a normal girl. Pretty, even. Her cheeks were flush, a soft rose colour beneath them, her chin ending in a subtle point on her cherubic face. Her deep blue eyes danced curiously around the room as if waking from a pleasant dream. The corners of her mouth began to curl up into a tired smile.

Angela bit her lip, her eyes turning moist.

But just as quickly as the girl's smile had appeared, it began to fade. She attempted to pull herself to her knees but stumbled. She tried once again—pushing herself from the floor—but her spine stiffened, her back arching awkwardly. The colour in her face faded from pink to grey and her eyes went black before she let out a horrible squeal. Her body shook and then dissolved into a syrupy streak, wet and slick across the floor.

"No!" Angela gasped and she drew back as the gelatine substance changed to ash—only a blurry smear of charcoal where the child had been moments earlier. Her breath caught in her throat and she closed her eyes, her cheeks flushed as she wiped the sweat and tears from them.

Eventually, she pulled the yellow legal pad from the burgundy briefcase and began writing. She ripped and folded the paper, jamming the sheets back into the bag.

Opening the chamber door, she slid her stocking feet along the cold floor, bent and scooped up her heels, staring for a long while at where the child had been. She turned away, flicking the light off, slamming the laboratory door behind her.

Chapter Twenty-Two

March 1995
Day 418 | Late Morning

The group spread out along the sloping shore of the creek. Stalks of bent and yellowed bulrushes transitioned to frozen mud and then into shallow icy-blue water. A thin crust of frost floated atop the waterway from the night's drop in temperature.

"Is she going to be okay?" Evelyn asked, staring anxiously at Maddy.

The woman's head was in the girl's lap, wheezing as she struggled to breathe. She had been in and out of consciousness since their early morning retreat, slipping into sleep for longer and longer periods of time.

Rachel nodded and yanked several rags from the backpack. She dipped each one into the cool water, letting them drip onto the snow before laying them across Maddy's face and neck.

"Wake up, Maddy," Rachel said. "Wake up. You need to drink." She gently shook the woman and squeezed several drops from the rags across her chapped lips. "That's it, drink up. The cool water will feel good."

Maddy's lips pulsed as the water dripped over the dried blood lining her cheeks and mouth, her teeth bleached pink.

She coughed, bringing up fumes of bile. Evelyn shuddered and turned her head away.

Further down the creek, Damien and Xavier sat on the bank, out of earshot from the others.

"It's close to noon," Damien said, looking at the sun creeping toward the mid-point of the sky. "We've been here for at least two hours."

"You think it's been too long?" Xavier asked.

"We've lost those things for now," Damien said, shivering from the winter wind. "But don't kid yourself—they'll find us soon enough."

"I know," Xavier admitted. "I just want Andrew to rest a bit longer."

"Do you think he'll be able to run?"

Xavier glanced toward Andrew. His brother was braced against a tree, legs splayed and eyes closed, the sticky tack of blood still on his fingers. His breathing had come in troubled bursts when they had arrived at the creek, shivering uncontrollably. Rachel had cleaned his wounds and strapped bandages to them so that over the last hour, his chest had calmed, his breathing now at a normal cadence.

Xavier let out a heavy sigh. "He's a tough kid. He hasn't had it easy, that's for sure."

"Oh yeah?"

"His real dad was shit-poor and then left the day after he was born. Didn't even hold him in the hospital."

"Jesus."

"Yeah, I think Andrew still feels that somehow. Like he carries the weight of it through life or something. He obvious-ly doesn't remember it but I think it left a mark on him."

"That's awful."

"I'm sure my father being cold and detached likely didn't make it any easier for him."

Damien nodded. "Look, I know he's tough," he said. "But when those things come for us, will he be ready to run?"

"Since day one he's been tough as nails because he had to be," Xavier said. "He's been a survivor his whole life. When the time comes, he'll be ready. If he needs to run, he'll run."

Xavier wiped a line of sweat from his grimy forehead as his gaze drifted to the women. "It's Maddy I'm worried about. I'm not sure if she'd be able to—"

"Water!" Andrew called out. His voice was hoarse and his eyes fluttered as he reached for the empty bottle from the backpack.

Xavier walked over and stared down at Andrew. Puncture holes peppered his chest, a mix of blood and sweat staining his damp shirt. A part of his left ear was bitten off, the skin crusted and serrated where normally it was round and smooth. A line of teeth indents snaked below his Adam's apple.

Xavier swallowed, pushing down the lump growing in his throat. He bent and grabbed the empty bottle and headed toward the creek.

"I'll come with you," Damien said. He rose from where he sat but Xavier motioned for him to stay.

At the water's edge, Xavier began to shake. He dug his nails into his palm, trying to focus the pain in his chest elsewhere. He heaved in stuttered breaths, his jaw trembling. It was difficult filling the bottle with his hands twitching, the quivering progressing up his arms and into his shoulders.

"He'll be okay," a voice said.

Xavier spun nervously but relaxed when Damien crouched beside him.

"As you said, he's a survivor," Damien said. "You both are."

Xavier closed his eyes and pawed at the last of his tears. "Sure, but I never dreamt we'd be trying to survive something like *this*!"

"None of us did," Damien said softly. "We're all just trying the best we can."

"I know," Xavier said. "But when he left for school last fall, we weren't on speaking terms. Some pent-up family bullshit we were dealing with, resentment that had built up over the years. So, because of that, it makes it harder to see him all clawed up and bleeding like that."

"I wouldn't stress it," Damien said. "You two care about each other. Amongst the bitterness, you can still see that."

Xavier reached down into the creek and splashed cold water upon his sweaty cheeks and forehead. A stream of it curled down the back of his neck, causing him to arch forward.

"I never had a brother so I can't really relate," Damien continued. "But you two have a bond. You can sense it. It reminds me of my father and uncle. Both of them could be cruel and mean to each other but you could tell they still cared a lot."

"Andrew and I definitely had our tense moments growing up."

"It happens, I'm sure," Damien said. He ran a hand through his oily dark hair. "You know, my uncle would visit us each June. One morning he would just be there, sitting at the breakfast table with my dad. The two of them would take Ev and I camping or we'd stay at our cabin a few nights. I forget the lake it was on—Lake Clearwater, or something like that. And it was my uncle, actually, who taught me how to shoot.

He taught me how to hold the gun, how to reload, how not to panic if I missed."

Xavier finished filling the water bottle as he listened to the creek trickle by. He took a large gulp. It was clean and cold and went down smooth.

"Last year was the first time Ev was old enough to go hunting with us," Damien continued. "It was just the four of us in the bush. We didn't let her shoot—as you know—but she still had a great time. We all had a great time."

"Sounds like a nice memory."

"My point is that even *they* fought," Damien said. "Some nights my uncle and my dad would drink too much and would start to poke fun and hurl insults at each other. It would get heated and they'd argue but you could see how much my dad missed him after he left. He would stand on our porch, looking down the driveway, as if trying to will him to come back."

Damien attacked an itch on his lower leg, pulling his sweaty sock over his calf once the tickle had subsided. Xavier spit into the grass, gazing beyond the creek.

"Listen," Damien continued. "When I saw you with my sister in the field yesterday … well, I know you were just trying to teach her how to shoot, just trying to help her. It's just that, well, she's all the family I have right now so—"

"You were protecting her as you should," Xavier said. "Don't stress about it."

"Anyway, I'm sorry for not trusting you. I think maybe if things weren't like this, like if we had met under different circumstances, then …"

"You're a good brother, Damien. She's lucky to have you."

Damien nodded and smiled softly.

"She's a good kid too," Xavier added. "Shy, but funny."

"Yeah, she's quiet around you guys. But Evelyn's always been pretty adventurous. All scraped knees and tangled hair. My mom used to say she was just a loud noise covered in dirt."

"Hmm, that's funny."

"Yeah, and my dad wasn't around much but when he was, he used to say she was like a tidal wave. Calm early on, but if she gets going—"

Xavier suddenly crouched low, staring ahead into the snow-covered brush. His arm jolted up and he chopped his hand through the air and Damien immediately dropped to his knee. Reaching for his gun, Xavier scanned the foliage on the other side of the creek. A crunch of snow caused his neck to twist as a flash of blue moved among the trees.

"Did you see that?" Damien whispered.

Xavier laid among the bulrushes and nodded. "We're being watched."

"By those crazy people?"

Xavier gave a sideways glance. "You wanna stick around to find out?"

"How about Maddy?" Damien asked. "She's not strong enough to run. If we need to go—"

A shout from behind spun them both around and they saw Rachel waving her arms. Xavier looked across the creek but no longer saw the spot of blue, only the muted greys and dark browns of the overhanging trees painting the wooded bank.

"Don't mention this to the others, it'll spook them," Xavier said. "But keep a close eye out. And have your gun ready."

Damien nodded and they both hurried toward Rachel.

"It's Maddy," Rachel said, panicked, staring up at Xavier. She reached for his hand. "She says she needs to tell you something."

She led them up and over the lip of the hill where Maddy was leaning against a large stone. She was covered in damp rags, her face missing chunks of skin, long gashes carved down her scalp.

Andrew pushed himself from the tree and gingerly made his way over to the rest of the group. He snatched the water bottle from Xavier and took a long drink.

Xavier crouched and cleared his throat. "What is it, Maddy?"

Maddy turned toward the sound, her pupils flickering until they were able to focus on Xavier. She sucked at the dry air, her voice cracking.

"I need to tell you something about my job," she started.

Xavier nodded and motioned for her to continue.

"Part of my job at the health unit was to organize the flu clinics. Back in November, our MOH made us use a different vaccine than normal, one with packaging I had never seen before."

"Hold on—what's a MOH?" Xavier interrupted.

"It stands for Medical Officer of Health," Rachel said. "Basically, the boss of the health unit—sort of like a CEO."

"That's right," Maddy said. Her brow cocked as she studied Rachel. "Anyway, I was preparing for one of the clinics when our MOH confronted me. She told me we were using a new brand of vaccine. This was odd because we've always used the ones shipped by the Ministry of Health. I kept asking her *why* but she never answered me."

"What'd you do?" Xavier asked.

"It all felt strange to me so I stole several of the original vials and took them home. At the time I didn't know why—something just didn't feel right. The next day my supervisor removed me from the clinics. I figured it was because I was asking too many questions."

Maddy's voice was shallow and hoarse and she paused every few words to catch her breath. Rachel nodded encouragement, caressing the woman's hand.

"The flu clinics went ahead with all kinds of promotion. There were posters at every office building with incentives: gift cards, movie passes, free groceries, you name it. They even had celebrities and athletes attend the clinics. All sorts of people came out. It was madness. After one week, the town had over 95% vaccination compliance. That level is unheard of."

"Why?"

"You just typically don't see those kinds of numbers. As I said, it all felt strange to me. So, I went home and administered the stolen vials to myself, my husband, and my son. I told them to keep away from the flu clinics."

Damien paced nervously a few yards away, gun poised at his side. Xavier sniffed at the air as if locating a scent. He ignored it and turned back to Maddy.

"Maddy, does this have something to do with what's going on in town?" he asked.

"What you need to know is that I saw a marking on one of those things," Maddy said. "One of those creatures."

"When?"

"It was on one of their wrists—on one of them you shot down in the forest."

"What was the marking?"

"I didn't get a close look at it then. But in the cellar, I saw a similar marking on that Jeremiah boy and I knew exactly what it was. It was a buck with antlers and I knew right away it was the logo from the new vaccines—the ones from the pharmaceutical company."

"Why was it on their wrists?"

"I don't know. Like I said, I was taken off the program. All I can think of is perhaps the staff stamped people with some sort of semi-permanent ink, probably to identify those who had been given the vaccine—"

"And those who hadn't," Andrew interrupted. He took a shallow breath and grimaced, releasing the tension along his ribcage. "Someone was tracking those who had received the vaccination to ensure full compliance."

"Are you saying all this stuff happening—all these people mutating into these, these creatures—that this was all done on purpose?" Xavier said. "That this was someone's plan?" Xavier shifted from Andrew to Maddy. "But who? Who would do this?"

"I don't know," Maddy said, her voice becoming weaker. "But I've never seen that logo before except on those containers. So, I think whoever owns that logo might be behind all this. I mean, the money spent on all the promotion had to come from somewhere, right?" She tried to lift her arm but grimaced, the muscles in her shoulder torn away.

"And to think ... all those people changing into those vile things," she gasped. "Some of those people were my colleagues. Some were probably my friends. And look what's become of them. They're probably all gone now. They're probably all—"

A tear dribbled down her scarred cheek. She looked up as if to say something but coughed several times, spitting up red phlegm.

"You're in a lot of pain," Xavier said. "It's probably best if you rest now."

He placed his warm hands on hers and repositioned her body against the stone. He laid a damp cloth over her wounds and shoved the backpack behind her head as a makeshift pillow. Maddy's eyes fluttered shut, her breathing calm and even.

"Damien and I will keep watch," Xavier said. "Try to get some rest. You're safe now, Maddy. You're safe here with us."

Andrew's breath caught in his throat and he knew right away by the angle of her neck. It had been nearly half an hour since he had checked on the woman and his eyes welled up as he stood over her. He reached down but was interrupted by Evelyn coming up the bank. When she saw Maddy's limp body, she wailed and threw herself onto the woman's lap, wrapping her arms tight around her.

Xavier and Damien rushed to the sound and after a moment, each of them bowed their heads.

Rachel followed the screaming from the creek and scooped the sobbing child into her arms. She held Evelyn tight, rubbing the girls trembling back.

For a long while, it was only Rachel's soft voice which could be heard amongst the trees, whispering over and over to the child. "It'll be okay, it'll be okay, it'll be okay."

Rachel wiped a mix of tears and sweat from her face; a smear of dirt rubbed into her cheek. She threw the compact shovel toward the backpack, staring at the small mound before her. She whispered a prayer as Evelyn prepared a cluttered bouquet of pinecones and hardy grasses to place on top.

Rachel swept the scene with her dark eyes before refilling the backpack. She shoved the rope, the bloodied damp cloths, and the shovel deep into the bag.

She stood and faced the others. "I know where we have to go," she announced.

She hoisted the backpack onto her slight shoulders and began moving south at a brisk march. Even as the red sun dropped behind the horizon, she didn't stop to look back at the others, all of them out of breath and confused, struggling to keep pace.

Chapter Twenty-Three

March 1995
Day 396 | Night

Angela spun the cordless phone on the massive glass table, rubbing her smooth cheeks and chin. Exhaling loudly, she spun the phone a second time. She looked across her living room and through her wide French patio doors into the dark night. Her brow furrowed, deep ruts carved into her forehead.

Finally, she snatched the phone and dialled the number from memory.

"Hey," she whispered. "It's me."

A surprised response came through the receiver.

"It has been a while. I've been distant, I know."

Angela paused as the voice spoke again.

"In all honesty, not very good … not very good at all."

There was some muffled talking from the other end.

"Yes, I know, there's a lot of sickness going around but it's not that, it's something else—"

Angela massaged her left temple with her free hand. "I've been under a lot of stress lately," she said. "I've had to make some … some difficult decisions. It's just become really confusing lately."

The voice came through the receiver and Angela listened

for a long time before speaking again.

"You know, it would have been Mom's birthday today," she said.

A faint noise came through the line.

"Anyway, I should go," Angela said. "But listen, I want you to know that I love you, okay? Whatever happens just know that. Know that I love you very much, Rachel."

Angela ended the call and returned the phone to the glass table. She reached inside the briefcase perched on the couch beside her and pulled out a small photograph, worn and folded in the corners, The photo held a frail Black woman within its borders, perhaps just shy of 70, laying on a hospital gurney. Tubes and hoses ran in and out of the woman, a cacophony of rudimentary plumbing, as she fearfully stared into the camera.

Angela put the photo down and began to tremble. She dropped her head into her hands, several tears dripping down her cheek and onto the polished hardwood floor.

Chapter Twenty-Four

March 1995
Day 418 | Night

I t was nightfall when the group reached the century home. The slanted gable roof stood tall, the expansive manicured grounds illuminated by the half-moon. The house was made of grey stone and brown bricks with narrow windows covering the front entrance. Heavy shutters hung outside, recently refreshed with a coat of ivory paint.

Xavier turned to Rachel. "Where are we?"

She ignored the question, leading the others over the stone wall along the back perimeter of the property. Andrew hobbled several steps behind as they shuffled beside the etched gardens, the shrubs and bushes still wrapped in burlap for the winter. The group moved toward the separated garage, a red-bricked structure with wood-stained doors and rustic metal handles. And there, the house spread out in front of them, a curved white-stone walkway dotting the driveway to the front door.

Andrew winced as his knees buckled. He fell forward but Damien caught him, easing him to the ground, leaning his back against the garage. He shivered continuously, as if the cold earth was seeping through his clothes and into his being.

"Rachel, where are we?" Xavier asked again.

"This is my sister's place." She remained fixed on a particular window along the far side of the house. "I haven't seen her in over a year but she called me out of the blue a few weeks ago. She sounded upset."

"About what?"

"She didn't say. But it was such a strange call. She said something about having to make tough decisions. Decisions at work, or … Anyway, I kept meaning to head over to her place but then all this crazy stuff started to get worse. By that point, I was too scared to even leave the house."

"Rachel, you're not making any sense. Tell me what the hell we're doing at your sister's house!"

Rachel wrung her hands and looked away.

"Look, we followed you all afternoon," Xavier continued. "And now you're telling us we're here because your sister was upset a couple weeks ago? And you don't even know why? You're going to have to give us more than that."

Rachel drew in a panicked breath. "I - I think she may have information about what's happening."

"How so?"

"I'm not sure, I just think she may understand what's happening to the townspeople, why they're changing into those things."

"And why would she know that?" Andrew asked, his injured leg splayed across the interlocking driveway.

Rachel stared at the ground and breathed through her teeth. "Because she's the Medical Officer of Health."

And in that moment Andrew understood why Rachel had seemed so familiar to him. He had sensed it when they first met and then again watching her sleep in the cellar. He had seen Rachel's sister interviewed on TV over the years, regularly providing health updates and public announcements. And now, with Rachel standing in front of him, the resemblance between the two was uncanny.

"Maddy's boss?" Xavier asked. "The same woman who threatened Maddy at her work? That's your sister? Why are you only telling us this now?"

Rachel turned away and remained silent.

Xavier cleared the tension from his voice. "Okay, well if you think she may know something, then let's go talk to her. Let's see what we can find out."

"It's just that," Rachel started. "If she does have information … well, I don't know how forthcoming she'll be with it."

"Why? She's your sister. Why wouldn't she tell you—"

"Wait!" Andrew interrupted. "Is she behind this?"

Rachel spun to face him. "She's not behind anything! She's a doctor for Christ's sake! I just thought she might have some information about what's going on, that's all."

"And you think there'll be information in there?" Andrew asked, motioning toward the house.

"Maybe … I don't know. I mean, we won't know for sure unless we go in."

"Is she even in there?" Xavier asked.

"Her car's not in the driveway." Rachel stood on her toes and peered into the glass cut-out of the garage door. "She's not parked in the garage either. She works long hours so she's usually out most of the day, always working late. It's pretty dark in the house. If she was home, there'd be lights on."

"What if she's sleeping and we startle her?" Xavier asked. "She could—"

"What if she's turned?" Andrew said. "What if she's already turned into one of those things?"

Rachel pressed her lips together and stepped into the shadows, a look of dread moving across her face.

"Okay, we'll go in," Xavier said finally.

"You're okay with all this?" Andrew huffed.

"If there's a chance we can find out what the hell is going on, then yes, I'm fine with it," Xavier said. "We might find something useful. I think it's worth checking out." He turned to Rachel. "So, how do we get in?"

She pointed toward the second floor on the far side of the house. "Her home office is that window. If there's any information, anything of value, it would be in there. We can get in through the side door. I know where she hides the spare key."

Damien reached down and hoisted Andrew to his feet. Andrew steadied himself against the garage, his leg swollen and throbbing from the long journey.

Xavier looked at him and then to Evelyn. The girl's hair was a knotted mess, her skin stained with dirt. Her eyes were frightened and red-streaked and her lower lip trembled. Standing amongst the adults, she was ever more a child, her slight stature staring up at Xavier.

"Andrew," Xavier started. "It's probably best if you and Evelyn stay here. I mean, you're in no shape for this and … and, well she's been through …"

His voice trailed off but Andrew knew what he meant. He had noticed the way Xavier's eyes had mellowed over the past few days, how his patience had grown—the girl's smile breaking down his tough exterior, Evelyn gradually carving out a tender spot for herself.

Andrew thumped to the ground. "That makes sense," he said. "We'll hold a lookout from here."

Damien piled the backpack and rifles along the side of the

garage. He handed his knife to Evelyn and both he and Xavier followed Rachel up the walkway, keeping tight to the high bushes lining the driveway. When they reached the side door, she upturned a stone from one of the gardens and removed a silver key. She approached the heavy oak door, a prominent frosted glass window carved into it.

She turned the key until the lock clicked, the sound amplified in the night air. Turning the squeaky handle, she gasped and stumbled backward into Xavier.

"What is it?" he asked.

"I think something moved in there," she said.

Xavier stepped forward and peered through the glass, straining to see. "I don't see anything."

"I think she sometimes has someone come in to clean the house and make meals for her."

"Like a housekeeper?"

"Sort of."

"Would she be here this late?"

Rachel thought for a second and then shook her head. "Likely not."

"Why didn't we bring the rifles?" Damien whispered.

Rachel turned on him. "We're not here to *shoot* anyone! Especially not *my sister*!"

Damien slunk back and Xavier turned the handle. The heavy door creaked open and one by one they slid inside under the dark archway.

Damien smacked the side of his flashlight and it sputtered to life. He followed the others down a short set of stairs onto the main floor. His foot stumbled on the last step and he lunged for the railing, his knee smacking the hardwood, the blunt sound echoing throughout the home.

The three of them stood ridged as a faint thud came from the floor above. Damien spun, swinging the beam up the stairwell and caught sight of a shadow darting along the wall.

"It's not your sister I'm worried about," he whispered.

He instinctively reached for his knife—the same knife he had unclipped and left with Evelyn moments earlier. Instead, he placed his hands on Rachel's shoulders.

"Where's the office?"

Rachel pointed down the dim hallway.

"Okay, lead the way. We'll be right behind you."

Rachel stumbled forward as Damien's flashlight flickered a few yards behind, up the high ivory walls and along the wainscotting clutching the ceiling. At the end of the hallway, she pushed open two large French doors.

Inside, she walked toward a massive desk and floor-to-ceiling bookcases. They were packed full of worn medical texts and academic journals. She moved her hand across the smooth wood of the desk until she reached several stacks of papers, scanning the first few lines in each pile.

Xavier stepped forward and pried open the large closet doors behind the desk, bending and shifting cardboard boxes and plastic containers. He paused when he spotted a narrow metal box tucked in the back. He stretched his large frame toward the container.

"I may have something here," he said.

He tried lifting it but it was made of thick steel, far heavier than its small size suggested.

Damien dropped to his knees beside him to peer inside the closet. "It's a safe. Any guesses on the combination?"

"1,2,3,4?" Xavier snorted.

"Looks like it's a six-digit code," Damien said.

Xavier turned the dial, trying different combinations of numbers, but the vault remained locked.

"Try 3-7-1926," Rachel said.

Xavier spun the lock until he heard a faint click. He pushed down on the steel lever and pulled the metal door open. He turned and surveyed Rachel.

"It was just a hunch," she said. "It's my mother's birthdate."

Xavier turned back toward the safe. He pulled out a slender manila envelope and handed it to Rachel. It had a grey logo of an antlered-buck staring straight ahead along the top.

"It's the same logo Maddy was talking about," Damien said.

Rachel removed a dozen sheets stapled along the edge. She began reading from the top of page one:

Copy 1 of 2: Highest security level - Confidential.

Natural observational study to assess the effects of pending drug, Lilasvir

Lead financier: Aaron Pak

Lead of operations: Alan Mackenzie

Hypothesis: Pharmaceutical drug, Lilasvir, to mitigate symptoms and potentially cure the Eastern Equine Encephalitis Virus (EEEV).

Study synopsis: Minute amounts of Lilasvir to be systematically added to town water

> *sources for a period of ten months. Sample subjects to be injected with traces of EEEV during month ten. Observational research to be conducted four to six-months post injections to assess full effects of Lilasvir.*

Rachel flipped to page two and continued reading:

> *Location of sample population: Town of Barn Wood*

> *Principal investigators: Dr. Simon Stone and Dr. Angela Till*

Rachel gasped. "Angela is my sister!"

Xavier stepped toward her and read over her shoulder. "Stone is *my* last name."

Rachel tilted her head, her anxious stare focused on him. "Do you know this Simon person?"

"No, we don't have anyone in our family with that name."

Damien shifted and cleared his throat. He motioned to speak but remained quiet, instead moving away from the desk, merging again with the shadows. A flick of light came in through the window but when he turned to peer out, the sky was dark once again.

Xavier scanned the rest of the second page before Rachel flipped to the third:

> *Origin and transmission of the virus: Transmission is through the bite of an*

infective mosquito. The virus is generally maintained within a bird → mosquito → bird enzootic cycle, with birds acting as the primary reservoirs and mosquitoes as vectors. This cycle has been observed in low-lying hardwood forests exposed to increased rainfall or flooding along with swamps and bogs.

However, confidential studies have shown the mosquito can act as a bridge vector transferring the virus to mammals, mainly white-tailed deer and equines. The virus is almost always fatal with the risk of death extremely high, the disease killing the animal from encephalitis within one week of exposure.

The mammals have always been dead-end hosts.

Until recently.

A thin line of sweat leaked down the side of Rachel's cheek as she continued to read.

Study details: *Beginning winter 1994, Lilasvir will be added to town-controlled sources of water. Regular monitoring of colour, taste, and smell to occur to ensure substance remains undetected. Ten months* *later, sample population to be injected with EEEV. Research to be conducted to assess the effects of Lilasvir on the virus. Analysis to be completed to compare results to control population.*

Study hypothesis: *The drug added to water supplies and ingested by the sample population for a period of ten months, triggered by EEEV, is sufficient to mitigate symptoms and cure the virus. If successful through natural experiment, the drug will have supportive data to proceed to clinical trials.*

Expected time to market: *24 months.*

Safeguards for information: *Only two written copies of study details produced. Principal investigators are forbidden to meet. All study details to be discussed in-person with the lead of operations only.*

Safeguards for substances: *Antidote has been included with the package. This is to be utilized if effects of EEEV in the sample population are unordinary or continue beyond twenty-four weeks, post-injection.*

Xavier reached into the safe and extracted a small box.

An image of skull and crossbones sat above a picture of a stencilled buck. He clicked the box open, a vial of milky liquid nestled within a layer of protective foam.

"An antidote?" he mumbled. "This whole time there's been an antidote?"

"But why are some people affected and not others?" Rachel asked. "How did the virus even get into their bodies?"

"The flu clinics!" Xavier said. "That has to be it! Maddy told us there were all sorts of promotion around them. The virus must have been injected there."

Rachel's mouth hung open. She eventually nodded.

"When we were going through one of the houses, I came across a pamphlet," she started. "It was advertising free gift cards and photos with celebrities just for getting a flu shot."

Xavier nodded. "Yes, and there was a photo taped to the fridge. It was of a man standing beside Tony *the Tank* MacAvoy. Behind them were rows of desks. They must have been in the flu clinic, set up to administer the virus."

"But how do you know when the photo was taken?" Rachel asked.

"It was date-stamped, November 21, 1994. The date stood out to me because I was away the last two weeks in November. I was getting in one last hunt before the snow came."

Rachel shook her head as she scanned the documents again. "I was away at that time too. Out of the blue my sister mailed me tickets, paid for a trip down south."

"Because your sister knew!" Xavier said. "She knew what was really in those needles! She flew you out so you wouldn't get the virus. Maybe she was protecting you."

"And look at this," Rachel said, pointing to a small footer on the documents. "It says here 'one of twelve.' But there's only seven pages here."

Rachel reached into the manila envelope but found no additional papers. There were however, excerpts from academic journals, faded and curling in the corners which read:

> … Human blood, when mixed with test drug Lilasvir over an extended period of time, shows promise … Properties and effects of activating agent still unclear and require further study …

She studied the articles. Many of them were illegible, but some of them contained the same smudged photo: a stocky, middle-aged man in a bleached lab coat. They read:

> … Head of pharmaceutical research fired for breaking ethics code … Conducting experiments on human subjects unknowingly … Researcher said to have gone too far with human testing … Continuously pushing boundaries …

> … "The substance works," Dr. Stone claimed during a recent conference. "We have proven effectiveness through mouse trials. We have an opportunity to change lives for the better. We simply need a human sample size large enough to corroborate our findings" …

… Research license revoked … Dr. Stone labeled a crackpot by peers … Has not been seen within the scientific community for years …

Trembling, Rachel dropped the news clippings. She took several quick breaths, steadying herself against the desk.

"They poisoned our town," she said quietly. "My own sister and this Dr. Stone guy. And all these other people named in these documents." She waved her hand across the pile of paper strewn across the desk. "They knowingly poisoned our town and everyone in it."

Her cheeks were flush and damp and she looked to Xavier with red-stained eyes; his own stared back, wide and frightened.

Chapter Twenty-Five

March 1995
Day 418 | Night

Angela sunk into the leather seat of her black Porsche and peeled out from the empty parking lot. For the past few weeks, she had been the only one utilizing the public health labs.

She sped through the deserted backstreets, the glow of the half-moon providing the only light. She whipped around a corner, the burgundy briefcase swaying in the passenger's seat.

She drove a few more kilometres, then turned, the car vibrating as it raced through the empty intersection. Yanking the steering wheel and forcing down the brake, the car weaved to a stop on the gravel shoulder as she threw the shifter into park.

Her head dropped between her shoulders and she wiped sweat from her forehead with the cuff of her blouse. "I don't understand," she whispered. "I just don't understand."

She sat quiet for some time, deep in thought, trying to make sense of her most recent calculations. The scratching of nails on metal began at the rear of the car so that by the time she heard the sound, the creature was already standing outside her window. A line of drool slid off its chin to the stones below.

Angela jerked up and jammed the shifter into reverse but

the gears didn't catch. Not taking notice, she forced the pedal to the floor but the car didn't move, the tachometer needle pinned, a high-pitched screech from under the hood.

The creature pounded its fist on the glass, dragging its clawed hand across the window. Angela stared up at it as the glass peeled away.

"Why are you like this? Why is this happening?" she shouted, her voice straining as she welled up. "What went wrong? I don't understand!"

The creature forced its long fingers under the window frame and began yanking the glass down. A swell of air passed into the car, Angela breathing in the potent smell of burning metal and decaying flesh.

She reached for the shifter and yanked at it again, this time the teeth of the clutch holding firm. She rammed the pedal down as the tires spun backward, spitting gravel into the air.

The creature turned and ran after the car just as a second figure emerged from the ditch. Angela hammered the brakes as both creatures crept into the hazy beam of the headlights.

From the muted glow, their features looked nearly human. There was nothing particularly strange about their shape. She could make out their ears, each normal in size, and their limbs were proportional to their bodies. The one which had emerged from the ditch was very thin and seemed quite young, the brow of her forehead taut, her skin supple, like that of a teenager.

But then the larger of the two opened its mouth and hissed, revealing a contorted line of fangs. Angela jerked the gearshift into drive and kicked at the gas pedal, swerving wide around the creatures. They chased for only a moment and then stopped—their yellow, crusted eyes following the rear car lights, bright red against the black night.

Angela drove for a long time, clenching the steering wheel. She turned into a winding interlocked driveway and turned the ignition off. She stepped out, her pumps coming to rest on the white-stone walkway leading to the front entrance.

She grabbed the briefcase from the passenger's seat but paused when she noticed a flash from a second-floor window. She spun and squinted toward the dark house and there it was again: a faint glow, like that from a flashlight, bouncing along the walls of her office.

She hurried up the path and then stopped. She fumbled with the lock on the briefcase, flipped it open and removed something. A glint of light moved across the stones below. She shimmied along the bushes leading to the side door, the shiny metal object disappearing in her hand.

Chapter Twenty-Six

March 1995
Day 418 | Night

At the back of the room, there was a faint thud. Damien moved toward the French doors, stepping under the office archway and into the dark hallway. His nose twitched, a subtle mix of wild orange and clove in the air.

His brow furrowed as he tried to distinguish the shape from shadow. The woman came into focus and he held her stare just long enough to see the handgun move from behind the briefcase.

Xavier came into the hallway but didn't see the woman raise the weapon.

Damien's eyes flitted between Xavier and the outstretched gun and he stepped between the two. His nostrils flared as the woman released a single bullet into his chest. He stumbled and cried out, reaching for the wall. The woman slunk from the dark and fired again, a second bullet ripping through Damien's lung. The boy wheezed, dropping to one knee.

"No!" Xavier cried, but retreated into the office when a third bullet ricocheted a few inches from his head.

"Get out! You are trespassing!" a voice hissed from the hallway.

Rachel stepped forward. "Angela?"

The woman skulked from the hallway into the office, the firearm still pointed at Xavier.

"You shot him!" Xavier roared. "You shot Damien!"

Rachel scurried behind the desk. "Angela, what are you doing with that gun?"

"Rachel?" Angela said. "What are you doing … why are you …" Angela twitched as if shaking off a bad omen. And then: "You're trespassing. All of you are trespassing!"

"I need to help him," Xavier yelled, jabbing his finger toward the hall. But still he remained planted.

"Angela, why do you have a gun?" Rachel asked again. "What the hell is going on?"

Angela glanced at the documents splayed across the desk. Twisting her neck to one side she peered toward the closet, the door of the safe ajar. She swung the weapon toward Rachel.

"How did you know the code?"

Rachel stuttered to the back of the room. "You're pointing a gun at me?" she said. "I'm your sister."

"How did you break the code?" Angela seethed.

"Y - you haven't been the same since she died," Rachel stammered. "I took a guess it had something to do with her."

"Haven't been the same? *Nothing's* been the same since she left!"

"She didn't *leave,*" Rachel said. "It wasn't a *choice*. She died. Sometimes people get sick and they die."

"She died far too young! She wasn't done being our mother! I still needed her."

"I needed her too. But there was nothing we could have done."

"Nothing we could have done? I'm a doctor for Christ's sake! Do you know how hard that is to live with? The kind of guilt I walk around with knowing I couldn't cure my own mother?"

Rachel grabbed her chest, struggling to breathe, as though months of neglect and cold detachment were solved in one short statement. Eventually, she found her voice again. "No one expected you to cure her," Rachel said softly.

Angela raised her head, her foreboding eyes meeting Rachel's frightened ones. She exhaled slowly. "It was a simple virus," she started. "A strain rarely passed to humans. One that up until now had always died with the animal. But not this time …"

She drew in a hurried breath, her voice rising in volume. "And I just have to stand by while her idiot doctor bumbles around with x-rays and blood samples. Taking his sweet time to diagnose, oblivious that the virus is rapidly weakening everything in Mom's body. Ten days! How does he explain that? She went from completely healthy to inside a wooden box in ten days!"

"No one wanted her to die," Rachel said.

Angela's shoulders shook. "She was our mother! Don't you miss her? Doesn't it tear you apart?"

"Of course, I miss her. I think of her all the time," Rachel said. "But eventually you have to accept what has happened and move on."

There was a seething silence from Angela so that Xavier hesitated before stepping forward. "I have to go help him," he said, pointing once again toward the hallway. "I have to go help that boy."

Angela tightened her hand around the gun and Xavier drew back. She stepped toward the desk, her eyes pinging from the confidential report to the articles shaming Dr. Stone.

"You've read all of it?" she asked.

"Yes," Rachel whispered, stepping closer to Xavier.

Angela sighed. "It's all gotten out of hand, it seemed to unravel so quickly. We were just trying to test a new drug. It was showing great promise. Something like this—if it had been approved several years ago—could have been given to Mom to slow the spread of the virus. Or even cure it. But time and again, the applications were rejected for human trials."

She dropped her gaze to the floor. "Of course, there were risks, but they all seemed minimal when the project started," she continued. "My role was to ensure all residents were given the virus to test the drug. But first, we had to get the drug into them. So, we liquified it, and I regularly added small amounts to the water supply. The drugs hadn't been approved yet but in order to get them to market, we needed data to support effectiveness in humans."

Angela was speaking quickly now, stumbling over her words.

"Generally, this strain of virus results in fever, diarrhea, maybe some vomiting. We assessed the symptoms as minor if it meant finding a cure. The company's plan was to observe the effects of the drug, and if effective, work backwards, getting everyone in town to consent."

"An experiment residents' didn't know they were a part of?" Rachel huffed. "There would be outrage. No one would agree to that!"

"The firm was *extremely* well-financed. If the drug made it to market there would be hundreds of millions of dollars to be made. Believe me, if the drug proved successful, the firm would find a way to achieve consent." Her eyes narrowed, the next words creeping slowly over her lips: "You'd be surprised what waving a few million dollars around can get you."

Rachel glared. "Is that how they got you?"

Angela rolled her eyes at the insult. "Given my position in the community, I was approached to conduct the experiment. The drug was in the water for nine, maybe ten months and then we infected residents with a large dose of the virus."

"It was done through the flu clinics, wasn't it?" Rachel said.

Angela nodded.

"And you sent me to Sarasota those same two weeks so I wouldn't be infected with it," Rachel added.

Angela nodded again. And outside the office, Damien howled.

"I have to go help him," Xavier said through gritted teeth.

But Angela didn't seem to hear him, her thoughts elsewhere. So, when she turned away, Xavier stepped under the archway and rushed to Damien's crumpled body.

The beige walls were stained with red splatters, illuminated by the moonlight peeking through the window. Xavier covered his nose, the stink of blood and bile oozing from Damien's chest. He propped him against the wall, the boy's breathing weak and shallow, his arms hanging useless at his sides.

He winced as Xavier pressed hard on his chest, attempting to slow the bleeding. With the other hand, he grabbed the boy's shoulder and Damien yelped in pain, squirming to get loose from the tight grip. Xavier held true and studied the shredded flesh. The puddle of blood pooling on the floor was deepening, a winding red ribboning across the floor. He scrambled along the hardwood and into the next room, frantically searching for something to plug the hole in the boy's chest.

From inside the office, Angela's voice rose again.

"But then something happened," she said. "The drug in the water reacted in an unexpected manner. It was a complete surprise. It didn't cure the virus as we had predicted. Instead, it *magnified* it. It accelerated the effects of the virus a thousand times over!"

"How so?" Rachel asked.

"I don't know for sure but my best guess is the pathogens evolved. They started to resist the safeguards we had put in place and began to wreak havoc on the hosts. Fevers led to migraines, migraines led to seizures, seizures led to hallucinations. Some of the subjects began displaying self-mutilating behaviour. We observed deformities of the skin and appendages. Over time, the virus began starving the body of oxygen so the host couldn't think straight."

"Is that why all these people have gone crazy?"

"Likely. The blood in the body began to transform into an ash-like substance. It clogged up their veins, pushing what little blood was left to an already starved brain."

"Your experiment resulted in them hunting us!"

"That completely surprised us as well. My theory is they hunted because they had such low levels of their own blood as most of it eventually thickened into a type of ooze. They probably craved the liquid form of blood. Somehow, they knew they needed it for their survival."

"But you have an antidote! Why didn't you just use that?"

"There was never an antidote. It was contrived, fabricated. An antidote was part of my demands before I agreed to the project. But what they provided ended up being sterile."

"You're lying! It's right there in the box!"

"Believe me—I tested it early on. It was spurious, a fake. I spent months doing tests, trying to concoct a true one."

"These people you're talking about—this firm you're working with—they're pure evil!" Rachel shouted. "They conduct experiments on people who know nothing about it. They lie about an antidote. And your partner in all of this has his research license stripped! Why would you ever partner with these people?"

"I never met the other researcher, it was never allowed," Angela said. "I was in charge of getting the drug into the water source and organizing the inoculation clinics. That was it. Dr. Stone was responsible for all things related to preparing the virus. Still, I wanted to know more about him. So, when this whole thing went sideways, I did a bit of digging of my own." She lifted her chin toward the clippings on the desk. "That's all of it—all I was able to find, anyways."

"This guy's a maniac and you still worked with him?"

"It was late in the process when I learned those things. Too late to stop what had already started. And there was a lot of money involved. So, I stayed quiet."

"But you called me weeks ago," Rachel stammered. "It was late at night. You sounded … confused … remorseful."

"I couldn't help Mom but … well, once this drug is proven effective, no one else will need to die from the same virus that took her!"

The beams from the flashlight bounced through the dining room as Xavier darted along the floor. He came across a pile of folded tea towels and rushed back to Damien. The boy was collapsed on the floor, his arm bent awkwardly, his facial features crooked and unnatural.

"Damien!" Xavier shouted.

He wrapped one of the tea towels across the boy's chest, applying a second one once the blood had seeped through. Damien had lost colour, his face flush, globes of sweat dripping along the creases of his forehead. His eyes were squeezed shut.

Xavier held him in his lap. "You need to wake up, okay? Everything will be okay, but you need to wake up now. Stay with me."

Rachel yelled from inside the office.

"But the drug doesn't work, Angela! The whole town is crumbling. Everyone's either unhinged or scared shitless. Is this what you wanted? Do you know how many people have been killed because of your million-dollar social experiment?"

Angela averted her sister's glare, instead studying the portraits and degrees hanging along the back wall.

"Help us!" Rachel shouted. "Angela, I know you are in a bad place right now, but—"

"And how would you know about that, huh?" Angela snapped. "Where have you been since Mom died? I've been in solitude for years with hardly a visit or phone call from you!"

"I'm sorry I haven't been around but I needed space. I was grieving too."

"Grief? You want to talk about grief? I've run through every therapist in a fifty-kilometre radius and no one can explain to me why Mom had to die!"

"Angela, I promise you, we'll find you the help you need. But right now, in this moment, you need to help us."

Angela snorted, shaking her head.

"How do we fix this?" Rachel asked, but again her question was met with silence.

"Listen to me," Rachel said. "There are so many people, good people out there, that needed our help. In fact, I just buried one of them." She paused, her eyes stern, her voice resolute. "But we have a chance to help the others. So, I need to know how to fix this."

Angela turned her back, her spine and shoulders rigid.

"What happened to you?" Rachel said. "We used to be so close. But since she died you've just … I mean, we've just … drifted."

Angela remained quiet and after some time, Rachel spoke again, gently. "She worked three jobs you know? She didn't want to tell you. She wanted you to focus on your studies. But she worked as a receptionist during the day, a waitress at night, and in a call centre on the weekends. All so she could afford to send you to medical school. And I was there the whole time. Watching her sweat, watching her skimp and save. Watching her go to work, even when she was dog-tired."

Angela's shoulders dropped. She leaned forward, the gun hanging loosely at her side.

"Most nights I watched her fall asleep at the kitchen table, our dinner going cold beside the stove," Rachel continued. "She was exhausted but never complained. Her arthritis had started to get worse around that time. But she kept telling me it was worth the effort, that it would all be fine in the end."

Angela's tongue travelled along her dry lips as though preparing to speak but she remained silent.

"She bragged to her friends that one day you would be a doctor," Rachel said. "*The first of our family,* she would tell them. She would tell anyone who would listen that you were the one who would bring us out of poverty. You would be the one who would use your love of science to help others. She was proud of you, Angela. So very proud of you."

The room grew quiet, an uneasy silence hovering between them. Angela crossed one hand over the other as a tear fell on the desk. As she reached up to cover her face, she inhaled deeply, the sound wet and hurried.

"I concocted a solution," she said finally. "Very recently. It took months of testing but I was able to create one. It won't cure the virus but it will mitigate the symptoms. The burgundy briefcase: it's in there."

In the hallway, Damien inhaled a slow shallow breath.

"Stay with me, Damien," Xavier said. "You need to stay with me."

The boy's head jerked forward. His eyes fluttered open, struggling to bring Xavier's chiselled features into focus. He reached out and caressed Xavier's strong jawline. He rubbed the stubble of black hair along Xavier's throat.

"Hey Uncle Joe," he mumbled. His voice was slurred and his head jutted forward, the weight of it causing his shoulders to buckle. He gasped as his lungs tried to draw air in.

Xavier pushed him upright, pressing against the wound.

"Damien—it's me, it's Xavier. I'm going to lift you now, okay? I'm going to get you out of here and we're going to get help."

Damien smiled a silly grin, a stench of bile drifting out from his bloodied mouth. "Is it June already?" he asked. "Have you come to take us camping?"

The corners of his lips were chapped with dried spittle, the hollows beneath his eyes moist and swollen and stained red. His neck twisted violently to one side as several loud cracks popped down his spine. His lungs wheezed but his chest did not rise again.

Months later, the sound Evelyn made would still haunt Andrew. The horrible noise which came out of her after Rachel hurled down the white-stone walkway and whispered into the girl's ear. He would try to erase the image of the child's knees buckling, her eyes swelling, and her body shaking. Andrew tried to block out her trembling lips, her mouth opening and closing but not making a sound, and then the vomit choking out of her, Xavier trying to console her as she thrashed wildly.

But in time, Andrew realized she wouldn't be consoled. The child was trapped now in her own thoughts, struggling to understand something that could not be understood.

In time, she would gradually come to accept that she was now alone. Her brother was on a different path, travelling down a different road. And where he was headed, she could not join him.

Chapter Twenty-Seven

March 1995
Day 419 | Dawn

It was minutes before daybreak when the group reached the cellar. Despite the creatures knowing about it, Andrew figured it was still the safest place to go. Even when Xavier spotted a shadow—a strange smudge of blue following them along the tree-line—Andrew still pushed the group forward. They travelled all night, hidden amongst the trees, listening for any grunting or growling, until they reached the underground refuge.

When they arrived at the cellar, Rachel pried the bolt open and lifted the large plank. She guided Evelyn down the steps, wrapping her tight in a blanket across the cold floor.

"You okay?" Xavier asked, turning to Andrew.

"I've been better," Andrew sighed. "But yeah, I'll live."

"Listen," Xavier started but then stopped. He swallowed several times, the words he sought not coming. "I'm just glad you're okay," he said finally. "After they attacked you, I was really scared you might not … that you might not make it …"

Andrew pressed his lips together and nodded. "It's okay," he whispered, his eyes red and misty. "I'm okay. We'll be okay."

He leaned into his brother, his head against Xavier's, like

two exhausted boxers spent from the match.

After some time, Rachel reappeared at the top of the steps.

"Evelyn's asleep," she said. "Thank goodness. She needs all the rest she can get. It will all come flooding back to her tomorrow, I'm sure."

Xavier nodded and then helped Andrew through the cellar door, hobbling down the steps until he came to level footing. Rachel was the last one down. She snapped the padlock over the bolted latch and laid out a blanket, smoothing the creases flat. After a while she curled into Xavier for warmth, his rhythmic breathing lulling both into a heavy sleep.

"We know you're down there!" the voice yelled. "We're armed and have you surrounded!"

Xavier shot awake as a thunderous thud came down upon the cellar door. It took several seconds for him to find the flashlight and shine it up the stairs. There was another loud bang as dust and debris shook loose from the door onto the steps.

"You're out-numbered!" the voice hollered again. "You come out or we're coming in! We won't ask again!"

Xavier handed the light to Rachel and shuffled her and Evelyn to the back corner. He dragged Andrew to the rear, linking his arms under his brother's scarred chest.

"How long were we passed out for?" Xavier asked.

"It had to be only a few hours," Rachel said.

Xavier kicked the burgundy briefcase aside and snatched his rifle. He tore open the backpack, toppling the contents onto the floor and reached for the remaining cartridges.

"Dammit. There's only three left!"

He fumbled to load the gun and clicked the safety but froze at the sound of the metal bolt grating across the wood above them. The door moved, but the inside padlock stayed true, not allowing the door to budge any further.

"Listen down there! Come out immediately or there will be—"

The voice was cut off and then there was shuffling overhead followed by the sound of a heated exchange. Eventually, a different voice drifted into the cellar. This voice was calm and soft with an even cadence.

"Hello in there. This is the police. We would like you to come out from there. You're not in any danger or in any trouble. We're here to help."

Andrew stared at Xavier and then turned to Rachel and Evelyn. No one spoke for a while.

"If they're infected, they wouldn't be able to talk like that," Andrew said finally, surveying the others. "Right?"

"I doubt it," Xavier mumbled.

"And we would be able to smell them, wouldn't we?" Rachel added. "With them standing so close, we'd smell them from down here, right?"

"Maybe not," Xavier said. "Remember, no one smelled them yesterday when they attacked."

Andrew lowered his eyes. "I did. It was faint but the smell was there. I was already through the door when I realized what it was."

Rachel shone the light up the stairs, the beam fluttering. Xavier studied the cellar door and then turned to Andrew.

"If I go up, can you cover me?"

Andrew shook his head. He was weak and tired from his injuries and the long journey back to the cellar.

"How about you, Rachel?"

Rachel adamantly shook her head. "I don't trust those things."

Evelyn rose to her feet and reached for the rifle. "I can."

"Ev, you sure? I mean I'm not sure you're ready—"

"Give me the gun," she said, her voice clear and firm.

Xavier hesitated a moment longer but then nodded, a slight smile teasing at his lips.

"Position yourself at the base of the steps," he instructed. "If anyone that isn't me comes down those stairs, you start firing."

Rachel placed a hand on Xavier. "Are you sure it's safe?"

"There might be only one way to answer that." He unsheathed his knife and nodded at Evelyn. "Okay, I'm going up."

Scaling the rungs two at a time, he jimmied the padlock and flung the door open. The rays from the morning sun bounced off the empty tins and jars scattered along the dusty floor. The light illuminated Andrew propped in one corner with Rachel kneeling beside him, shielding her eyes from the glare.

But the sun also shone on a smaller silhouette, the outline of a child, crouched at the base of the steps. She was pointing a rifle, hands steady, eyes locked down the scope, her stare fierce and unwavering.

Xavier was above ground for a long time until he finally

showed his face at the cellar entrance again. It was red and blotchy, wet streams carving uneven lines through the dust on his bearded cheeks.

"It's okay. We're safe now. It's over."

He waved the others up and one-by-one they emerged, each one squinting as they came above ground. They were greeted by a dozen officers, their bright blue shirts tucked into their black wool dress pants. One of the officers kicked mud from his combat boot, an assault rifle held at his side.

A portly older man, nearly out of breath, approached Andrew. He pawed at his salt and pepper hair, trying to cover the bald spot in the centre of his head.

"I'm Staff Inspector Tom Everett. We're glad we found you. Is everyone alright?"

Andrew recognized the voice as the kinder of the two which spoke to them from outside the cellar. The man placed his chubby hand on Andrew's shoulder.

After Andrew nodded, the Staff Inspector moved toward Evelyn but drew back when his eyes met hers. She was filthy, her eyes bloodshot and stained red, slack skin gathered beneath them. She was muscular yet very thin, her ripped pants held loosely to her waist by a beaded belt, a frayed shirt hanging off. She wrapped her arms across her body and shivered.

"Bring some blankets over," Everett hollered.

When they arrived, he wrapped Evelyn tight, kneeling in front of her, rubbing her shoulders for warmth.

"How did you find us?" she asked.

Everett tilted his head away, the girl's breath an acrid stench, a smell similar to sour milk.

"We've been following you since we spotted you near the creek. The one along the back here, a few kilometres in," he said.

Xavier stepped forward. "It must've been your uniforms we spotted by the creek yesterday and again in the forest last night. I saw your blue shirts among the trees but at the time, I didn't know what it was."

"Most likely an over-anxious rookie going headfirst into the forest before waiting for back-up," Everett said. He gave a sideways glance to one of the officers who turned away and trounced off.

"We were looking for safe passage into town when my rookie spotted you by the water. He followed you. Eventually, he turned back to issue the report. But not before you spotted him, it seems."

"Why didn't you come sooner? People in this town have gone crazy and have been hunting us for weeks," Andrew said.

"As soon as we learned of suspicious activity in the area, we dispatched a team."

"*Suspicious activity*? These things are out to kill!"

"To be honest, at the time we didn't know much," Everett said. "Only some questionable reports of people getting sick and some fighting among residents. We figured it would be handled by your regional division."

"Well, it wasn't," Xavier said.

"No, I suppose not. It wasn't until some of your local officers made it out to us that we learned more. They told us residents were acting strange and some were resorting to violence. Yet, the situation still seemed minor and so it took a while to prioritize the calls. We didn't *really* know what was going on until we tried to get in."

"You drove your police cars in?" Xavier asked.

"We tried. I sent two cruisers to investigate. But they radioed in saying there were hundreds of people blocking the road. They reported residents lighting barrel fires, throwing planks of wood at them, metal bars, all sorts of things. As you know, there's only the one road into town so I ordered the officers back. It was only when they returned that I learned more about the situation."

"What did they tell you?"

"My guys said the residents seemed possessed. Reports of deformities. And that none of the residents were right in the head."

"Yes, we've unfortunately experienced all of that," Xavier growled.

"To avoid a confrontation again, I figured the best way would be on foot through the woods. But it proved more difficult than I had imagined. As the days turned over, I reconsidered our tactics, including trying to get in again through the main road."

"What happened when you tried again?" Andrew asked.

"In the end, we didn't attempt it," Everett said. "I didn't want to engage in a gunfight or put my officers in danger without knowing the full situation."

"So, you came in through the woods? How long were you set up there for?"

"A few days. We were about to change our approach but then caught a glimpse of a few of you by the creek. We followed, hoping you would lead us to something useful, some information or answers."

Rachel lowered her head. "There were six of us at the creek," she said. "But one didn't make it. We had to bury her there."

Everett pressed his lips together. "Yes, we know. I had a

team sweep the area after you left. We came across the mound of dirt and figured as much. I'm sorry for your loss."

"How long did you follow us?" Andrew asked.

"Right up to the house you stopped at. Again, we didn't have the full story so we surveilled from a distance. We closed in when we heard gunfire."

Xavier glanced toward Evelyn but she looked away. "It was her brother who was shot in there," he said.

"Yes, we came across the body when we raided the house. We spotted you fleeing the property so sent a couple guys ahead to follow you. The rest stayed back to survey the scene."

Rachel stepped forward. "It was my sister's house. She's the one who shot the boy."

Everett drew back. "Your sister? That woman is your sister? In that case, we will need to take you in and question you in private. You may have knowledge which will be useful to us."

"What will happen to her? To my sister?" Rachel asked.

"In terms of …" Everett paused to reach into his jacket and pulled out a notepad, his thick fingers flipping to an earmarked page. "In terms of Dr. Till, she came willingly. Surrendered without a fight. She even showed us documentation outlining the entire scheme. The water tampering, the fake flu clinics, the secret accounts set up for payment. She handed over files incriminating her and the financiers. She's on route to our headquarters now and she'll be processed there."

"But what will happen to her?"

"It's hard to say. We haven't seen a case like this before. Tampering with government records, crimes against public interest, medical negligence leading to death." Everett flipped the page of his notepad. "And if it's proven that she pulled the trigger on that boy, she can be charged with manslaughter."

"Even though we were trespassing?"

"It's an ongoing investigation so I've likely said too much already," Everett said. He leaned back, his boots worn and canted at the heel. "It's a complex case to be sure. We'll just have to wait and see how a judge assesses it."

Rachel hung her head, stepping beside Evelyn.

"We have the antidote," Andrew said.

"Yes, Dr. Till told us it was with you. We need to get that from you so we can replicate it. We're hoping to process it through our forensic assessment centre to learn more about it."

He turned to Rachel. "Sorry to say, but given the circumstances, your sister is not considered a trustworthy source. So as of now, we're treating her claims about an antidote with extreme caution. We'll do our own testing. If it comes back clean and is in fact what she says it is, then our forensics division will work with the labs to produce a permanent antidote."

He stepped back, his head swivelling as he took the group in. "If you don't mind my asking: why weren't the four of you infected?"

"None of us were given the virus. Evelyn lives on the outskirts and the three of us were all out of town when it was distributed through the flu clinics," Andrew said.

Everett looked away, chewing on his lip, his bushy brow furrowed. "Surely there are others like you, then? Others that were out of town when all this happened? Others that weren't issued the virus?"

Andrew shrugged. "There could be, I suppose. But those creatures are ruthless! If they saw anyone normal, I'm sure they'd attack."

Xavier cleared his throat. "We've searched a lot of homes around here and have been in and out of that forest nearly every day for weeks. Aside from Dr. Till and us, we haven't come across anyone else that wasn't infected."

"Yeah, and Maddy—the lady who was with us at the creek," Andrew explained, "she said vaccination rates were well over 95% this year."

Everett nodded, turned his back, and began speaking with the other officers. After a short time, he turned back to the others.

"Still, we're going to send out search parties to see if we can locate others who may have managed to survive," he said. "Even though you haven't come across any, there could still be some out there."

He cleared his throat and dropped his voice. "I realize you've been through a lot. But you obviously know how to take care of yourselves as you've survived this long. We could use your tracking skills to find and capture any remaining infected persons. Not to kill them, mind you. I believe enough of that has been done. But rather to find them and administer the antidote, when it's ready."

"Well, first things first: my brother's injured and needs to be looked at," Xavier said. "He needs medical attention right away."

Everett hollered to one of the officers who unpacked a large first aid kit.

"My men will treat him here as best they can," Everett assured him. "And then we'll get him to a hospital outside of town as soon as we have safe passage out of here."

"Once he's stitched up and on-the-mend, we can help you track and capture," Xavier said. "We, unfortunately, seem to have a knack for attracting these things."

Everett scanned the body-strewn yard. "Yes, I've noticed."

"And we'd like the boy, the one shot in the house. We'd like him returned so we can conduct a proper burial."

"I'm sure that can be arranged after forensics gives the go-ahead."

Rachel wrapped an arm around Evelyn but the girl remained stoic, staring at her frayed boots poking out from beneath the blanket.

"We need to start testing that antidote," Everett said. "You need to hand that over to us now."

Xavier nodded and descended the cellar steps, waiting a moment to adjust to the darkness. He jostled the metal container from the burgundy briefcase and removed the glass vial. Pulling the seal off, he reached for a Mason jar from one of the racks. He tilted the tube, a few murky drops squirming into the glass container. Screwing the lid tight he placed the jar into the backpack. He resealed the remaining liquid in the vial and returned it to the metal container, clipping the latch shut.

Hoisting the backpack over his shoulder, he tucked the metal container under his arm and then bounded up the steps, squinting as he returned to the brightness of the sun.

Chapter Twenty-Eight

April 1995
Day 427 | Afternoon

A strong breeze jostled the wind chimes above Rachel's head as she gently blew on her cup of coffee. She adjusted the wool shawl around her shoulders, the crisp April air a reminder summer was still several weeks away. She turned to Xavier and Andrew, both seated on the front porch of her century home.

"She's still in shock," Rachel said. "Doesn't talk much either. Still processing everything, I suppose."

"Damien's death?" Xavier asked.

"Yes. And Maddy's. Plus running and hiding from those things for so many nights. She's very tired. Been through a lot for her age."

"It's a lot for *any* age," Xavier said. He slid his backpack off and into his lap, burrowing his shoulders into the stiff wooden chair. "Has she been with you since we came out of the cellar?"

"Of course. She never leaves the house. Only leaves her bedroom to eat or use the washroom."

"You think she'll be okay?" Xavier asked.

"She's still trying to find her way, I guess. Find a new path now, one without her brother." Rachel paused to take a sip. "God, I don't wish that walk on anyone."

Andrew peered into the high grass lining the meandering laneway, weaving from the road to the bricked path. He noticed the trees overhanging the eaves were starting to bud, a whiff of lavender on the breeze. The smell reminded him of Juliana, her thick red hair diffusing the floral scent as she laughed along to his stories on the plane. He scratched at a deep scab along the side of his face, yellow and black bruises still prominent along his neck where the creatures had buried their claws and teeth. A lopsided bandage covered his left ear where one of them had bit it.

Rachel cleared her throat and turned to him. "Have you been out there this whole time? Hunting those things?"

"It took about five days for the antidote to be tested and replicated," Andrew said. "Which was good, because I needed time to heal. But yeah, ever since they got the solution over to us, X and I have been out every day."

"Any luck?"

"Some. Everett is leading logistics and tracking progress of all the teams. He thinks we've inoculated about a tenth of the town. Still a long way to go."

"Where are you finding them?"

"Anywhere it's dark and cramped, really. Barn lofts, attics, closets. X has a knack for it. He can usually smell them when we're close. Maybe it's because they smell as bad as he does."

Xavier scoffed and rolled his eyes.

"It will take a while to get them all," Andrew continued. "But Everett has requested reinforcements to help with that. He thinks they'll be here within the next few days."

"When will you be done?" Rachel asked.

"I'd say we're on track to find and cure everyone by end of summer."

"Cure? I thought my sister's concoction was a *good-for-now* type of thing?"

"It is *good-for-now*!" Andrew chuckled. "Everett said his forensic department is still doing tests on it. Although they say the original solution from Angela was quite accurate. It turns out it was close to something permanent."

"Well, I suppose that's one good thing to come out of this whole nightmare."

"I know your sister contributed to all of this," Andrew said. "But recently, I mean … she's also sort of helping to solve it."

Rachel nodded and shifted in her seat, the cool breeze moving her hair across her face. She took a sip of coffee. "How are you doing health-wise?" she asked.

"I'm getting there," Andrew said. "My leg still bothers me but the cuts are more or less healed. I had over a dozen stitches put in along my side but I'm getting my full range of motion back."

"He can still shoot," Xavier grumbled. "And for the time being, that's pretty much all that matters."

"You should still rest though, don't you think?" Rachel asked. "Is it safe for you to go out? You might be putting too much strain on your body."

Andrew adjusted the bandage along his ear. "Nah, I need to be out there, I need to be helping. I need to see those things change back to the people they once were."

He exhaled through his teeth, watching a song sparrow hop from one branch to the next. "I owe Maddy that much. Or maybe it's just guilt from shooting so many of them down."

"You didn't have a choice," Rachel said. "It was us or them."

"I suppose. Still doesn't make it any easier though."

"Will you go out again soon?"

"Everett wants us to head out tomorrow for another stint," Andrew said. "Besides, being out there, finding others—it gives me hope for my parents."

Xavier pointed toward the rifle leaning against the siding. "Did you learn to shoot?"

"Not well," Rachel moaned.

"I thought you didn't trust guns?"

"Well, those things are still out there. I needed something in case they came around here."

"I can teach you how to shoot sometime if you want," Xavier said.

Rachel nodded, a coy smile parting her lips. "That'd be nice."

Xavier rose from his chair and motioned toward the screen door. "Mind if we go talk to her?"

"Evelyn? Sure, go right ahead. She's upstairs, first door on your right."

Xavier slung the backpack over his shoulder and made his way up the narrow stairwell, Andrew hobbling behind. He knocked gently and when there was no response, pushed the bedroom door open. Evelyn was lying face down on the bed, a pillow wrapped around her head.

Closing the door behind them they crept into the room. There was a worn chest of drawers pushed to one corner and a standing mirror in the other. A graduation photo hung over a wooden desk, a young Rachel beaming with her arms wrapped tight around Angela. A smirk graced the older sister's face, the mortarboard and tassel of her cap askew.

Andrew leaned into the wall as Xavier sat down on the

yellow comforter folded under Evelyn. "Ev?"

She shifted at the sound of his voice but continued to hold her face in the pillow.

He reached out and placed her hand in his. He moved his index finger from her wrist through her palm and up the length of her pointer finger, just as he had done when he had taught her to shoot.

"Are there any markings still from the gun?" He flipped her hand over but she yanked it away.

"Listen, Ev. I know it hurts now but it's going to get better." He made figure eights along her spine as he gently rubbed her back. A faint metallic smell wafted up from her skin. A tremor trickled across her shoulders as she sniffed into the pillow.

"It's okay, Ev. It's all going to be okay."

He sat silently at the foot of the bed for some time. Eventually, he reached into the backpack and pulled out a Mason jar and needle. He unscrewed the lid and dipped the point of the needle in. There was a slurping sound as the liquid was sucked up the barrel of the syringe. He rolled her shirt up and Andrew noticed several pinpoint scabs peppered along her spine, identical to the ones he saw down Damien's back.

"Hold tight a sec," Xavier whispered, and he pressed the needle firmly into her back.

Her head shot up and she howled in pain. Her legs thrashed and kicked as Xavier removed the sharp instrument. He wiped at it and then returned it to the backpack.

"What in the world was that?" Rachel yelled as she burst through the bedroom door.

She knelt to caress Evelyn, trying to calm her writhing body.

"You're infected, Ev," Xavier said. "But I think you've known that for a while."

"What in the world are you talking about?" Rachel shouted.

"I gave her some of the antidote," Xavier said. "I stole some from your sister's solution."

"This is insane!" Rachel said. "You're diagnosing people now?"

"Rachel, it's okay, please calm down," Andrew said. "X and I took some as well earlier this week. As a precaution, after the attack."

"But why her?"

"Evelyn's walked with a limp since we came across you guys in the woods. We've come to learn it's one of the symptoms of the virus. We watched her closely but she never healed. The injury just got worse."

"But she doesn't look anything like those things," Rachel said.

"We think the virus was already in her when we met up with your group. It was already taking root."

"I caught the scent of it by the creek," Xavier said turning to Evelyn. "It was faint but it was there. You were beginning to smell like them. You were slowly changing."

"Were you ever bit by one?" Andrew asked. "You got blood on you from one of them in the cellar but you were limping before then. I think exposure to their blood may have accelerated your body's response to the virus. But we don't know why you had those symptoms in the first place."

Evelyn clenched her teeth and blinked her watering eyes. She laid back down, turning toward the wall, and remained silent.

"We go out again tomorrow with the police teams," Xavier said with a heavy sigh. "We'll be gone for another four or five days, but Andrew and I will check on you after that."

He slung the backpack over his shoulder and twisted the door handle.

"You should start to feel better soon," he said. "Goodbye, Ev."

"It was our third night in the forest," Evelyn said. Her head was still turned but her voice was strong and clear. "Damien tried so hard to stay awake. But by the third night, he was just too tired. He fell asleep. We both woke up from a scratching sound. I don't think the thing saw us at first. Damien stood up and shot it. It was the first one we had seen up close. It was so scary looking—drooling everywhere and it stunk so bad!"

Evelyn rolled over to face the others.

"At the time, we didn't know there was always more than one—that they travel together. So, we fell asleep again. That's when the second one attacked. The noise woke me and I saw it was on top of Damien. He was screaming and he kicked it off. It went after me and scratched me. I was bleeding badly."

Evelyn rubbed the swollen scar carved into her forearm. "Then Damien shot it. I asked him if I would get infected, if I would turn into one of them. He told me not to tell anybody. He told me he would find a way to help."

Evelyn sniffed, silent drips of tears travelling down her cheek, the pillow now moist.

"The next day I was so sore and tired. My knees hurt so bad. I tried to walk, but it was too painful. I could only limp. So, he carried me a lot of the time. He wanted us to move around. He said it was safer that way, that they couldn't track us that way. So, we never stayed in one place for very long. He tried so hard to keep us safe."

Rachel held the small girl, rocking her on the bed. She whispered into her ear as Evelyn shook, sobbing into Rachel's shawl. After a few moments, Rachel laid her down and drew the comforter over her.

"Get some rest now," Rachel said.

"The antidote will help heal your body, Ev," Xavier said. "It will get better. From now on, things will get better."

Andrew and Rachel slid out of the room. Xavier followed close behind but paused at the sound of Evelyn's tired voice.

"Thank you," she said. "Thank you for always looking out for me."

She smiled weakly, rolled over, and fell into a deep slumber.

Chapter Twenty-Nine

April 1995
Day 447 | Dusk

Andrew nudged the door with the toe of his boot, the barrel of his rifle pointed straight ahead. The hinges whined as the door tilted open, the glass closet in the foyer smashed to pieces. A tremor shuddered through him as he surveyed the damage.

Ribbons of drywall peppered the floor leading to the staircase with several of the steps torn off. The wood panelling was stripped, many electrical outlets pulled from their mounts.

The wrinkles across his sweaty forehead crumpled as his eyes flitted around the century farmhouse. He looked back at Xavier and the three constables. "What do you think?"

Xavier clutched his rifle tight to his body and sniffed the air. "The smell is strong. This house is active."

"How about we skip this house?" one of the officers said, a metal container tight under her arm. "At least until tomorrow. When there's more light."

Andrew read the lapel of her uniform. "Powell, is it? Listen, one of those things is here. Let's save it and then call it a day, okay?"

Powell wiped her forehead, her dark skin sheen with sweat. Andrew looked at her steady and eventually she nodded. She raised her arm at the armoured van parked at the end of the laneway and the driver flashed the headlights.

"Protocol says police should clear the house first, but …" she trailed off, nervously looking up at Andrew.

"Protocol went out the window when feral lunatics started chasing us," Andrew muttered, stepping through the threshold.

"Everett thought this might work," a second officer said coming into the farmhouse, the name *Lawson* sewed into his uniform. He was stocky and pale and he extended a six-foot rod with a noose dangling from the end.

"They're not stray dogs! Have you even seen one of these things?" Xavier said, turning on him. "You go ahead and put your trust in that catch pole if you want but I'll put mine in *this*!" He bounced the heel of his hand against the stock of the rifle.

"We're not here to *kill* them. We're here to administer the antidote," a third officer said. He was tall and lanky with the name *Prasad* stitched into his arm.

"It's just a precaution," Xavier grumbled. He rubbed the coarse tufts carpeting his cheeks and throat. He stepped through the front archway, his boots scraping along the floor.

Andrew was already across the main room, the area half-filled with shadow. He remembered when he went back through his own parent's house the night his flight landed. He had expected the house to feel warm as it once had: the familiar smell of his mother's baking, cinnamon buns in the oven or a fresh loaf cooling on the counter. Echoing and unfamiliar, he was instead met with overturned furniture and smashed windows, rips in the drywall where claws had sliced through.

He examined similar marks now, his finger rolling over the

deep indents. The markings were low on the wall as though a child had dragged a pitchfork above the baseboards. A tint of red caught his eye and as he stepped closer, he saw smears of it upon the strands of frayed rope.

"Fresh blood," he whispered.

Prasad hustled over. "What's that? What did you say?"

Andrew raised his finger to his lips to signal silence and gestured to the corner of the room.

Prasad shuffled closer to examine the moist stains. His eyes widened as they caught on two parallel tracks dug into the floor. The hardwood splintered beside each groove as if something heavy was forced across it.

He twisted toward Andrew. "Wh - what is this? What's this mean?"

Andrew drew out a slow breath but said nothing, slipping into the dining area. In the same room, Lawson jimmied around a wooden table, the far end of it smashed through the drywall. A curio cabinet laid in the middle of the room, shards of crystal-ware and broken china scattered along the scratched floor.

Lawson focused on a gaping hole in the wall. "Are they that strong?"

Andrew examined the wreckage, a look of uneasiness seeping across his face. "They get stronger the longer the virus is in them. The further along it is, the less human they become."

Lawson stepped forward, the glass shards popping from his weight. Andrew jerked at the sound then paused at a different noise: a faint shuffle, right above his head.

"X!" he hollered.

Xavier ran into the dining area. "I heard it too!"

"Powell, we need that solution!" Andrew ordered.

Powell flipped the latch of the metal container and removed a long instrument filled with a cloudy liquid, her panicked eyes fixed on the steel needle. She gasped as something scurried upstairs.

Andrew followed the sound with his stare.

"Let's go! We're losing the light!" he said.

Andrew's rifle vibrated as he climbed the stairs. Lawson followed a few steps behind, the beam from the flashlight needling into the darkened corners. A door shut and the officer swung the light as a shadow disappeared into one of the rooms.

"Stay calm," Andrew whispered.

A line of sweat dribbled down his pudgy cheeks as Lawson swallowed and nodded. Andrew adjusted the strap of his gun and inched toward the bedroom, the roar of blood in his ears.

"This is where the noise came from," he said.

He pushed the door open. He retched and grabbed at his stomach from the stink of metal and vomit. And then the panic coiled up him as he spied the woman slumped in the corner.

Lawson covered his mouth but couldn't muffle the scream.

"It's okay! She won't hurt you!" Andrew said.

The woman stared straight ahead without blinking, her face blue and moist, purple bruises along her wrists and forearms. Her legs were stretched out in front but sat at odd angles to each other as though they had been removed and then carelessly put back on.

"H - how do you know?" Lawson stammered.

Andrew focused on a thin line across the woman's neck, the skin bubbling around it. He had seen similar trauma when his traps malfunctioned: a hare or otter caught in the twine, the air choked out of them, the blood vessels seared under the fur.

He shuddered, a sensation of spiders crawling across his skin. "Because she's dead," he said.

He moved into the hallway and edged into a second room, followed by the others. He stepped around the overturned lamp and moved toward the bed, pushing on the mattress with the butt of his rifle. A bookcase laid on the ground: figurines, sports cards, and comic books scattered along the area rug.

Gone were the posters and pennants once tacked along the wall, now punctured with holes and claw marks. Shattered glass and splintered frames were kicked into the corner. A wooden memory box sat broken in half: *Daddy and Me* sloppily inscribed along it.

Andrew motioned toward the closet door. Lawson grasped the handle as Xavier raised his rifle.

"Open it and get the hell out of the way," Xavier said.

Lawson exhaled. He yanked the handle and threw the door open. He shrieked and stumbled backward, the flashlight dropping and rolling across the floor.

Andrew stopped the spinning flashlight and shone it into the closet. His breath caught as the light rested on the child.

Damp hair hung over the boy's face. Wide hazel eyes, dull and lifeless, looked out between the loose curls. A rope was cinched around his neck, a splatter of blood caked the skin just below the teeth marks pressed into his throat. His arms were bound behind his frail body as he slumped in the chair. His chest was still, his legs hanging inches from the floor.

"We're too late," Andrew said. His voice broke and he

gagged as he brought the light away.

He knelt to help Lawson up, handing the officer the flashlight. Andrew ducked through the bedroom doorway but a voice caused him to stop.

"But how did the door shut?" Lawson said. "We heard it close. When we were coming up the stairs. If the boy's dead, then who closed the door?"

Lawson leaned into the closet and there was a flutter of movement. At first it appeared the boy's shoulders were quivering, a slight bounce to them. But the movement wasn't from the boy but rather something moving up from behind. Lawson jerked the flashlight as a fist unfurled atop the child's shoulder, red liquid streaming along the palm and fingers.

It wasn't the boy's eyes that blinked but a second set, flicking back and forth behind the chair. Lawson staggered and screamed but the creature was already crawling over the child and out of the closet, its limbs bent and arachnid.

Powell spun to see the officer's head thrown against the wall.

"Jonathan!" she screamed, as the creature lunged and bit down into Lawson's chest.

It raised its head, bloody saliva and bits of blue uniform chocked within its teeth. Lawson wailed as the creature dug into him with its claws.

Xavier tackled it to the ground, gripping the creature's wrists as it thrashed wildly. Andrew dropped a knee onto it, the length of his rifle pressed down across the creature's neck.

"We need that needle now, Powell!" Andrew yelled. "Into the spine! Stab it right into the spine!"

The creature screeched, its head twisting, its yellow eyes full of fear and hate, its black tongue flicking side to side. A nauseating stench passed through the room as Powell drew her arm back and drove the needle down.

Through its ripped shirt Andrew could feel sweat pooling along the creature's neck as it squealed and shook. Soon its breathing slowed and Andrew watched as it began to calm— its clenched hands loosening, its pointed nails regressing. Eventually it stopped twitching and laid still.

Andrew flipped it onto its back and watched as it coughed and wheezed. The creature was more man now than beast. His eyes shot open.

"Y - you were poisoned," Powell stammered, looking down at the man. "We've just treated you." She bent and helped him to his feet. "It may take a while for you to remember things ... for you to feel normal again."

The man's eyes rattled around the room but stopped on the closet. He drew back and covered his mouth.

"Who is that? What happened to that boy?"

Powell pointed across the room. "Sir, this is Constable Prasad," she said. "I'd like you to go with him. Everything will be explained to you. We have treatment and counselling prepared for you outside."

She spoke into the police radio strapped to her vest and the armoured van crept up the gravel driveway.

The man tilted his head to get a better look at the child.

"Who is that? Wait, is that my—" He began to well up. "Please someone tell me who that is. He looks just like my—"

"Sir, why don't you come with me?" Prasad said. "We can explain everything outside."

The man stuttered down the hall, bracing himself against the tall officer, anxiously looking back over his shoulder.

Andrew stood over Lawson. "Fill the needle again, Powell.

He's been exposed so we'll have to do him as well."

Andrew flipped the officer onto his front as Powell bent to one knee. "Sorry, Jonathan," she whispered. "Hold very still."

Lawson yelled and shook, sucking at the air as Powell plunged the needle into his spine. After some time, his eyes fluttered open and Andrew brought him to standing.

"Here's one more for you," he said as Prasad returned up the steps.

Prasad wrapped Lawson's arm around his shoulder and guided him down the stairs. "Are you okay?"

"What the hell happened?" Lawson slurred.

"One of those things jumped right at you!" Prasad said. "It bit you and knocked you into the wall. Those two fellas saved your life!"

Powell hollered down the stairs. "He'll need medical attention just like the others, Prasad. Treat all the cases the same."

Andrew noticed she was trembling. "You okay?" he asked.

Powell bit her lip but remained silent. Eventually, Xavier turned toward her.

"What happens to the boy?" he asked.

"They'll send a second unit to pick him up," she said, her voice weak. "They're collecting all the ones that … that didn't make it. They'll dispose of him correctly to ensure the virus doesn't spread any further."

"I don't think that's how this virus works," Andrew mumbled.

She turned away and spoke into the police radio. "They're asking for me outside." She handed Andrew a second radio. "Stay tuned to that. We'll call you if one of the other teams identifies another active house."

She hurried down the steps but then stopped. "I'm glad you agreed to do this. You both should be proud of what you did today. You saved that man. You did good." She turned then, disappearing out the front door.

"Not good enough," Xavier mumbled.

"The boy was dead before we got here," Andrew said. "There wasn't anything we could have done for him."

Xavier nodded but said nothing.

"They feed on each other when they're scared," Andrew added. "We've seen this before."

Xavier sat down on the hardwood and laid his rifle across his lap. His head slumped forward.

"Why can't we find Mom and Joe?" he said, his voice catching.

"I don't know."

"We've searched dozens and dozens of houses! Where the hell are they?"

"I, uh … I don't know anymore, X. I just don't know."

"No answers this time, huh?"

Andrew closed his eyes and hung his head.

"I thought *Mr. Fancy School Boy* always had the answers," Xavier mumbled.

Andrew drew in a shaky breath. "Sorry I act that way," he said softly. "Like I've got it all figured out and …"

He trailed off and they both sat on the bedroom floor for some time, the stress and adrenaline of the day slowly leaking out of them.

Eventually, Andrew leaned forward and peered into the closet. Blue and green shirts adorned with superheroes hung from wire hangers, dirty laundry shoved into the corner. Assorted baseball hats and empty shoe boxes lined the shelf above, a tiny lacrosse stick and rubber ball leaning against the back wall.

The boy had almond-shaped eyes and hairless cheeks—a glossy shine to his smooth brown skin. A web of crusted spittle had gathered along the boy's chin, just below his chapped lips. Ignoring the rope, Andrew imagined the boy sitting peacefully, waiting for the school day to end or for his father to get home from work.

Xavier frowned, pausing a long while. "He looks a little like Damien," he said.

"Don't do that," Andrew said. "That's not fair. Don't do that to yourself."

Xavier shook, a quiver travelling along his bottom lip. "He looks just a little younger than Damien."

"Don't do that, X—"

But a lump drew up in Andrew's throat, pushing down any words he had hoped to say. He wrapped his arms around his brother and held him close as tremors travelled through Xavier, his shoulders heaving, his cries low and guttural.

Chapter Thirty

May 1995
Day 455 | Morning

"You guys let me know if you need anything," Rachel said, standing in the doorway of Evelyn's room.

Xavier and Andrew hovered over the twin bed in the corner, Evelyn sitting up and propped against a pillow.

"Sure thing," Andrew said.

"I'll be in the kitchen," Rachel said. "Just finishing up some cinnamon buns in the oven."

"Oh, I may need some of *those* when they're ready," Xavier said.

"I'll see what I can do," Rachel chuckled as she closed the bedroom door behind her.

Evelyn was curled tight in a ball, the yellow comforter tucked tight under her chin.

"Warm enough?" Xavier asked.

She smiled and nodded.

"How do you like staying here?" Xavier asked. He dropped the backpack to the floor and dragged a wooden chair toward the mattress. "Rachel taking good care of you?"

"She's nice, but—"

Evelyn went silent as she spotted the backpack. Xavier followed her line of sight.

"It's okay, Ev. No more needles," he said. "I promise."

Still, she winced as Xavier reached into the bag. He carefully pulled out a flat brown paper bag folded and taped near the top.

"We did bring you something though. A small gift, something Andrew and I thought might help you."

She took the bag and sliced the tape open with her fingernail. Reaching in, she pulled out a handmade willow hoop, a woven net of colourful feathers and beads. She held it up to the light.

Xavier shifted in his chair. "We bought it from an elder. It's a dreamcatcher."

"I know what it is," Evelyn said. "My mother used to make them for Damien and me. When we were younger."

"Rachel told us sometimes you wake up screaming," Xavier said. "Said she tries to calm you but …"

"I get nightmares too, Ev," Andrew said. "Ever since the forest."

"A dreamcatcher is known to stop nightmares," Xavier said. "It catches the bad spirits and sends them away, or so the guy told us. So, we thought it might help."

Xavier smiled softly, the raw tension that consumed him in the cellar gradually slipping away.

Evelyn reached up and hung the dreamcatcher from the bedpost. "It's beautiful," she whispered.

Xavier stood to help, nudging it with his finger so the intricate stitching spun round and round. The motion made Evelyn giggle.

"So, is it *that* bad staying here?" Xavier asked.

"No, no, it's good," Evelyn said. "It's just that, well, Rachel's really busy. She's always working or busy and I think

I might … I mean, I might just be getting in her way. I think I make her tired."

"Oh, I'm sure she's fine," Andrew said. "She's just not used to having someone your age to take care of, that's all. And she's probably still worried about you."

"Well, she's a lot nicer than when she was in the forest!" Evelyn said. "She hardly talked to me at all!"

Andrew laughed. "I don't think any of us were the best versions of ourselves out there."

Xavier leaned back in the wooden chair. "Ev, there's something I've wanted to ask you for a while," he said. "But I'm not sure whether you're ready to talk about it."

Evelyn sat up straight and nodded for him to continue.

"Okay, well, when Damien sacrificed himself for me, he was … I mean …" Xavier closed his eyes and exhaled softly. He swallowed down a lump of pain, still frayed and raw, his emotions smouldering just below the surface. "As you know, I was with him when he passed on," he continued. "He was bleeding badly and after a while, I mean, I think at some point he knew he wasn't going to make it—"

"I wanted to run to him!" Evelyn said. "I could see him through the window. I wanted to run but then the lady's car was coming up the driveway! I shone the flashlight at the window but no one saw me!"

"It's okay, Ev," Xavier said, placing a hand on hers. "This isn't your fault. None of this is your fault."

She turned to Andrew. "Do you remember? I wanted to run and throw rocks at the window but you called me back. You said we needed to hide behind the garage where she couldn't see us."

"Ev, we all tried our best—"

"I saw the lady pull something out of her bag and then go to the side of the house," Evelyn said, sniffing. "I wanted to come to you. I wanted to tell you she was coming!"

Xavier sat down at the foot of the bed. "It's okay, Ev. You did everything right."

She sobbed and smothered her head in the pillow. "Then why does it feel so wrong? Why does it hurt so much?"

Xavier rubbed her shoulders. "We all miss him, Ev, and no one more than you," he said after some time. "You need to know that we're here for you, okay? If you need anything, anything at all, Andrew and I are here for you."

She nodded as she pulled her sleeve across her damp eyes.

"Ev, I need to ask you a question though," Xavier said. "But you let me know if you're not ready to answer."

He paused until she motioned for him to continue.

"When I was with Damien in Angela's house … well, I think his vision might have been going. He started rubbing my face. And then he called me Joe. I figured he was hallucinating. But since then, I've wanted to ask you: do you have any idea why he would call me that?"

"He was probably confused. You do sort of look like our uncle though. Maybe that's why he called you that."

"And your uncle's name is Joe?"

"Yeah, but we only see him once a year. He stays with us in June for a few weeks. He usually takes us camping."

She swatted her oily bangs from her forehead.

"Each time he comes he asks me to make him bracelets," Evelyn continued. "I always use red or yellow string 'cause he likes those colours best. He told me once he was going to use the string as bait because the bright colours attract the fish! But I think he was just being silly."

Andrew grew tense remembering the bright thread worn above his mother's ankle each summer, a similar splash of coloured strand below Evelyn's calf when they first met in the forest.

"Evelyn," Andrew said. "What's your father's name?"

"Simon."

"And your last name?"

"Stone"

Xavier sat up straight and shuddered.

"It's the second researcher from the documents Rachel and I found in Angela's office," he said, turning to Andrew. "And Joe was muttering the name Simon around the house after he contracted the virus. I thought he had just lost it but—"

He paused, rubbing his chin. "But why wouldn't Joe ever mention him? Why have we never heard of him?"

Andrew screwed up his face, his heart pounding. His mind raced, his thoughts split between the past and present, like a cleaver had just hacked out a new truth.

"You told me this Simon guy had his medical license revoked," he said to Xavier. "You read something like that from the news clippings you found in the office. You told me he was shunned by the research community?"

Xavier nodded. "Yeah, that's right."

"Well …" Andrew started but then stopped, trying to hold onto a drifting string of logic. "Maybe Joe was embarrassed of him," he said. "Or maybe Joe knew something. Perhaps he knew what this guy was really involved in."

Evelyn looked back and forth between the brothers, a puzzled look across her face. "Who are you guys talking about?" she asked.

Xavier paused for a moment before returning to her.

"We're trying to figure that out as well, Ev. Joe is my father's name. And I think I look so much like your Uncle Joe because, well, *your* Uncle Joe is *my* father."

"What? But how? What does that mean?"

"What it means is … I think we're cousins."

Evelyn drew back, her grip tightening around the blanket. A quiver moved across her lower lip but she bit down hard on it before it spread any further.

"But why haven't we ever met?"

"That's what we don't understand," Xavier said. "Did your dad ever tell you about us? About our family?"

"No."

"Did he ever mention what he does for work?" Andrew asked.

"Not really. He does science for the government, or something. Or maybe that was an old job, I can't remember. He doesn't really tell anyone about his work."

"Did you notice anything different about him over the past few months?"

"I mean, he wasn't home much. My mom told us he was just working late or meeting with other business people. Why?"

"Well, your dad was named in some documents Rachel and I found in her sister's study," Xavier said. "Your dad might have done some … what I mean is, your dad might be in trouble."

Evelyn placed a hand at her neck, her breathing intensifying, her cheeks blotted red.

"Did anything strange happen the last time your Uncle Joe was at your house?" Andrew asked.

"No. Well, actually, I do remember one thing," Evelyn

said. "I remember my dad and him getting in a big fight. And after that, we didn't see my dad very much, like even less than usual."

"Anything else?"

"I remember the night that Damien and I went into the forest. My dad came home really late. He was really loud and it woke me and Damien up."

"Do you remember when that was?"

"It was a while ago, the beginning of March, maybe. It was the first time he had been home in a very long time. He was really skinny and had a beard."

"What was he like? Did he act different?"

"He was really angry. My mom and him got in a big fight. In the morning, my mom was gone. I asked my dad where she was but he wouldn't answer. He said he had to go to work and that he was dropping us off with someone he knew."

"Did he tell you anything else?"

"I asked him so many questions but he didn't answer me. And he was talking to himself a lot, like he was thinking about a million things at once. He dropped us off on someone's driveway and drove away. But Damien said we weren't staying."

"The people just let you leave?"

"We didn't even go up to their house. Damien picked up our bags and we walked back to our house."

"You *walked* all the way back? How long did that take?"

"I think two days. We had to sleep a night in the forest, I remember that. But we go camping all the time, so Damien knows how to build a shelter, how to build a lean-to. He knows how to do those things in the woods."

"Yeah, I don't doubt it," Andrew said.

He remembered when he first met him: Damien firing a

warning shot at he and Xavier—the boy taking it upon himself to hunt and feed for his sister and two strangers. And then when the creatures attacked, how Damien moved just like Xavier, like a smaller shadow, his motions and rhythm the same. It was no wonder they were related.

"But, Ev," Andrew said. "What happened when you got back to your house?"

"It looked like it had been robbed," Evelyn said. "Things were thrown everywhere. There were claw marks on the door. And it felt evil, like a bad spirit was there, or something."

Her eyes met Andrew's and he nodded, remembering the eerie feeling walking through his own home the night the cab dropped him off.

"So, Damien grabbed food, his gun, his knife, and we left again," Evelyn said. "He told me it would be safer in the forest."

"That's when you came across Maddy and Rachel?"

"Well, we were on our own for a few nights before we met them. We met Maddy first. And then a few days later we found Rachel. She was crying by the creek. She didn't say hardly anything the first few days. She's much nicer now."

Xavier swayed at the foot of the bed as if about to be sick. "It doesn't make sense," he said. "It still doesn't make any sense. Why wouldn't we know about them? Why would Mom and Dad keep them from us?"

Andrew shrugged and sat silent, a thousand questions circling the air like a cloud of gnats on a humid night. He laid a hand across his brow, his breathing deep and steady. "It's a lot," he said. "This is a lot to think through."

Just then Rachel called from downstairs. "Evelyn, there's someone here to see you."

Andrew shook his thoughts away as Xavier helped the girl out of bed.

"Wow, you have a visitor," Andrew smiled. "You're becoming famous—the girl who put up with Xavier Stone for five straight days in a cellar! No one has ever put up with him for *that* long!"

Xavier huffed as the three of them came down the stairs toward the foyer, the bright midday sun shining through the front window. At the base of the stairs, Staff Inspector Tom Everett beamed, a line of sweat carving a path down his pale, pudgy cheeks.

"It's very good to see you up and about, my dear," he smiled at Evelyn. "Rachel tells me you're recovering well, that you're on the mend."

Evelyn smiled sheepishly and then turned her gaze toward the floor.

Andrew extended his hand. "Good to see you, Staff Inspector."

"Looks like you're on the mend as well," Everett said.

"Slowly getting back to normal."

"So, you fellas ready for another round?"

"Why? What's the update?" Xavier asked.

"We want to do a sweep of the north side," Everett said. "Several homes and old barns up that way."

"Yeah, I know the area. How's the rest of town?"

"Some areas took more of a hit than others. The grocery store and downtown strip are trashed. It'll take a few months to get everyone and everything back to normal."

"Reinforcements come in yet?"

"Not exactly. My supervisor still isn't taking this thing seriously. So, it would be good to have your help for a few more weeks."

"We can help," Andrew said. "Has there been any word on our parents? Or Evelyn's?"

"Nothing. A team has searched both your houses."

"And?"

"Evelyn's house was deserted as was yours. We've put out internal notices across departments and have multiple units engaged. We'll let you know as soon as something comes across the wire."

Everett removed his stiff-brimmed hat and dragged a sleeve across his damp forehead. "Now for you, my dear," he said, looking directly at Evelyn. He struggled to lower his heavy frame to one knee.

"We need to figure out a more long-term arrangement for you. I'm afraid Rachel isn't well-equipped to care for a child for such a long period of time. So, we need to explore other options. What I was thinking is—"

"I'm staying with Xavier," Evelyn said.

Everett drew back. "Oh, I don't think you understand how these things work. What we need to do is contact your next of kin to—"

"Until you find my parents, I'm staying with him!" she said. She reached up and grabbed Xavier's hand. Everett stood and turned to Xavier, his eyebrows raised.

Xavier smiled. "It's fine. She can stay with Andrew and me back at our place, at least until we figure out something better. Besides, I may very well be her next of kin. We just sort of found out we're cousins."

Rachel cocked her head. "You're what?"

Andrew laughed. "It's new information to us as well. The last few weeks have been … interesting, to say the least."

Everett stepped back to take both Xavier and Evelyn in. "I didn't notice it before but looking at you now, there is quite a similarity between the two of you," he said.

He adjusted his black wrinkled pants and navy-blue shirt, the seams stretching to cover his wide midsection.

"This is not normally how these things work," Everett said. "But for the past five weeks I've been chasing virus-infected lunatics around this town so I'm a bit short on normal lately. I suppose she can stay with you until we find something more suitable, something more permanent."

He twisted his wrist, glancing at the silver timepiece. "I should get going. There are several teams still out there who will be radioing in soon. And then I've gotta talk to some Brad Moseby fella, a local journalist here who's been nagging me for an interview. Wants to know all about our progress and such."

Rachel nodded, handing him his coat. "Well, thanks for stopping by," she said.

Everett wrestled into the jacket then turned back to the brothers. "Fellas, I'll be expecting you 6:45 a.m. for a briefing tomorrow. We want to get a full day's search in so we will roll out at 7:00 a.m. sharp."

Both Andrew and Xavier nodded.

"Oh, and by the way, I gave someone the address here, someone who's been trying to track both of you down for a few days. I hope you don't mind. He was quite adamant to speak with you directly. He should be around this afternoon, would be my guess."

Everett turned to leave but paused to reach down and tou-sle Evelyn's hair.

"Good luck, my dear. You've been through a lot, but I see

great strength in you. And I believe you will be just fine when all this is over."

With that, the portly inspector turned and staggered down the long driveway to his police cruiser, the dust stirred up from the tires hanging in the cool spring air long after the car disappeared.

Chapter Thirty-One

May 1995
Day 455 | Afternoon

From Rachel's porch, Andrew saw them approaching. The man raised his arm. "Staff Inspector Everett thought I might be able to find you here," he called out. He was a burly man, measuring close to Xavier's height. He had a rust-coloured beard and a plaid flannel shirt snug tight to his broad shoulders. He gripped the hand of a young teenage boy.

"I'm Travis and this is my son, Jacob," he said when he was just a few yards away.

Andrew reached out to shake his hand. "I'm Andrew. This is my brother, Xavier."

"Yes, I figured as much," Travis said. "The Staff Inspector speaks highly of you two. He tells me you're helping bring this whole thing to a stop."

"We're doing what we can," Andrew said. "Making a bit of progress each day."

Travis eyed some of Andrew's scars. "Looks like you got banged up out there."

Andrew smirked. "A little. I'd imagine they look worse than they actually are."

Travis averted his eyes, studied his boots for a moment.

"In speaking to the Staff Inspector, I learned that

Madeline Stover spent some time in your company," he said. "Is that true?"

Andrew nodded. "Maddy was with us for five days before she—"

"I was her husband," Travis interrupted.

"I'm so sorry," Andrew said. "We did everything we could to save her. There were so many of them, so many of those creatures. When we were finally able to—"

"No, no, I didn't come here for an apology," Travis said. "Quite the opposite, in fact. I owe both of you a huge debt of gratitude for what you did for her out there. Everett tells me you protected her until she … well, that you protected her as best you could."

Travis took a deep breath and closed his eyes. "It was all so confusing those last few days, wasn't it?"

Andrew regarded him but said nothing.

"She told me to go, told me to take our son, that we needed to leave town," Travis continued. "Said she was going to stay to help at the clinic. I figured she'd be safe and that she knew what she was doing. She always seemed to know what she was doing. She was confident that way."

Travis shifted his gaze down the driveway and then turned, resting his eyes on his son.

"Anyway, I wanted to come out here to thank you both in person. I wanted to thank you for looking after her for as long as you did. Both Jacob and I are eternally grateful."

He forced a smile and turned away, guiding his son to the pickup truck parked at the end of the laneway.

"She was incredibly brave!" Andrew shouted after him. "She was scared—all of us were—but Maddy was very brave. She was courageous, right till the end."

Travis and Jacob stopped and turned back.

"We'd still be hiding from those things if it wasn't for her," Andrew continued. "They'd still be hunting us. She led us to the answers we needed. You should know that. We wouldn't have figured out how to cure those things without her. You would have been proud of her."

"Oh, I've always been proud of her," Travis said, his eyes misting over. "Jacob and I have always been *very* proud of her."

He turned then, squeezing the boy's trembling hand in his, the two of them shuffling slowly toward the truck.

Chapter Thirty-Two

August 1995
Day 545 | Evening

Andrew strummed his fingers on the metal tabletop, his palms sweaty, his knee juddering underneath the restaurant booth. He fussed with his mop of curly hair, still damp from the shower he rushed through to arrive at the bistro on time. He took a sip of water, rearranged the salt and pepper shakers, checked his watch, fidgeted with the collar of his wrinkled golf shirt.

The bells over the front entrance chimed and he sat up straight and stared toward the door at the woman coming through. He sheepishly smiled and waved.

She skipped over to the table, her red mane curled and set along her slight shoulders, her dark jeans snug against her thighs. She smiled back and slid into the bench across from him. A hint of lavender drifted off her skin and the scent brought Andrew back to the airplane, the fall from the sky, and the easy banter and playful laughter they shared afterwards. Once again, he immediately felt a pull toward her.

"Why hello there, stranger," she said, placing her handbag on the vinyl-covered seat beside her.

"Juliana," Andrew said. "Wow. It's good to see you. Like *really* good to see you."

Juliana glanced around the small diner. "Well, this place is cute."

"Yeah, it's been here forever. Came here a lot when I was a kid. Best ice cream sundaes you'll ever have!"

"Hey, I'm just impressed you finally invited me to your home town. I thought I scared you away after we almost died together. Do you remember how crazy that was?"

"Yeah, of course," Andrew laughed. "Hard to forget."

"Maybe not as scary as when you got lost in the woods with your brother as kids!"

"Oh, still remember that, do you?"

"Yes, of course I still remember that story!"

"Yeah, you're pretty much the only person I've told that to."

"I was actually thinking of that story lately. Thinking about the plane. Thinking about you."

Andrew stifled a smile and an awkward moment dangled between them.

Juliana tilted her head. "What happened to your ear? And I don't remember that scar on your neck."

"Oh, that? Yeah, that's a whole other story," Andrew said, nervously rubbing the wound.

Juliana cleared her throat. "Hey, well let's get some drinks, shall we?" She raised her hand as a server scurried over.

"Welcome to Brenda's Bistro. Are you ready to order?" the server asked.

"Hi, yes, I'd like a tall glass of your house white," Juliana announced.

"Certainly," the server said, then turned to Andrew. "Anything for you?"

"Just a refill on the water thanks," he said.

The server nodded and disappeared.

"Ah yes, now I remember," Juliana said, her faint Irish droll nipping at her words. "I forgot you're a *straight-up-water* type of guy. I tried to get you drinking on the plane but you weren't having any of it!"

Andrew smirked. "I just try to keep it simple, I suppose."

"Well, I'm drinking!" Juliana blurted out. "But I guess you already know that about me, don't you? I'm sure I was quite the drunk by the time that plane landed."

"Hey, I don't blame you. That was quite an event."

The server returned and placed the drinks on cork coasters, moisture dripping down the side of each glass. Andrew chugged the water, the cold liquid drenching his parched throat. He returned the glass to the table and anxiously rubbed his hands together.

"It's crazy seeing you again," he said finally. "Thanks again for meeting me here."

"Of course! I wanted to see you again. But hey, why did it take you until August to call?"

"Oh, I got caught up in some stuff pretty much the minute our plane landed."

"I thought maybe you lost my number."

Andrew dug into his pocket and pulled out the piece of paper with Juliana's name and phone number on it, the corners folded in, the paper crumpled and tattered.

"Wait! Is that the same—is that the same paper from the plane?"

"Sure is. Held onto it this whole time. Can hardly read it anymore."

"You could have just written my number on a new piece of paper, you know?" Juliana giggled.

"Nah, wouldn't have been the same. Wouldn't have been as special as the original."

"But this one's almost illegible. It looks like it's been through war!"

"Just about," Andrew mumbled.

"Here, let me write you a fresh note, one that doesn't look like it's been through the wash a dozen times." She reached into her bag and pulled out a pen and paper. "That's what happened, isn't it? You just forgot to take it out of your pocket and you ran it through the laundry, didn't you?"

"Not quite," Andrew said.

She took her time writing a lengthy note, her pen carefully swooping across the page. Near the bottom, she scribbled her number and signed it once again with a heart. "Now don't ruin this one, okay? And I expect you to use it more often than the first note I gave you."

She laughed as Andrew nodded and reached for it. He read the note slowly, a smile forming as his eyes moved across the words. He folded it and carefully guided it into his pocket.

"I should really get *your* number," she said. "This way I don't have to wait another five months for you to call!"

"I'll be quicker this time," Andrew said. "Four months max."

Juliana playfully made a face.

"So, what about you?" Andrew asked. "Are you still taking a break from being a lawyer?"

"I just recently started practicing again—just part-time for a small firm," Juliana explained. "But it's good, something to get my feet wet again. The staff are really friendly, so that's nice."

"Less shady than your last gig?"

"Hell yeah! I'm staying away from pharmaceutical law for a while. Just working on simple civic cases—that's more my speed right about now."

"That's good. I'm happy for you."

Juliana smiled. "So, what's next for you now that summer is almost over? From what I remember, you still have one more year of university, right?"

"Yeah, that's right. I'm still deciding if I should go or take a year off."

"Why would you take a year off? Don't you want to finish your studies as quickly as possible?"

"Originally, I did. But I feel my brother could use me around the house a bit longer to help fix it up. We've had a … a busy summer, so to speak."

She paused to take a sip of wine then tucked a loose strand of hair behind her ear. "Look, I know we still don't know each other that well, but the way you talked about school on the plane, well, don't you think you'd really miss it if you took a year off?"

"I'm just feeling I need to be around more. Just to help out and … Anyways, I have a couple more weeks to decide, so we'll see. Besides, I might stay back a little longer so I can date."

"Oh, really!" Juliana blurted out. "Well, excuse me, Mr. Casanova. You're just going to spend the next few months dating all the girls you see?"

"Not all of them," Andrew chuckled. "But there is one. There is this one girl I might try to date."

Juliana drew quiet and smiled, a pink blush unfurling across her cheeks. "Well, if you do decide to go back to university, it's only a short plane ride away," she said. "I mean, for the sake of this mystery girl you're interested in."

Andrew laughed and took another swig of water. Juliana adjusted in her seat, fiddling with the sliver pendant hanging loosely off her neck and draped over her tight black sweater.

"So, it took you forever to call me, so what'd you get up to?" she asked. "Anything exciting happen over the summer? Do these scars have a story?"

Andrew gave a hearty laugh, gently stroking the scratch down his neck. "Umm, you may need to order another glass of wine because I definitely have a story for you. One hell of a story, for sure."

Chapter Thirty-Three

February 1994
Day 1 | Before Dawn

Angela sat idle inside her grey sedan, her gloved hands clenched tight around the steering wheel. From the empty parking lot, her tired eyes surveyed the web of steel pipes and squat industrial buildings which sat beside the towering water silo. In the dark, the looming pillar seemed to callously stare back at her from behind the high chain-linked fence. She scoffed at the 'No Trespassing' sign.

The car had been parked for a while, the engine now cold, sheets of mushy slush gathering along the windshield and hood. She swung the car door open, her heels slipping on the sleet-covered asphalt as she stepped out. She shivered and buttoned the top clasp of her checkered pea coat just as the wind picked up, a squall of icy snow biting at her gaunt cheeks.

"Jesus," she muttered.

She reached into the car and removed a large black duffel bag, heaving it from the rear seat. She shimmied into the shadows along one side of the building, the sign 'Town Water Services – Employees Only' secured onto a hidden door. She scanned the empty lot once more, then crept inside.

The slam of the door echoed throughout the dank, dark

hallway. Scrunching her nose at the sting of chlorine, she followed the red glow of the emergency lighting strips down a long hallway until she reached an oversized door, several deadbolts denying access. She pulled out a set of keys, each one numbered sequentially, and clicked the locks open.

"Seems like you are useful after all, Mr. Mackenzie," she mused, jingling the keys then returning them to her coat pocket.

She pushed through the heavy door into a massive room full of thick metal pipes where a grid of channels and conduits pulsed with the sound of moving water.

Eyeing something across the room, she skirted along the cement floor, past the filters and disinfectant basins, and stopped at a giant water storage tank. She dropped the duffel bag to the floor, unzipped it, and removed two large jugs of blue-coloured liquid, a strange logo of an antlered-buck plastered on one side of it.

Heaving one of the jugs to her chest, she unscrewed the top, and hoisted it onto the metal barrier surrounding the water tank. She moved to tip it over but then stopped, her hands suddenly shaking, a few drops spilling onto the floor.

"What am I doing?" she muttered, returning the jug to the bag. "This can't be the way. I - I can't do this."

She screwed the cap back on and stood motionless for several minutes, stoic, staring into the dark. She closed her eyes and exhaled loudly, grabbing at her hair and stomping the floor, seething, an internal struggle unravelling. Finally, she looked up, her eyes red and swollen.

"I just miss you so much!" she cried out, the noise echoing within the dim industrial space. "I'm sorry I wasn't good enough! I'm sorry I couldn't help you!"

Her breaths came out in heaves, her voice breaking. She pulled out a small photo from inside her jacket and stared at it, wiping at her eyes.

"But I can make it up to you," she said, drawing in a ragged breath. She gently kissed the photo, worn and folded in the corners, then returned it to her jacket. "I'll make it up to you, Mom."

She reached down and again unscrewed one of the caps, a potent smell of aluminum spewing forth from the jug. She hauled the large container onto the railing, tipping the contents into the storage tank. The liquid swirled and mixed, quickly diluting then disappearing.

She reached for the second jug and emptied its contents, watching as the chemical mixed seamlessly—now undetectable—with the water in the tank. A sly smile passed over her as her eyes followed the piping that led from the tank to a second cistern, 'Potable drinking water,' displayed in bold black font along the side.

"I hope you can overlook the methods," she said. "They're just a means to an end. Sometimes you need to break a few eggs to make an omelette. You taught me that, remember, Mom?"

She threw the empty jugs into the duffel bag and zipped it up, dragging it across the massive room.

"I have to do this every month?" she said. "Jesus. I'll have to think of a better way than this!"

Her gaze caught upon an upright elongated cistern with the word 'Fluoride' printed in large black font across it. A heavy plastic tube fed into it from a much larger tank above, the mouth of it wide enough for the two empty jugs beside her. Her eyes widened at the possibility.

"Hmm, that could work," she muttered to herself, then scurried out from the room, locking the bolts behind her. Marching down the hall, she flung the side door open and trounced to her car, tossing the duffel bag into the rear seats.

She stepped into the car, slamming the door behind her, and cranked the engine. "Okay, Mr. Mackenzie, it has begun," she said. She grinned, wide and empty, then slid her gloves off.

She coiled her fingers tight around the steering wheel and firmly pressed down on the gas, the rear of the sedan drifting on the ice and snow as she skidded out of the parking lot, peeling away into the cold February dawn.

Chapter Thirty-Four

August 1995
Day 555 | Evening

"It's hard to believe six of us spent almost a week down there with little more than a few tins of beans," Xavier said, motioning toward the cellar.

Evelyn turned and smiled. "I know," she said. "Hard to believe."

The warm August air blew up from the south, gently rocking the pair perched on the swing-chair. Xavier was nursing a lager, Evelyn an ice-cold lemonade. They sat staring out from the deck into the lush foliage surrounding the house. The tall ash and ironwoods creaked from the breeze, the long grass nearly covering the cellar door sixty yards away.

"Beans and *fisher meat*," Xavier added.

Evelyn swivelled to face him, a look of horror on her face. "Was that what those meat-sticks were? *Fisher meat?*"

Xavier nodded.

"Fishers?" Evelyn screwed up her face. "As in those things that look like weasels?"

"Those are the ones. Although, I think they're more rat than weasel."

"Gross!" Evelyn shouted. "That's disgusting."

Xavier chuckled as the girl shook her shoulders,

pretending to dry heave. Andrew slid through the screen door, a glass of ice water in one hand, a bowl of washed cherries in the other.

"Is he making you sick with one of his outlandish stories again?" he teased, tossing a cherry into his mouth.

"He told me what the meat really was in the cellar!" Evelyn exclaimed. "You never told me it was fisher!"

Andrew chuckled. "Be glad it wasn't snake like my stepfather made. I'd eat fisher over snake any day of the week!"

He leaned his sinewy frame against the doorframe and took a long drink. After a few moments, he turned to Xavier.

"I just got off the phone with Rachel," he said.

"How's she doing?" Xavier asked.

"She's still dealing with it all, says it plays over and over again in her mind. She said even though it's been months, the visions still creep up on her."

"Yeah, I could imagine. We'll probably all be wrestling with those images for quite a while."

"She told me Angela has since been charged with multiple offences. Said she has a court appearance next month after they conduct a psychiatric evaluation on her."

"Okay. Where are they holding her?"

"She's in a cell at the local station for now but will likely be relocated after the court date. Rachel visits her occasionally. Says Angela's finally speaking to her again, so I suppose that's a good thing."

"Is it?"

"Well, Rachel says Angela's struggled with mental health issues most of her life but is now just starting to show remorse for what she did. So, I suppose *that's* the good thing."

"Remorse doesn't bring people back from the dead."

"No, I guess not. The whole thing is taking a toll on Rachel though."

Xavier nodded but said nothing, peering into the thick stand of trees bordering their property.

"She figures she'll be up soon for a visit," Andrew continued. "Said she'll pop by in a few days."

"That's good to hear. She hasn't been up this way in a while."

Rachel had been to the farmhouse a handful of times since Evelyn moved in with Xavier and Andrew. The odd weekend she would come over for brunch carrying sliced watermelon or a basket of warm cinnamon buns. Occasionally, she would find an excuse to drop in on her way home from work early on a Friday, uncorking a bottle of red to share on the rustic patio set.

"You should give her a call," Andrew said. "I think she'd like to hear from you. She asked how you were doing. It sounded like she could use some company."

Xavier looked away and took a long pull from his bottle, the amber liquid swishing through his teeth. "Yeah maybe. Maybe I will," he said.

Andrew shuffled toward one of the empty deck chairs, a slight stutter in his step. His movements seemed carefully planned as he gingerly crossed the stained planks of wood, his injuries still not fully healed. A stubborn scar curved down his neck, pulsating as he chewed.

"And Evelyn," Andrew continued. "Rachel wants to take you out next time she's here."

"She does?" Evelyn said.

"Says she wants to do a bit of shopping with you, buy you something nice for the start of school in a few weeks."

"Oh, I can't wait!"

Xavier stood, downing the last of his beer. "Well, that's good to hear. A new school dress will be great because, to be honest, I'm getting tired of you always borrowing mine."

Evelyn shifted around to face Xavier but his back was turned, already half-way through the kitchen screen door.

"Was that humour?" Andrew called out after him. "Was that a sad attempt at being funny?"

He turned and winked at Evelyn. "Well, my dear, your presence seems to have brought out a different side of him. It seems he's not meant to be a grumpy old hunter the rest of his days after all. Maybe his true calling is stand-up comedy!"

Evelyn laughed and Andrew realized it had been the first time he had heard the sound since Damien's passing. She gulped at her lemonade, the ice cubes crashing into each other as she put the glass down on the wooden table.

"Are they opening the schools, then?" Xavier called out from the kitchen. "After this summer, seems to me the kids around here might be too traumatized for all that."

"I read about it in *The Chronicle* yesterday," Andrew hollered back. "Some town official said they just want to get things back to normal. Feel it will be the best for everyone if schools and workplaces resume as soon as possible."

"Makes sense, I guess," Xavier said.

"They've set up a hotline as well," Andrew said. "For residents to call if they see anything suspicious, like anyone acting … crazy."

"And what if someone calls?"

"Said they have lots of the temporary antidote still and will send the cops out in the event anyone sees one that might have been missed."

Xavier returned to the deck with a fresh beer. The cap hissed as he twisted it off and tossed it on the table. "Yeah, and that probably just means the cops will come knocking here again, asking you and I to help," he said.

"Aren't you too young to drink beer?" Evelyn interrupted with a sheepish grin.

"What are you talking about? I'm the ripe age of 20!" Xavier said. "Besides, after what we went through these past few months, I think I've earned the right to a few drinks!"

"Yes, and his truck got smashed to pieces, remember?" Andrew said. "And nothing makes a man sadder than a wrecked truck."

Evelyn giggled. "Oh yeah, I almost forgot!".

"Suppose you'll have to go by Randy's Auto Shop then, see if he has any cheap pickups for sale," Andrew said.

"Yep, just add it to the list," Xavier moaned.

His gaze drifted toward the empty driveway, but then looked up as a flutter of birds flapped overhead, their last dart through the orange sky before settling for the night. They landed on a branch and hopped among the lush foliage of a leaning oak.

The phone rang and Andrew pushed himself from the chair and moved inside. After several minutes, bits of conversation floated out to the back deck: *"Thanks for calling… Grab another drink … Would be good to talk again …"*

Xavier shrugged Evelyn's curious eyes away as Andrew lumbered back to the deck. He had his rifle tucked tight under his arm and when he sat down again, he began polishing the stock and barrel with an oily rag.

"Who was that?" Xavier asked.

Andrew put the rifle aside and pulled a crumpled note from his jean pocket, then passed it to Xavier.

"Juliana? Who's Juliana?" Xavier said. "And what's with this heart over the 'i'?" He passed the note to Evelyn who snickered at the handwriting.

"I met her on the flight back in March," Andrew said. "We had quite the adventure together on the plane."

"More exciting than what we went through here?"

"Well, not that exciting. Anyway, I met up with her again last week. She just called to see if I wanted to grab another drink sometime."

"Juliana? Sounds like a summer fling."

Andrew smirked but said nothing.

"Besides, look what shape you're in," Xavier continued. "You're still limping and the scratches on your face haven't even healed."

"Exactly! You see, I'm in need of my own private nurse!"

Xavier rolled his eyes as Andrew eased himself back into the chair. "She's actually a lawyer," Andrew said. "Smart and quick-witted."

"So, you guys a thing now or something?"

"Is she your girlfriend?" Evelyn teased.

"Nah, just meeting for coffee, that's all," Andrew said. "But you'd like her, X. She's funny and kind and pleasant—basically the exact opposite of you."

"Jesus, now who's the comedian," Xavier said, shaking his head. "So, I imagine you'll be heading out for school soon?"

"Not sure. I was toying with the idea of taking a break."

"Why?"

"To keep looking for Mom and Joe. Maybe stick around here in case something comes up."

"Ev and I will hold down the fort here and will let you know if any news comes in."

"Just doesn't feel quite right leaving knowing they could still be out there, you know?"

"Not sure what else you can do here. I'll stay tight to Everett—anything comes up, I'll call you."

"We'll see. A bit more time together, just the three of us, might be good. Until things settle down here a bit."

"I think you should go."

"It's just school. It'll always be there."

"But you love your studies."

"Sure, but the last time I left wasn't in the best way. So, I want to make sure it's good this time. I mean, that you and I are good."

"You need to go, it's what you're good at."

"I believe *Mr. Fancy School Boy* is the term you used."

Xavier smirked. "You're smart, I get it," he said. "That's your thing. Besides, you knowing about viruses and everything kind of got us out of this whole mess."

"I think we have Maddy to thank for that. She led us to most of the answers."

Evelyn smiled softly then cast her eyes to the ground, something about the woman's name causing her to look away.

"Besides," Andrew added, turning to Xavier. "Rachel told me it was you who pieced together what was really going on at those flu clinics."

Xavier shrugged. "I think we all contributed in our own way."

Andrew mulled the words over for some time and then: "Listen, just so you know, I don't think I'm better than you."

Xavier sat up straight. "I didn't mean it that way," he confessed. "When I said that, well … it came out all wrong, that's all."

"No, no, it's okay. I know that I haven't been the best brother. How the way I act can push people away."

Xavier let out a heavy sigh. "Joe made such a big deal of it when you got accepted to that gifted high school and then the university overseas," he said. "He's actually been making a big deal out of a lot of things our whole lives."

He took a drink and adjusted his dusty cargo pants.

"When you got that scholarship he thought I would be jealous," Xavier continued. "Or that I was being left behind. You don't need to worry about that. It doesn't matter anymore. You need to go back and finish your degree. It's who you are."

Andrew turned and regarded his brother. "Thanks, X. That means a lot."

"Of course. So, when does the term start?"

"If I go, I'd need to leave in a week."

"You need to go."

Andrew smiled. The wind had calmed, the sun starting its slow descent behind the trees. The cicadas were beginning their nightly chorus and a pair of eager bats sagged and flopped like drunks.

"My course syllabus was just mailed to me," Andrew said. "Wanna know what I'll be studying my final year? Antidotes."

"Figures," Xavier grunted, shaking his head. "So, one more week, huh? Good, then you have plenty of time for one more hunt."

Andrew motioned to speak but he could tell Xavier's mind was already elsewhere, his thoughts likely bent on flushing out deer and trapping hare. It was as though the smells of forest oils and woodsmoke were already seeping back into his skin, flooding back into his being.

"Heard any news from Everett?" Xavier asked after some time.

"Spoke with him last week."

"Any news on the antidote?"

"Said his forensics department is still working on it, still working on a permanent solution. Should be ready any day now … or so he says."

"What in the world is taking so long? Hell, in less than three months the town flu clinics will start up again. Maybe just line everyone up again and inoculate them there!"

"I have a feeling compliance will be lower this year," Andrew teased. "Anyways, Everett said there are rumours that our initial sweep of the town might have missed some. A few may still be in hiding."

Andrew shuddered at his own words, a fragmented memory of the cab driver's warning so many months ago.

Something creepy is going on in that town.

"Man, I thought we were done with all this," Xavier sighed.

"Everett said he hasn't seen proof yet himself," Andrew said. "But he's hearing whispers, random reports of some deep in the forest, or around some abandoned campground or something."

"Ha! I knew the cops would have to come sniffing around here again. So, Everett's banking on the Stone brothers to come to the rescue again?"

"Looks that way." Andrew said. "Might be headed for another feral winter." He shifted to Evelyn. "Would you be ready to go out there again?"

"She better be," Xavier said. "She's got one of the best shots I've seen. Far better than yours!"

"Wow," Andrew said. "Again, with the comedy!"

He spit the last of the cherry pits into his palm and tossed them into the grass. Leaning back in his chair, he drew in a deep breath, the moist evening air tickling his throat. He shifted as he heard the faint sound of claws digging for grubs along the side of the house, a nocturnal forager gathering its meal.

He turned again to Evelyn, her skin dark with a healthy glow, her body fit and defined. He noticed how she now resembled a young woman, the summer bringing about changes in her.

"Would you be okay to go out there again?" he said. "Back in the forest?"

Evelyn closed her eyes. A breeze lifted her hair across her cheeks, the dark strands coming to rest on her shoulders. She brushed her fingertips along her wrist, across the centre of her palm, and up toward the tip of her pointer finger. She repeated the motion, following the same path Xavier had shown her months earlier.

Her eyes wandered across the backyard, pausing on the wooden cross and pile of stones at the head of Damien's plot, the leaves of the forest rustling behind it. She breathed in the warm August air, adjusting the string of bright yellow and red along her ankle.

She looked to Andrew and smiled. Andrew shifted towards her but she was already pushing off the deck, laughing as she grabbed his rifle and bounded through the long grass, her body rushing toward the skinny birch and tall maples.

Epilogue

November 1995
Day 636 | Early Morning

Alan Mackenzie raised his fist and pounded on the cabin door, much louder than the first time. Once again, his knock was met with silence. He lowered his arm and adjusted the clasp on his cufflink. The wool collar scratched at his neck, the tightness of his overcoat constricting his ribs. He looked back at his driver, Milton, and shrugged, brushing the November snow from his shoulders.

He raised his arm a third time but lowered it upon hearing a clunk of metal from the other side of the door. The sound of rapid clicking followed, gears spinning, and then the heavy door tilted open. Two sharp black eyes peered out from the dark, trying to adapt to the sudden light.

"Alan! Do come in," a man with a nasally voice said. His glasses fogged up with the rush of cold air.

Alan hesitated, holding firm to the porch. "Mr. Pak sent me. Said you have some news to share?"

"Yes, yes, that's correct. Please, do come in."

The man angled the door just wide enough for Alan to jostle his heavy frame through and then slammed it shut. The same clicking and clunking sounded as several locks were secured. He shone a beam of light at Alan who drew back, raising his hands to his eyes.

"Oh, sorry, I didn't mean to blind you," the man stammered. "Here, come this way, I have so much to show you."

The man limped down a stairwell through a dark hallway and descended a second set of creaky steps.

Alan felt his way along the wooden railings as best he could in the dim lighting. He scuttled along the floor, the surface changing as he walked. It started as plush carpet and then hardwood and then transitioned to cold cement. By the time the pair had reached the second landing, sharp gravel was pushing through the bottom of Alan's polished dress shoes. He paused outside a locked door, moaning and screeching coming from the other side of it.

"What the hell is in here?" Alan asked nervously.

"Oh, not that door, my friend," the man said. "We'll save that surprise for another time. Come, just a little further now."

Alan sneezed and brushed the grey dust from his dress slacks. They continued walking in the dark and as they turned a corner, Alan sniffed the air, screwing up his face. "What is that awful smell? It smells like burning metal! Did something catch fire?"

"This way," the man said, losing patience. His hand pressed against the coarse cement wall, stabilizing his crooked gait. He continued at a quick pace, scurrying like a rat in a tunnel.

"This may all be normal to you, wandering around a bunch of dark tunnels," Alan said. "But remember, I've never been to this cabin way out here in the boonies. And I have a very busy schedule today, a number of business appointments to attend to."

"It's only a little further," the man said excitedly.

Alan followed until they turned a second corner and both came to a steel door. The man fumbled through a set of keys and slid one through the hole. He used his shoulder to heave the door open and pawed at the wall until he found the light switch.

Alan squinted at the bright light as he began to make out shapes in the massive room. He looked up and observed the unusual height of the ceiling—at least twice as high of a normal living space. A long wooden desk with several microscopes was pushed against the far wall. Binders and papers were strewn across its surface and along the dusty floor. A white-board filled with formulas and equations filled the space above the desk. A towering oval glass dome took up the remainder of the room, a deep cavity clawed into the earth. The room was dank and musty and Alan surveyed the space with a crimped brow.

"How can this be?" he asked, staring at the staggering height of his surroundings. "Are we underground?"

"Deceiving from the outside, isn't it?" the man chuckled.

Alan turned and, in the light, took in the full appearance of the man. His cheeks were ashen, covered in a patchy beard, the skin along his neck grey and drooping. He was short and skinny with thick veins meandering from his bicep to his rigid forearms. He adjusted his bifocals, tucking several frayed strands of grey and black hair behind his ear.

"You look different," Alan said. "Something's off. You don't look well."

The man chuckled. "Oh, you don't need to worry about me. But please, come this way."

The man guided Alan to the opposite side of the glass dome toward the desk, a black raincoat and Tilley hat hanging from the office chair. A bright yellow and red bracelet was pushed into the corner of the desk, a checkered shirt crumpled into a ball.

A number of jars haphazardly lined a shelf a few feet above the desk: a dead mosquito frozen in golden sap filled one of them, a deer hoof severed and submerged in liquid lodged in another. Two full vials of blood stood erect in a plastic rack, the initials 'D.S.' scribbled on one, 'E.S.' on the other.

But it was the sudden whirring that caused Alan to turn. He leaned closer to the centrifuge, several other vials of sealed liquids vibrated at lightning speeds.

"What's in these?" he asked.

"I'll explain those in good time," the man said. "But come over here. This is what I want to show you."

The man turned a key and switched a lever. A metal door separating the glass dome from the far wall began to rise.

Underneath the door, Alan could see a pair of massive bare feet, coarse black hair sprouting from the toes and fingernails. The feet began to shift back and forth, bouncing from one foot to the other. As the door reached the halfway point a high-pitched squeal filled the room. Alan dropped to his knees, cupping his ears and squeezing his eyes, choking on the sudden stench of metal and fire.

The squealing stopped and Alan opened his eyes and cried out. The beast charged and ricocheted off the fortified glass, crashing to the concrete floor. It sprung up and spread its arms wide, dragging its yellow claws along the smooth glass, frosted shavings spilling to the floor.

"What is that?" Alan shouted. "I thought they were all cured?"

"Everyone thought that," the man said. "You, the newspapers, even the cops."

"The police did sweeps of the town all summer long," Alan said. "Are you saying this one wasn't caught?"

"No, no, this one was caught, along with all the others. The brave Staff Inspector Everett and the heroic Stone brothers I kept reading about did a fine job of capturing them."

Alan swung his arm toward the dome. "Then how do you explain this?"

"The so-called antidote was never a permanent solution," the man said. "Both you and the Staff Inspector knew this. But as residents turned back to normal and the heart-warming family reunions were played over and over on the news … well, it seemed everyone conveniently forgot. Everyone assumed it had worked just fine."

"But it did work just fine," Alan challenged.

The man smirked and glanced toward the glass dome. The creature was hunched over and drooling, its arms long and spidery, almost reaching the ground from where it stood.

"Evidently not," the man sneered.

Alan gasped. "Wait, are there more of these things?"

"Loads more!" the man squealed. "In fact, I have dozens behind that panel just over there. How do you think I do all my testing?"

"Testing? What testing? What are you talking about?"

"He's one of hundreds that were captured and given the antidote over the summer—an antidote which is now wearing off."

"Wearing off?" Alan paused to allow his thoughts to catch up. "So, these people will be reverting back to those … those *creatures*?"

"Depends on how their bodies react to the antidote," the man said. "The young ones are especially prone. Not all of them will revert. But enough of them will."

"What do you mean, *enough*?"

The beast charged the glass and Alan shrieked, the thud of the creature's body shaking the perimeter of the dome.

"Do they frighten you, Alan?" the man asked.

Alan pressed his lips together as his chest heaved up and down, his normal pink hue slipping from his cheeks.

"It's interesting you're scared of them," the man continued. "After all, they're your creation."

"What in the world are you talking about?" Alan boomed. "I didn't do this!"

"You recruited the investors that funded the research. It was you who wanted to find a cure for this virus. It was your greed which pushed people to continue with very dangerous experiments."

"There were miscalculations, sure. But I'm not a doctor. I'm not a scientist. How was I supposed to know these things? I didn't have control over *this*!"

"No control? You had plenty of control!" the man shouted. "Control over the purse strings, control over the experiments, control over the greedy drive of your investors. Hell, you even had control over the woman! Leveraging her emotional vulnerabilities, twisting her grief to line your pockets!"

"How in the world do you know about her?" Alan said.

"Okay, okay, well if you're not *solely* at fault, Alan, then let's agree that you and Dr. Till are *partially* at fault. We can blame the pair of you for countless deaths. Is that better?"

The man scrunched up his face and took a step closer. He was several inches shorter than Alan but still stared at him with piercing eyes. Alan stood motionless, sweat gathering along his brow.

"Tell me this though, Alan. How is it that she serves a jail sentence and you are here standing before me, free as a bird?"

Alan clenched his fists. "You know damn well why that is."

"Ah, yes. Mr. Pak. The classic stay-out-of-jail card: rich friends in high places!"

"It's more complex than that and you know it," Alan said. "But how did you learn of her?"

"I've been studying this virus for quite some time, long before your funded experiments. Long before your secret boardroom meetings and dates at the local diner."

"Boardroom meetings? Diner? Wait, do you mean *Brenda's Bistro*?" Alan looked to the floor, lost in thought. "Wait, I remember now ..." he said, his voice trailing off for just a moment. "There was a man that came into the diner that day—the same day Dr. Till and I met there for a meeting. It was me, her, and one other man sitting in the corner."

Alan scanned the room. His breath caught as he took in the black raincoat and Tilley hat. "He had that same coat and hat! It was you?"

"What was it you said to her?" the man said. "Do you remember? I'm paraphrasing, but it was something like, *'if you can't hurry science, then we will find someone who can.'* Oh, it was quite poetic! I had to stop myself from laughing off my chair right then and there!"

Alan took a step closer to the exit. "H - how did you know we'd be there?"

"I've been tracking your courtship for a while. In fact, the woman nearly spotted me outside the nursing home but I was able to get away."

"But why were you following her?"

"I needed to learn her role in the project, her motivation

in all of this. And most importantly, I needed to understand why her chemical solutions were flawed, why her concentration levels were off."

The man stepped toward the control panel and lifted a different lever. A small hatch at the back of the dome opened and inside stood a single vial, a cloudy solution of grey and red.

"Drink that!" the man shouted to the beast.

The creature glanced at the test tube but remained still.

"Drink it! Drink that! Go get it and drink it!"

The creature eventually ambled to the vial and smashed it on the ground, licking the liquid off the concrete floor.

"It listens to you?" Alan said, mesmerized by the scene unfolding before him.

"To a certain extent. Now watch this, Alan. Watch very closely."

The creature began pacing back and forth, squeezing and unfurling its fists. It started to grow taller, its slumped shoulders now round and erect. Soon, its muscles were firm where seconds earlier they had been stretched and flaccid. And after a few more seconds the creature resembled less of a monster and more of a teenaged boy.

The young man shook his long-matted hair and peered out, the colour of his skin changing from a pasty grey to a healthy olive tone. His eyes were no longer muted and vacant, but now a deep brown, wide and curious.

"That's incredible! He's cured!" Alan said excitedly. "But how is that formula different from the solution the police administered?"

"Because I've tested it, Alan! Something you had no patience for!" the man shouted bitterly. "I told you I've studied this virus for years—for almost my entire career! I've tested it over and over and over again. Believe me, what you see in these vials is a *permanent* antidote!"

"Well, this is very good news. If you have a cure, then why not hand it over to the authorities?"

"Well, it's a touch more complicated than that," the man snickered.

"If it's money you're after I'm sure the government will pay you. You'd probably be compensated quite well to inoculate all the residents of Barn Wood."

"The long game has never been your strong suit, has it?" the man sneered.

"I don't understand."

"I suppose if *you* were in charge, then we would hand the antidote over to the authorities for a meagre payout. But then I would only have the population of Barn Wood to cure and what's that from a numbers point of view? Several thousand people, at most? You're a numbers guy, Alan. Where's the financial gain in that? What type of respect would I earn from that?"

Alan took the pocket square from his suit jacket and dragged it across the damp crevices along his forehead.

"Even look at the flaws in your original plan," the man continued. "Research a cure for a virus that only a small number of people will ever contract? And a virus that's only transferred through horses!"

"There are other vectors that can transfer the virus. Horses are only one of them," Alan said.

"How many horses are running around the city, Alan? Out here in hick-ville, there are plenty of them. But drive two hours south and there's not a horse in sight! You and your team of rich idiots set out to find a cure for a disease nobody even gets!"

"We had reason to believe the disease rate would increase—promising data to show it was growing. The virus was mutating, and in the scientific community, there was still no known cure for it. It was a sound financial opportunity."

"There's no money in it, Alan!" the man shouted. He moved toward the cluttered desk and studied the formulas strewn across the whiteboard. "But stopping a pandemic in its tracks? Well, *that* commands money! Mayors and politicians would pay a lot to end something like that!"

"Barn Wood is not considered a pandemic," Alan countered. "It's a major problem, certainly. But an event that affects a small population in such a secluded area wouldn't be classified as a pandemic."

"You're right, Alan. You're absolutely right. A true pandemic would involve many more people. It would need a much larger ... *client* base."

"Client base?"

"It seems I need to simplify it for you, Alan. You see, while you and Dr. Till were testing for a potential cure, I was travelling to other towns—spreading trace amounts of your test drug through dozens of water sources."

The man paused to adjust a calculation on the whiteboard.

"So, when all these people who have been drinking tainted water are then given the virus as the activating agent, I won't have politicians worrying about only Barn Wood. I'll have them throwing money at me to cure people across dozens of towns. We are talking tens of thousands of people! They'll be begging me for a cure. And that cure will come at a very steep price!"

The man waddled over to the control panel and yanked down the first lever he had pulled earlier. For a second time, the panel at the back of the dome clunked open. A creature stood hunched over, its long fingers ending in jagged claws. The beast was excessively tall, nearly seven-feet, and its skin was bleached white as a ghost. An albino. It paused for only a second before rushing toward the teenager, throwing him against the glass. A thundering echo reverberated across the room.

"What are you doing?" Alan shouted. "Stop it! Tell that thing to get away from that boy!"

Gnashing its teeth, the creature plunged its pointed claws deep into the boy's side. The boy wailed as the creature opened him with a sweeping slash then reached down and tugged the large intestine free, its claws slicing their way up through the abdomen.

Alan shrieked as an organ splattered against the glass. "Tell it to stop! It will listen to you! Make it stop," he pleaded.

The sobs from the boy quieted as the creature repeatedly brought its arm down onto his chest, his sternum snapping, several ribs clicking as they came loose. Through the blood-smeared glass, Alan could see the boy's legs go limp, his head drooping to one side, his bright brown eyes now dull.

"You've gone insane!" Alan yelled. "You murdered him! He was cured and you had that thing kill him!"

"He didn't pay to be cured," the man said gravely. "No payment, no cure."

The man walked over to the desk and scribbled into one of the notepads.

"Two years ago, you paid and arranged to have an entire

town ingest an unproven drug through their water taps and then infected them with a dangerous, untested, volatile vaccine. It was a chance for you and a few friends to make some money. A ridiculous amount of money to be sure, but only if it worked."

"We were very close to something permanent!"

"Yes, but through that same transaction, Alan, you paid for other things," the man said. "You paid for risk. You paid for fear. And you also paid for chaos. And now, you will get what you paid for, Alan. Because there will be risk and there will be fear and believe me, there will be worlds of chaos."

Alan trembled, his voice barely above a whisper. "What have you done? Simon, what have you done?"

The creature looked up then from the exposed organs, thin strips of wet fabric between its fangs, red saliva pooling on its swollen chin. Simon stepped forward and peered into the dome, a toothy grin creeping across his face.

The beast stared out, its eyes content, as though satisfied with its work of torn limbs and bloody tendons. It moved its mouth, its pointed teeth jutting out from its jaw—a sickly smile eerily resembling that of the man on the other side of the glass.

Acknowledgements

This project began in 2014 as a short story. Novelist Sharon L. Crawford—who led the East York Writer's Group of which I was a member of at the time—encouraged me to read the story in front of the assembled. It felt good to voice the story into existence. Strange, but good.

So, I wrote another. And I read another.

Years went by and with them came the realization that I had accumulated many short stories. I began stitching them together. Maybe, just maybe, I had enough material to work with. Maybe, just maybe, this could be something.

I want to sincerely thank my editor and publisher, Alanna Rusnak, of Chicken House Press, for seeing my passion for writing and valuing my voice. She has heaped a great deal of confidence upon an introverted, timid writer. She's passionate and clever and scrappy and I'm so grateful she's in my corner.

I wish to thank those who assisted with early reviews of the manuscript, providing invaluable advice and direction: writer and poet laureate Jillian Morris, playwright and fiction writer Janet Wilkinson, novelist J. T. Maxwell, along with many members of the East York Writer's Group.

To Kimberly Vincent for the perfect author photo. To Joe Sisto for legal counsel.

My parents, Herb and Janice, and parents-in-law, Chuck and Linda, have spoiled me with unwavering support. Even when my work was shit.

My siblings, Dallas: heart of our family and constant cheerleader; and Andrew: overly generous with smile and laughter.

My extremely talented children, Asia and Will. I have strived to be a strong role model to you so let this book be a lesson: follow what you believe in with everything you have.

And to my wife of twenty years. We became best friends in elementary school and have never faltered since. You have my heart.

Lastly, to you, the reader. You could have picked any book in the world but you chose this one. I am truly honoured you decided to spend your time with Andrew and Xavier and Rachel and Evelyn.

Want to know how it all ends? So do I. Let's finish this journey together.

With love and humility,

Ben

Watch for Book 2 in the Feral Winter Series:
MUTATE – coming 2025

About the Author

Benjamin Rempel is a Canadian writer and essayist. Nominated for several literary awards, his work has appeared in *The Toronto Star, Blank Spaces, Fifteen Stories High Anthology*, among others. His short story, *In Search of Damien*, upon which this novel is based, was a finalist for the Rising Spirits Writing Award. A graduate of the University of Waterloo, Rempel lives in Collingwood, Ontario, with his family. He can be found at benjaminrempel.com.

www.ingramcontent.com/pod-product-compliance
Lightning Source LLC
Chambersburg PA
CBHW021413010826
48972CB00014B/1828